T0077622

Carmen Dreams

Learn the Truth About Life

Kerit Johnson and Chantilly Harrell

iUniverse, Inc.
New York Bloomington

Copyright © 2010 by Kerit Johnson and Chantilly Harrell

All rights reserved. No part of this book may be used or reproduced by any means, graphic, electronic, or mechanical, including photocopying, recording, taping or by any information storage retrieval system without the written permission of the publisher except in the case of brief quotations embodied in critical articles and reviews.

iUniverse books may be ordered through booksellers or by contacting:

iUniverse
1663 Liberty Drive
Bloomington, IN 47403
www.iuniverse.com
1-800-Authors (1-800-288-4677)

Because of the dynamic nature of the Internet, any Web addresses or links contained in this book may have changed since publication and may no longer be valid. The views expressed in this work are solely those of the author and do not necessarily reflect the views of the publisher, and the publisher hereby disclaims any responsibility for them.

ISBN: 978-1-4502-5076-4 (sc)
ISBN: 978-1-4502-5077-1 (ebook)

Printed in the United States of America

iUniverse rev. date: 08/17/2010

To my beloved daughters. Tatisha, Tiffany,Anesha,Ashanti,Stephanie,Keara and Sonya.I love you all. Special love to my mother Sandra and cousin Kim. A special thanks and love for my friends that was always there for me and characters of my story. Patricia,Chantilly,Keisha,Cathy,Dana,Nancy,Julie,Carmen,James,Veronica,Carlos,Lola,Jannelle and Rick. I LOVE YOU ALL. Thank you.

Prologue: The End: 6:45 am 12/21/12

I can't believe what I'm seeing! Before my eyes, chaos and destruction have been released to wreak havoc and my hometown of Spanaway, Washington is ablaze. Everywhere, as far as my eyes can see, the fire rages! Civilization as you have come to know it has collapsed: a nuclear bomb with one hundred times the power of the Hiroshima bomb was dropped and around the world, flaming, lifeless corpses are burning! My nose is assaulted with the raw stench of burning human flesh. I was born on your planet and had the greatest family a person can ever have. Horrendously, they met their ends in a gulf of flames; left to burn in their beds until the last of the material matter that was them was charred to dust. It is unfathomable that this was once planet Earth. Your culture, your way of life, the knowledge and technology that you have amassed, has all come to an abrupt and horrible end.

I am safe here, inside The Legendary Diamond Shield of Atlantis. It protects the mansion, but I have not seen my Mistress. The house is pregnant with a heavy silence, surrounded by its protective encasement. From the windows, the dazzling white and deep orange flames lick at its impenetrable walls. The remnants of the cosmic blood that had rained from the sky earlier this morning is now sizzling and bubbling from the heat of the nuclear fire. Not only does it protect us from the wicked flames that seek our demise, but even more, it is barricading us from the fall-out radiation and volcanic ashes. I pray that the poor souls, who were lucky enough to survive the blast, were fortunate enough to make it to one of the arks. The arks from the realm of E'ly sent to protect the precious few. All others will be sure to succumb to the radioactive contamination that will follow on the heels of the demented flames.

The horrors that I have survived should never be relived; but I must let the new seed know the truth. Locked safely away in my glass case, bid by my master not to leave, I stay here to bear witness to the aftermath. Mistress Pat has seemed to go mad with the turn of recent events. Last, I saw her, she had an insane gleam in her eyes and she was running from the room screaming her children's names, hatchet in hand. She had tried to hack her way into my sleeping chamber but the glass is impermeable and she had no success. I have no idea where she ran to, but I pray that she and her children are safe.

This will all still be your future by the time you read this. None of this will have occurred yet for you. I must write what will be so that there will be more survivors. After the madness,

1

there will be a new scroll for the new seeds to follow. If you choose to believe what is written here and heed its warning. Once the radiation is gone, I'm not sure I will stay here in your future. Knowing what is to come and being helpless to stop it, only a messenger of the doom to come. I'm not sure I want to go back. My advice is simple, stay close to the world oceans. However, to go back and relive this Revelation again is unthinkable. I am an abomination. Nueden doesn't want me and Sotterus fears me!

Scripture 1: The Curse of the Hubriser

There is a very old saying my readers. Be careful what you wish for, you just might get it! This book is written only for the survivors! If you are reading this scroll, you are a survivor from the end of days. I must write this scroll so that the new seeds of the future will know the truth and have something to believe in. Just like my predecessor's did for you.

I still haven't gone outside yet because the air isn't safe to breath. I'm pretty sure there wont be much left to see after yesterday anyway. Instead I stay tucked in my haven. Waiting to see what fresh horrors may unfold. I do not know if the terror of darkness will grip me as it has for the past three weeks. I still haven't grasped what all has happened in such a short period and I often wonder if I could have prevented the events that followed. I know that is only childish musings and like we all must do, I push these infantile thoughts from my head. They wouldn't help you now anyway.

I am doomed to live the Curse of the Hubriser! Yes, my readers. The legend is true. The stories you read and the movies you see bare striking resemblance to the truth. They are the watered-down truth from lore and myth that was forgotten in centuries long since past. I would wish my curse on no one else, even knowing that my life will never be the same. If you could recognize the nature of the universe and the cosmos withheld no secrets from you, would you be the same person that you are now? I don't think so. I would hope not. The constancy of man's existence on earth, the date of Earth's last day; I know it all. I know that Earth is not alone in its planetary evolution and that there are many more planets, identical to yours in every way. Well, maybe not every way as you very soon will also learn. Your not as special as you think you are.

Before you discount all I am going to tell you as the delusional ravings of a mad woman, let me first tell you who I am. My name is Carmen Dreams and this is my testament, or should I say your fate! If you wish not to know your destiny, stop reading when it is written the seventh hour in my dreams: the hour of Repent! On the other hand, maybe I should just start from the beginning.

Scripture 2: The Keeper of the Spanton Spells

When the antiquities trader got off his private jet in Spanaway, Washington it was thundering and lightning. The rain was pelting him so hard; it was painful to his skin, even through his clothes. This was no normal rainfall, he knew. The atmosphere was filled with static and he felt nervous. From the corners of his eyes, he saw moving things in the shadows. Shadows that were flying over the airport skies. He started to feel that the Creators knew what he was doing; the clouds in the sky parted in darkness with the sibilant sounds of whispers: then the wind kicked up a notch. Kirk Bailey a Native American from the Kituwah bloodline knew he was running out of time. He looked at his watch and realized the portal of madness would soon be open. Out of anxious habit, he absent-mindedly touched the solid gold handcuff that secured the gold armatura to his left wrist. It was etched all over with symbols that he had never seen before or after he had come into possession of the armatura but he knew it to be an ancient language. The rain continued the relentless assault and he quickened his step across the tarmac.

As he crossed to the waiting limo, the refueling truck was making its way to his jet. The truck slowed as it passed him and he watched as the driver stared straight through him with eyes aglow. He couldn't have said they were red or orange, green or blue. They were eyes the color he knew not off and he was sure that unseen forces were at work around him. He quickened his gate; he did not want any delays to keep him from getting away from this god-forsaken city. He could not stop the anxious feeling roiling around in his gut and he tightened his grip on the armatura.

"Hurry, drive me to Mistress Pat's Mansion now!" Bailey ordered. "Right away sir." the driver said. "How long will it take to get there?" "Not long sir." "Damn you, I said how long! I'm running out of time!" "Ten minutes sir". Bailey looked out the back window and saw clouds that were pitch black and racing behind them. "They know, O God, they know!" he screamed! "Who know?" James asked. "The Them!" "Them sir?" James asked. He was confused but he kept driving. "Drive faster! In God's name, please! Drive Faster!"

James stepped on the gas; dark clouds enveloped the luxurious sedan in what appeared to be thick black smoke. He started having difficulty seeing the road; the other vehicles on the road started to slow down and witness the supernatural. As James watched his crazed passenger in the rear view mirror: Bailey bid the gold armatura to open and spoke the verbal charms for Tranise. Tranise is the Angel of Cosmic Wind Spells.

When this powerful angel is called upon; she creates winds that you have no categorization for on your planet. A full gale of her power can literally blow you apart! As Tranise appeared in the pitch black sky her beauty lit the night with beams of red, blue, yellow and amber. It was an amazing sight to behold and nearly every car on the road had come to a complete standstill; every car that is besides the limo transporting Bailey to Mistress Pat with a protective shield around it. James tried to weave the limo in and out of the mass of cars stopped on the highway but it was useless. The car was too big and the traffic had become too congested so he too pulled over to watch the show. Some of the braver souls had even stepped outside of their cars to witness the spectacle. Others watched from the safe confines of their cars in disbelief. The wind started to gust high and the power of Category six winds was unleashed to the night. Cars started to blow off the road and people standing outside became flying debris. Anything that wasn't rooted to the ground had to succumb to the powerful force of the winds that Tranise's power had unleashed. The limo was protected by its cosmic shield that Bailey wished upon. A foreboding evil mass possessed with sinister intelligence swooped around the trees to hide; much like the thick black smoke that had enveloped the sedan. Tranise waved her light and the powerful wind blew down the trees; leaving the mass with no place to hide. The wind increased and the evil clouds of darkness blew apart and disappeared. The spell of Tranise surrounded the limo: her brilliant, compelling power entered through the window and returned back into its nest. He bid The Armatura closed without batting an eye.

James couldn't believe what he'd just seen. The fact that the power he had just seen had exited and then returned like a dog on a leash to Bailey unnerved him to his soul. The fact that all that power had parked itself in a strange gold box sitting in Bailey's lap didn't help any either. He was shaking from head to toe and what he really wanted to do at that point was bolt out of the car and run for his life. What the hell had that been and who the hell was this guy that he was taken to his mistress.

Kirk Bailey had sat through it all. He didn't even bother to look out the window and see what was transpiring. He had seen it all before and he trusted Tranise to do what it was he had summoned her to do. None of it was new to him; it only served to make him more anxious to rid himself of the armatura. His uneasiness did increase however because he knew that he had just broken one of the Celestial Rules. The Angels of Spanton were never to be exhibited before the humans on Earth. They had been born from the cosmic dust of I AM and it was for the very sanity of humans that this law even exists. Bailey knew he had been damned since he had first signed for the stone four years ago this day: breaking the cosmic law now couldn't hurt. He sensed the waves of fear coming off of the driver and he ordered him to get to going. James was too scared to speak, hell, to even move if truth be told. He jumped at the sound of his passengers' voice but then he started the engine, put the car in gear and flew at break neck speed to get them to his mistress. The cosmic shield released itself as the car pulled off. A short time later, the limo was pulling to a stop. Ashen faced and looking like he had just seen a ghost, James jumped out of the driver seat and opened the door for Bailey to exit.

Scripture 3: The Mansion of Pain and Pleasure

The circular driveway of Mistress Pat mansion was elegantly lined with manicured trees and shrubs. Stone gods and goddesses stood sentinel between the shrubs and trees providing an impressive grandness to the front entrance of the mansion. It looked like heaven on the ground, as though it was waiting for those stone deities to come alive and take up residence at any moment. The front is marble white and navy blue. It has four three-story pillars to attest its beauty; and it is surrounded by forty wooded acres with a giant maze in the back made for someone to get lost in.

The owner of this magnificent estate is Mistress Pat. At thirty-four, she is what dreams are made of. Her skin is flawless in its beauty; its café-de-leche color was accentuated by her rich coal hair with striking streaks of red that framed an angelic face. Angelic face or not, she outfitted that five foot nine inch frame in leather: the tighter the better. Her life's passion had always been the collection of precious gems and artifacts. This had made her a very, very wealthy woman. However, as a girl, she had reverently wished to be a mother and she had two beautiful children named Sonya and Carlos. Sonya is very beautiful at seventeen; she want to be a movie star one day. Carlos is eight years old, full of life, and as adorable as he can be. On this hallowed eve of delivery, she had sent them away to be safe with family. She didn't expect any danger but Bailey had sounded terrified when he had phoned and she would be cautious.

Paul the butler opened the door to let the sweating Bailey inside the mansion. Paul had been in Mistress Pat's employ for six years. His devotion to her was unquestionable and he would be in her service until she saw fit to let him go. If left to his own devices, he would be with her until the day he died. If his ivory white pallor didn't make you pause, then certainly his bearing would. He made you think of an undertaker because the expression on his face never gave away what he was thinking. His lanky, six-foot frame stayed outfitted in the finest suits that money could buy and he had been grateful that his Mistress had never insisted that he wore a standard butler uniform. You see, his taste had always been for the finer things in life. Nevertheless, he lacked two things that made sure he would never amass any personal wealth on his own: the desire to be successful and the wherewithal to see a plan through to completion. No, he would much rather enjoy someone else's wealth and after Mistress Pat had offered him a job six years ago, he knew he would never want for anything again. In return, he was hers for eternity.

Paul looked past the sweating Bailey to James sitting out in the limo. James usually came inside the house after his pick-ups and it didn't escape Paul's notice that James hadn't budged from the car. He just sat their looking up at the house with a look of sheer fright on his face. In fact, James was wondering at that very moment what his mistress had gotten into. He glanced up at the sky and saw the strange dark clouds that had engulfed them on the airport were coming back. Like severed arms and legs, the mist began reattaching itself into one whole piece and James watched transfixed as the foreboding mass swooped behind trees and buildings in the skyline as it got closer to the mansion. He couldn't suppress the cold shiver that ran up his spine when a terrible thought raced through his head: the clouds were alive! Alive and stalking the keeper of Spanton spells with intelligence so sinister, he was certain they were possessed with a mind of their own.

Meanwhile, Bailey had been escorted to the library where he sat and waited impatiently for the mistress, constantly checking his watch. "Butler where is she, you must bring her now!" He demanded. At that moment, Mistress Pat walked into the library to greet him. "Hello Mr. Bailey, I'm please we can finally meet". Bailey jumped out of his seat, ran over to Mistress Pat, and handed her The Scroll of Spanton. He wanted to get right down to business; he had no time for niceties. "Mistress Pat this scroll must be signed by the new owner of the stone in order to possess the Spells of Spanton." He explained. "What is this scroll Mr. Bailey?" She asked. "This is what you asked for; please sign now: their coming for me!" He yelled. "I asked you for the Evolutionary Stone of the Hubriser." "I have the forsaken stone and can't wait to give it to you; but you must sign the scroll first! Please hurry they're coming!" He shouted. "Who's coming?" "O God you don't ever want to know; they're not like us, they are the creators of this universe." "This universe?" She said confused. Mistress Pat feared that she might be getting in over her head; she looked at the scroll and saw it appeared to be very old. The papyrus that it was made from was dried and rotting at the edges. "What do I need to do?" she asked. "I can't say until you sign the scroll, there are rules that must be abided by and that is the first rule." Mistress Pat looked at Bailey and saw the look in his eyes: this was a desperate man. She wanted the stone for her priceless divinity collection. "Let me see the stone", she demanded.

Just then, the trees in front started to lean towards the mansion; their roots were trying to come out of the ground and blood started to drain out of the barks. The evil clouds of darkness surrounded the mansion. Trailing tendrils tried every crack and crevice in the house, trying their best to find a way in. James had seen it coming and was cowering on the floor of the car. Praying to the God, he didn't believe in, that whatever sought entrance to the house wouldn't find him. Kirk looked out the panoramic windows of the library and could see big, black, almond shape eyes staring at him though the mist and screamed "Good Lord, they're here!" and he opened the armatura.

The Evolutionary Stone of the Hubriser is spectacular to behold; it generates colors that you the people of the Earth know not of. Inside the stone, there are amazing spells placed by I am. It has the power to take you to a world where dreams come true. Just then, an oak tree fell to the ground and started to roll towards the mansion: blood splattered on the windows to the library. Bailey screamed! Mistress Pat was taken back by the simplicity of its light and didn't notice anything! "I'll sign." She said excited. Bailey put the scroll on the desk and the voice of a ghostly dragon yelled. "The Revelation Of The Leader Which I Am Gave Unto Him!" She looked around the room and said. "What was that?" "Sign, Sign!" Bailey screamed; she signed. At that moment, a clap of thunder like the sound of many bombs shook the state of Washington. The deep voice in the cloud of darkness screamed out with the sound of many waters! "To Shew Unto His Servant's Things Which Must Shortly Come To Pass," and it vanished. The trees turned back up in place: the sap stopped coming out of their bark. James peeked out from below the car window; he was thinking about quitting his peachy job. Then everything got quiet and calm. Kirk took a deep breath and said "Thank you Mistress Pat. You have no idea what you just did for me; I am finally free. May Who You Believe to Be God watch over you my child." "What is this all about Mr. Bailey, explain to me what I need to know."

Scripture 4: The Four Celestial Stones of the Cosmos

Bailey wiped the sweat from his eyebrow and sat down; the relief he felt could not be described. The universe had literally, just been lifted off his shoulders: knowing the future of humanity was no longer his problem. "Tell me Mr. Bailey, what is it I need to know." She was desperate to learn about the stone. "You don't realize the power that you now have Mistress Pat." "This power, where does it come from?" She asked. "It comes from the Stone of the Hubriser; it is one of the Celestial Stones. You have The Spells of The Cosmos. You are the keeper of the Spanton Spells." He explained. "What do you mean one of?" "There are four stones." Bailey told her.

He is telling the truth: there are four stones. The first stone is The Stone of the Hubriser. By outward appearance the stone is a solid round diamond the size of a softball; it has the power to open the door to dreams. In this amazing world, angels rule with awesome magic and spells. It takes you to The World of Spanton where wishes come true. When you live your fantasy, you must be out of the keepers dream before the eighth hour. The eighth hour is the Hour of Madness and that is when The Mist of Darkness comes to harvest your ethereal soul. This stone gives you the power over Light and Darkness: this is Supreme Power to have.

Next, is The Stone of Perfection. The Stone stays suspended in infinite animation around its owner. A bowling ball sized planet; it exhibits cosmic intelligence. Its atmosphere is acidic and is savaged by preternatural lightening strikes. The Stone has the ability to absorb anything around it and make it into Spectacular Spells of Perfection. When the planet is under commandment, a lustrously golden man angel materializes! He is a towering menace standing over twenty stories tall and he is called by the seeds of Spanton The Profective.

Beware of the third stone: The Stone of Jinni. This stone is a crystalline Arabic oil lamp with a radiant iridescence. Its ancientness is incomprehensible to your version of "time". Far into the oceans abyss, a netherworld protects the lamp. The Stone of Jinni's ability is to transform into a very extraordinary genie: yes my readers, I said GENIE. This apparition has total authority over the Spell of Suetonius the Twelve Caesars. An exhibition of twelve powerful spirits that cannot be restrained. Belief for you can be a luxury, but I live with the truth. One day very soon, the verity of what I tell you will come out. My curse is living with seeing how you will all end. It is The Day of Rapture that you must fear; and when that day arrives: you will finally understand why all of this is what it is. I cannot reveal the date of this future event; I must write this book as fantasy or your Government will not allow this book to be published. For some reason your world governments have an understanding about keeping the public in the dark. They say it's to keep the world from going mad. But the truth must be told. The C.I.A. initially disregarded the "tales" of people who had escaped my dreams. Now, they know what is fact and not merely "tales" from delusional people.

The Divine Stone of Mirabilia is the last and final stone. In the shape of a hexagram, it is a fiery red ruby the size of a human heart. Beating with the blood of The Twelve Disciples, it sits on a one-foot tall pillar coated with platinum. The pillar is filled with plutonium and if exposed to evil; it will spontaneously exterminate anything within a two hundred mile radius: ensuring complete and total devastation of all roguish and vile demoniacs. Protection of The Divine Stone of Mirabilia is paramount for when it is combined with the three other Celestial Stones; it summons a flock of superior angels that manifest supreme scriptures. The protector of the stone two millennia ago was The Messiah, The Son of "I AM" and he named them "A Fold of Sheep You Know Not Of!" They have the supreme power of inscription spells. There is a revelation that the Spantonites dare not to speak of; this revelation imbues that when the Divine Stone of Miriabilia is found, The Day of Rapture is at hand.

Bailey looked at Mistress Pat and said "It's now 10:34pm; in ten minutes the door to The World of Dreams will open for you." "Open where?" Mistress Pat asked. "Right here in your home; upon making your first wish to the Hubriser Stone: you will be the new Angel of Dreams. This gives you the authority to allow anyone to live out his or her deepest fantasies while you slumber. You must know that what I tell you next is of the greatest importance." Pat looked at Bailey as if he had lost his mind. "The fantasy may not go beyond seven hours and fifty-nine minutes; or the Mist of Darkness will take the fantasiers immortal soul. At the eighth hour of fantasia, The Fog of Evil will come. They must allot themselves at least one minute to escape or madness will follow." Bailey knew the horrors of having to see thoughtless numbers of people lose themselves to the pits of hell: he shuddered.

"I must warn you that when you're ready to give away the stone to its Replacer, The Mist of Darkness will try to stop you." "Stop who, me: what did I do?" "You will know the answers to The Secret Book of Spanton. The secrets must not get out to the outer world; they will deter you from exposing what you know at all costs." He explained. "The outer world, what's that?" "Earth." Bailey replied. "Earth Mistress Pat." The four stones are doorways to the Realms of Spanton." Bailey sits down on the desk. "I know you see on TV, videos of u.f.o.'s.; a lot of those tapes are fake." He stood. "But some of them are not; we on earth think you have to travel through space to find other worlds: it's not done just like that. It is as easy as walking thru a door: believe me when I tell you child. The Them are The Creators. They were here before us and will be here when we are but a memory to time; but Mistress Pat as you will find out, it is all true. It's written in the Scroll of Spanton." "Scroll of Spanton; Book of Spanton, what the hell are you telling me Mr. Bailey?" "The scroll tells us about what was and what is and what will be. Each stone has its own scroll. The Book posses the secrets of powerful spells with Angels of light and darkness to call upon." The only thing is that The Book hasn't been seen in over two thousand years since the death of Jesus Christ."

The scroll tells of the great Leader and his twelve most worthy disciples. The worthiest of these, was entrusted with the keeping of the stone. Upon his martyrdom, his body was transported to Spanton; the stone also now rests with him. The eternal resting place is a cave the Spantonites call Mount Alpha Omega. The legend says that he was able to foresee the future of the earth and how it ended. Before his death, he wrote it all down and it was copied and written in the Book of Revelation.

Scripture 5: The Abduction

Mistress Pat looked scared. "What are you saying Bailey, that I'm going to learn the truth about life?" He looked her directly in the eyes and said. "All I can say is that you'll soon fully understand why the knowledge you gain must be kept secret. You have the cosmos, the doors to what we call Heaven and Hell in your hands" Just look into the stone and make a wish and it shall be. Good luck Mistress Pat, use your ultimate authority judiciously." Bailey said with caution.

Sometimes it is best not to know the truth. Ask yourself; would you really want to have direct cognition of all the mysteries of the universe? In essence, there was no mystery. It is best my readers, not to know these things. You normal human beings do not possess the extrasensory perception required to reason beyond your ordinary senses. Upon signing the scroll, The Replacer is gifted with the Gift of Awareness. It is irreversible and even when the next Replacer has signed the Awareness never fades: it should be called the Curse of Awareness. All in the eye of the beholder, I suppose. What is sad is that your own world leaders keep very important secrets from the public. Your planet is going to do what's normal for a planet its size and perform it's task that is very important in winter two thousand twelve for its body. You must understand that man is not needed for your planet to exist. You do more harm than good for the earth. What you call earth will and must clean itself from deadly viruses like it always do. Humans who are living in two thousand twelve will be recycled. They won't tell you because it will cause mass panic around the world: so you go on not knowing and enjoy the last days of your life.

Magnetic fields surround magnetic materials and electric currents in your planet and are detected by the force they exert on other magnetic materials and moving electric charges. The magnetic field at any given point on earth is specified by both a direction and a magnitude; it takes twenty six thousand years for the magnetic fields to go haywire within your planet. It really doesn't affect the earth at all, because all your planet has to do is correct itself.

The cataclysmic pole shift hypothesis is how your planet does this. None of you was here 26,000 years ago to witness this event: lucky for you. The conjecture that the axis of rotation of a planet has undergone relatively rapid shifts in location, creating calamities such as massive floods and large-scale tectonic events. This type of event would occur if the physical poles had been or would be suddenly shifted with respect to the underlying surface over a geologically short period. It's like a hiccup to your planet.

There is only three human beings on your planet that know about the Book of Spanton. This secret makes knowing about u.f.o.'s not so important anymore. There are secrets far more classified then u.f.o.. Your government is just getting the smartest and most important people for this day in a sad attempt to keep them alive. Truth be told; maybe it's best this way: but for those who want to know the truth. I was sent to tell you this so you can choose to believe in him and die in peace or not believe and; well why don't I just finish telling you what will happen to you.

Bailey knows, he has a reverential awe for The Them. For the rest of his days he will look over his shoulder with trepidation whenever the wind blows or the sky darkens. Safe is a word that has no meaning for him. He will never be "safe."

The stories about people who just disappear without a trace are true. But something that I can divulge to you is that they aren't disappearing. The Them just take back the souls that escaped and destroy the stolen remains: you the people of the earth have no idea what's going on.

Let me tell you a little about when I was human living on your planet. My cousin Kim and I are like sisters. Or should I say were? We were both born on the first day of the eleventh month in the year of the Gregorian Calendar. This is the day after All Hallows Day, what we observe as All Saints Day. We entered the world at exactly forty-four seconds past midnight. Our mothers were identical twins who married identical twins. Born under alternately hallowed circumstances, our mother's were born on December twenty-first, our father's December twelfth. We were all born on the same hour on the clock twenty two seconds apart. I am the first-born, of two first born. I wanted for nothing. After my father's death, I was lost and Kim brought me back from depression.

We grew up together in an upper class community called Royal Street in Spanaway; right next door to one another in fact. We could see each other from our bedroom windows and we were each other's closest companion. The kinetic bond that we shared grew as we did. She got me into trouble for smoking a joint in the girl's restroom at school. I was the one who snuck us into an eighteen and older club and got us busted by security. We were only sixteen and our parents were called. They were furious does not justifiable portray how pissed they were; our punishment was volunteering at a teen runaway shelter. As though that wasn't punishment enough: we were made to give away ten things of the others and well, we were spoiled little rich girls to the tenth degree. We did more crying and screaming over what ten things were being given away of ours; I cursed her and she cursed me and that was the last time I talked to Kim.

When she had chosen my tenth item, a fifteen-hundred dollar pair of pink six-inch strappy leather Jimmy Choo stilettos, I was enraged. She was a bitch and everything else under the book. I fumed off to my bathroom and slammed the door. Swearing that I would never talk to her again. I heard her slam my bedroom door and after I had collected myself; went to cry more on my bed. She and I had never gone more than sixty minutes without talking to each other and the fact that I hated her so much at that moment, meant that I couldn't call her and tells her how much I hated her for giving away my favorite pair of sandals. That Bitch! I digress readers; forgive me Kim wherever you are, I love you.

I couldn't bring myself to stay mad at her. Early the following morning, around one o'clock, I phoned her. Just to hear her voice; hear her curse me back, just say hi. I heard that characteristically sarcastic Kim voice say, "Are you still mad about the sandals, Carmen?" Then there was a strangled sound and I heard Kim scream "Oh My God!" I was desperately screaming her name but all I heard was silence on the other end of the line and the sheer horror of her scream in my head. I looked out my bedroom window and there was a startling, radiant light emitting from her room. I could vaguely see shadows of what I initially thought were people but the posturing; their movements were all wrong. I ran downstairs and out the front door; across the yard I ran, my legs churning: propelling me to go to my sister's side. If not sister by blood then she was by soul. Through her front door and up the stairwell my legs carried me plummeting into her room as if mad and all that was there was her cell phone. Sitting on the floor, my memory made me see Kim sitting there as she had been a hundred times before. Legs crossed, beautiful black hair shining in the picture window, gabbing away: but she was not there. I screamed.

The police searched for Kim for weeks; bulletins were up across the globe, asking for any information leading to Kim's return. We offered a five million dollar reward on GSPAN: No charges, no accusations: just for her to be returned, alive and well. Kim disappeared on January first, in two thousand and one. I now know this to be the first day of the twenty-first century, the first day of the third millennium. The knowledge I have gained has delivered me with peace as to Kim's destiny. It is an added burden that I bear that I cannot share this with her parents, my aunt and uncle. It is a tangled web that I have been immersed in my readers and I pray that "He Who I Believe To Be God" has mercy on my soul for extending their anguish. The savage torment of not knowing. And they will never know, because I can never tell. Eight years have lapsed, and this burden never lightens.

Bailey looked at Mistress Pat with sadness in his eyes and said, "I'm sorry to tell you but when you let people enter your dreams, you must take their soul for The Them." "TAKE THEIR SOULS FOR THE THEM,WHAT KIND OF MADNESS IS THIS! WHO ARE THE THEM?" She shouted.

Bailey started walking back to the front doors; he did not need Paul to show him the way. He would tunnel out of there if he thought it would carry him to the furthest reaches of the earth faster than his private jet. His express desire was to be away from the stone; away from Mistress Pat and the responsibility that he had just unloaded on her. He wanted away from her questions and away from Spanaway, Washington. What he truly wanted he could never have: and that was a way to unknown. The knowing is what would ensure Bailey would never see his sixty-fifth birthday. He was just forty now and he would never see his unborn daughter marry and bear him a grandchild in his spitting image. His was to know all but never know the joy of being an old man; senile in his chair: arm in arm with his childhood sweetheart.

"Damn you Bailey! I said tell me who are The Them; I have grown tired of your vagueness and will not tolerate it any longer! Tell me what I demand to know!" You'll soon find out my child, you'll soon find out." The pity in his eye sent a chill down Mistress Pat's spine. "Tell me Pat; Do You Believe In God?" "Hearing all of this, I guess anything is possible." She said sounding exasperated. Bailey walked thru the double French doors, sauntered down the steps of the mansion and slid into the backseat of the waiting car. James slammed the door shut and hopped into the already running limo. Kirk Bailey sat back in the seat and let out a deep breath that he hadn't been aware he was holding. "Airport driver! Quickly!"

In fact, it was denial and his eagerness to rid himself of the stone that led to the clouding of his Gift of Awareness. Had he been more in tune with this, he would have foreseen that his private jet would "run out of fuel" thirty aerial miles from the island of Montserrat. Bailey would never return to his private refuge there; he would not sleep in the arms of his very pregnant wife and feel her beating belly. Bailey should have foreseen this, but it was his destiny to not see: perhaps that was best.

All that was found in the wreckage was bits of the propeller, a seat and the wing of the plane. If you check the longitude and latitude of where the wreckage was found, you will learn that the plane went down dead center inside of The Bermuda Triangle. A body was never found: just that wreckage and Bailey and his pilot were gone. I'll let you in on another little secret friends, Bailey was more important to The Secret than he could imagine and they had lain in wait for him to enter The Outer Bounds. The pilot was just in the wrong place at the wrong time. Unfortunate really, but what The Them demand must be delivered!

Scripture 6: The Transformation

Mistress Pat stood next to the gold armatura bewildered. Could everything that she had just been told be true? And what had he really told her anyway? Her mind was spinning with the implications that Bailey had just leveled on her: had she just become all-powerful? It had occurred to her while Bailey was spinning that fantastic tale that he might not be all there: I mean, come on. She hadn't seen any "Awesome Power" displayed to her, but what if Bailey wasn't crazy. What if everything she had just been told was true. She glanced down at the gem-encrusted watch on her arm and noted that it was ten forty two pm. If what Bailey had said were true, some strange happenings would be starting to occur in less than two minutes.

Mistress Pat couldn't stop time; nor could she revoke signing for the stone. The second hand on her watch inched maddeningly fast towards the forsaken time. She stole herself for what would come next. It was at that precise moment that she began to feel lightheaded; she started to faint but gripped the armoires edge and righted herself. Paul hurried to her side and asked, "Mistress, are you not well?" The concern in his voice was sincere and she knew it. However, she had the responsibility of keeping those under her care safe. Though he served her, he was not her servant: neither did she treat anyone in her employ with such despicable cruelty. Whatever happened next, she wanted Paul safe from harm. " Paul, I want you to leave this room immediately. You are to wait for James' return: after that, the two of you are to go immediately to Sonya's guesthouse and lock the door. I will come for you as soon as I can. Go now!" Paul left running from the room and closed the doors. He wasn't about to leave his mistress alone however and he stayed just outside the doors of the library to wait for whatever happened next.

She opened the case to see the stone: it was now ten forty four pm. The stone began to radiantly glow; it was as though millions of brilliant prisms of light were being emitted from the diamond: The Stone of the Hubriser. The giant movie screen began to warp its shape: a doorway materialized inside of the screen and radiated sparkling hues that she had never seen before. She started screaming and thought to herself, "I'm getting the fuck out of here." She was scared shitless. No if, and or buts about it. She ran out of the library and locked the door behind her. Gripping the doorknobs, she was breathing heavily and she struggled to calm herself: she began thinking of a way to get her ass out of this curse.

She also noted that she felt different. She walked over to one of the giant mirrors lining the entry hall; she was physically the same. She was still gorgeous but she felt an electricness. As though hundreds of protons were firing throughout her body, parts of her body that she didn't even know she had. She thought to herself that it might be safer to let someone else enter the dream portal: she wouldn't or couldn't risk herself. James and Paul were out of the question. Whom could she get to fill the responsibility that she had just been laden with? Carlos and Sonya were too important to risk their mother become the Angel of Dreams. She looked into the Stone of the Hubriser brilliance and wished, "I wish for someone to take on this task for me: I Wish To Meet The New Angel Of Dreams." She walked back into the library and put the stone into the armatura and closed it. The doorway was there: still emitting its awesome color. Mistress Pat unclasped the gold handcuffs from the armatura and walked out of the room.

The doorbell rang. Who would come to her house at this hour? The entry hall was longer than a city block and the click-clack of her black leather Pradas rang across the Parian marble floor. Paul opened the door: what he saw was a very striking woman. Her hair was a lustrous black on black and her skin was the color of milk and honey. Her eyes were Egyptian and the depth to them was entrancing. Paul's height made him peer down at her. He thought she couldn't be more than five feet and ten inches. She was slender but not thin; lean best described her. She looked like an Egyptian Goddess: as though Cleopatra had tried to reincarnate herself in this young woman. Her eyes were a translucent hazel. As she fidgeted outside of the door, Paul noticed that with the play of light and shadows her eyes changed color. Her red Dolce suit was two-piece and form fitting; it accentuated her small, muscular thighs and played up her ample breasts in the way only a tailor-made suit could do. Peeking from under her 1933 Marie Claire red velvet hard round brim hat, she knew what it was like to have money. "Madam, I am certain that you realize what late hour this is so, what is your name?" Paul asked. She was divine and he felt compelled to assist her in any way he could: if only she would say her name.

If you haven't guessed, this is when my life changed. I was driving down Mountain Highway, from taking my best friend Julie back home. We had stayed late at the library and I thought it would be able to get me home quicker than Pacific Road. It must have been around ten forty something because I was talking to my mother for the umpteenth time in the last five minutes. She was hounding me by asking how much longer it would be before I got home. Nothing had ever really been the "same" after Kim's disappearance and I had to constantly fill the void that my dear cousin's absence had left. I had just told my Mom I'd see her in fifteen minutes when everything stopped at the same time! The car lost complete power and came to a jerking stop. My screensaver is a picture of me and Julie and after I said hello a couple of times and got no answer; I looked down and it too was dead. I recall thinking to myself, "What fucking kind of dead zone is this?" I looked out the car windows and up a long driveway was a mansion that deserved to be on "Lifestyles of the Rich and Famous." All I wanted most at that time was to use the phone and surely, there was a phone to be had up there. I got out of my BMW; locked it and ran up the winding drive and changed the course of my entire life. I rang the doorbell, and when the man I presumed to be the butler opened the door; I told him my problems.

"I'm so sorry to bother you this late, my name is Carmen and my car stopped on the road in front of your home; it won't start. To aggravate matters further, my cell phone died. I had noticed some strange lightening in the sky right before everything died on me so I guess it's just some freaky electrical storm: it's somewhat funny though because I see you people haven't lost any power up here. You have a wonderful home here by the way." I did know what time it was and I wanted to sound as non-threatening as possible. "Well, this never happened to me before and I would really like to call my mom and tell her what's happened: if you don't mind." "You wish to use the phone miss Carmen?" Paul asked. The sound of my voice made Paul unnervingly aroused and he turned his body so that the lower part would be blocked by the doors. He could not hide the eagerness in his gaze however and his eyes uncontrollably roved my body. "Yes please." " Miss Carmen, there is a phone in the sitting room, please follow me."

The butler strode purposefully down the hallway and I quickened my gate to match his. As I followed, I couldn't help but be impressed by the sheer grandness of this place. There was a feeling of enchantments about, and I couldn't help but be also astonished by the original works of art that hung the walls. "Wow, that's a Da Vinci" and I gasped, "Is that Giotto's, The Lamentation." "Yes miss Carmen it is. My mistress is very generous and she lends her paintings to any society with an interest in preserving the arts." The butler replied. "Now I know this is Picasso, how did she get such paintings?" I kicked myself in the mouth. Foot in mouth disease had always been my primary illness, well, no need to break from the status quo. I sure miss myself when I was human: sorry back to telling you the truth about life. "The Mistress." Paul fumbled in his head for the right words, "is a collector."

Mistress Pat watched this mesmerizing stranger enter her home and could not help noting what a lovely young girl she was. Could this be her wish? Had it been that easy to selfishly save herself from the task she had been charged with? Mistress Pat thought to herself, "This is too damn amazing; if it wasn't happening to me, I wouldn't believe it." She watched the delicateness and grace of the young woman as she walked briskly behind Paul. She had been bred and not born. It was evident in the regalness she exuded and the feminine; come hither sway of her hips. They were such that a queen would be envious. And as queen of her castle, Mistress Pat stood a bit taller and felt a small twinge of envy spark her brown eyes. Priorities must always dominate pettiness though and as she continued to watch their progress down the hall, she noticed that Paul's penis was markedly erect. She smirked inwardly and thought, "I guess he finds our visitor most enticing as well."

She met us midway down the hall and said "Paul I'll help our pretty guest." "Yes Mistress Pat." He walked hurriedly away to leave us alone. "My dear, are you aware that your prettiness rivals that of any model walking the runways: for surely that is what you must be?" The mistress asked. She was a seducer, a master negotiator. What she wanted she got and she wanted me. I would be the next Angel of Dreams. Every fiber in her screamed that this was why I had been sent. It was fate but she inherently knew she must work quickly.

"Heavens no! I'm too shy for that line of work." I giggled and Mistress Pat couldn't help but to giggle with me. Pat thought to herself. "Priceless, she is shy with a beauty that Snow White would have killed her for. She is absolutely priceless." "Your home is so lovely." I said looking around as I speak. "Thank you. What is your name love?" "Carmen, my name is Carmen Dreams Mrs.:" I was blushing an awful scarlet red. If the niceties this beautiful rich woman was bestowing on me weren't enough, I noticed the butler had had a hard on when he rushed away. I was still wondering what kind of naughtiness the mistress of the house and the butler must be into when Mistress Pat placed her hand on my shoulder and remarked, "You have the most remarkable eyes." We had come to the locked library door and stopped. "I can't quite tell what color they are, look deeply into my eyes for a moment: and did you say your last name was Dreams?" "Well yes I did, but you can call me Carmen." Mistress Pat knew unequivocally that the wish had been granted. The epitome of fantasy was standing in her foyer and as she stared into the ever changing eyes of Carmen Dreams, she said a prayer of thanks that she had been delivered. I stared back, transfixed at the mistress of Paul the butler and could only wonder.

"My dear, I have a position that just recently opened on my staff; I think it was destiny that caused your car to stop and I know you would fill the position perfectly. Money as you can see is not a problem and everything you need will be provided: can I consider the job taken?" The mistress offered with a enticing grin. "Wow this place is so awesome." I said. "What would you need me to do?" The mistress walked over to me and stopped so close to my face that I could smell her dinner of black caviar, truffles and rye bread: there was something sweet, probably butter. She said, "Whatever it is I desire, my dear. Whatever it is that I desire." Mistress Pat felt the power of the cosmos ignite within her soul. She looked straight over my head and her body had gotten stiff. She relaxed and she held up her middle finger with finesse and blew. A red mist began streaming lazily from her finger. The Book of Spanton recognizes this as The Orgasmic Hells Curse. I shrugged her hand off my shoulder and backed slowly, nervously away. I began to feel very strange and weak and fell to the floor. A feeling of euphoria swelled within me and I fell deep into a prophetic trance.

I was writhing on the floor in the most intense ecstasy that I had ever experienced: I had had orgasms before; however, this was unlike any sensation I can describe! As I thrust my fingers deeper and deeper into my slick wetness, I began moaning in a voice that sounded like mine but wasn't. I was lost. Over and over, the orgasms rocked me. My stomach clenched and unclenched and I began to dread the next shocking wave; but not more than I wanted to feel that next earth shattering spasm. As a Cosmo chick, I knew what multi's were but what I was feeling was not multi-orgasms. This was other worldly stuff and the heat that was spilling from my tight, wet hole was blazing. My heart felt like it was between my legs; beating out of control.

Mistress Pat unlocked the door to the library and retrieved the Stone of the Hubriser. I was still writhing on the floor in the hall with my pants and panties down to my ankles. The erotic sensations shooting throughout my body were disabling. I tried to rise; but couldn't. When the heat from my juicy snatch became too hot, I took my fingers and licked them clean. Three of the fingers of my left hand claimed the inner realms of my wet folds and the other two fingers rubbed my pearl faster than I could have thought possible. I took my right hand and savagely pistoned my vice like anal hole. As I fucked myself harder and harder; Mistress Pat walked towards me with a shining stone and tried to place it on my forehead. I pulled my fingers away from their relentless torture of my womanhood to stop her. Mistress Pat grabbed my hand and began to savoringly lick every bit of cream from my fingers!

I had never been so sexually aroused in my life. My vagina was throbbing with the need for something hard: Long and Hard; short and hard: Just hard. And fast! I needed someone to touch my body in the places that my useless fingers were not able to go. I gazed at my new mistress and the heat in her eyes scorched me through to my very being! I saw me riding her face and the intense ecstasy she could give me and I her: I was home. Whatever my mistress desired was done. Mistress Pat watched in wonderment while licking the red mist off her Cursed middle finger and pulled the gold cuffs from her pocket. She bent down on her hands and knees and grasped the wrist of the hand that was tearing my buttocks in two. She secured the cuff to my wrist and just then, the stone's energy faded. And I too along with it.

Scripture Seven: The New Seraphim of Dreams

Mistress Pat looked fixedly upon the place where I had been only moments ago. She waived her hands through the area, as though they would feel what her eyes could not see. "She just disappeared!" "She just freaking disappeared! This is unreal!" She jumped up from the ground with the dormant stone in tow. She had no idea what had just occurred. She had to piece together more of what Bailey had told her; and fast. "I wished for someone to replace me as being the Angel of Dreams. And just like that Miss Carmen Dreams was delivered unto me." She unlocked the doors and strode to the desk where the gold case lay and placed the stone back in its perfect nest; which the World of Spanton recognizes as The Impenetrable Armatura.

I watched her from afar my new mistress. I could not help her yet; I myself was under transformation. Her thoughts were now mine just as her every command would be my whim. I saw and felt her grapple with reasoning and uncertainty: Power madness and humility.

Mistress Pat thought, "Bailey was rather vague in the light of all of this strange shit."

"Strange as all of this is however, my next wish is important: I can feel it. But what do I need to wish for next?" She reasoned. "I have power over good and evil, no, he said Light and Darkness. He also told me that The Mist of Darkness will harvest the eternal soul of whoever has entered the keepers' dreams; at the eighth hour." He had stressed that, she thought. She knew what her next wish must be.

She gazed upon the stone and said. "I command the governor of the Mist of Darkness to bring himself to me!" She did not know where those words had come from and yet she heard herself sound as though she had spoken them eons ago; when the earth was yet not thought of.

An alarming red mist emerged within the stone; then a face appeared: If a face is what your eyes would want to make of what it was seeing. The countenance of this figure was offensive: to the senses, it was debilitating and it was especially hard on your sight. In simple words, this demon monstrosity was hideous. Mistress Pat imagined; feared really, that what she saw must only be a foretaste of what true Darkness looked like. The beast looked as though it had been boiled at an unfathomable temperature; then had the skin pulled from its flesh: inch by agonizing inch. It was the truest blood red that Pat had ever seen.

In the World of Spanton, they know him as Devy: Master of the True Mist of Darkness. Ruler of the Underground, some angels refer to it as the Devil's Playground: and not that bullshit you see on cable. He is the catcher of souls for Mistress Pat. His Army of Dark Angels is a nightmare that you would never want to experience. At the eighth hour, his army is unleashed and it cannot be quelled with anything but souls. The torment and havoc that they cause, readers, I shudder. I have born witness and I cringe now in remembrance. For those of you who still do not believe: you will. In the end, everyone will come to believing: knowing what I know now, you should have done what was asked of you. It was a very simple task he asked of you; but the non-believers will learn when it is too late.

Hell is a real domain. It is not what we have been taught to believe. Your shameful tongues lack the dexterity needed and your written language the alphabets required to call it by its true and rightful name. You as people talk and write to understand each other. So stagnant in your development are you. Newsflash readers! Talking and writing is archaic to true intelligent life. For the sake of your own understanding (mine too if truth be told) I will call it Section Zero. Section zero is a burning star. A star that has burned prior to the existence of time and is the size of a million Jupiter's. Imagine what I tell you next; there are a billion stars spanning across your universe. To add to the vastness of that, there are a billion more universes containing their own infinite number of stars. All cradled in their own existence of dark matter. I'll pose the question; as I'm sure you have." How can you walk around there on Earth and not see something so massive?" Simple. It all exists beyond your existence. You can only see what lies right next door to you, and then most of it through a haze. It takes your most expensive technology just to catch an x-ray of infrared light from the next galaxy. Even then, that light is from hundreds of eons of light years ago. Section Zero is a realm in another universe where the souls of the people of earth go. It is an autopsy of the good you brought and the evil you fabricated upon your world. You call your planet Earth; it was given a true name before you were ever thought of. The Book of Spanton recognizes your protector as Aissen.

Why do people die and go to such a place you ask. Why judgment, child. Judgment. Everything that you have done in your life must be accounted for. To some, that thought may be comforting for they have lived lives of peace and goodwill; but to others, the thought is a nightmare. Vlad the Impaler, Manson, Hitler, Caligula and Dahmer to name a few. The screams of those whose tortured souls will never rest yell out from Section Zero. In whatever manner, all souls must be explored. I tell you this readers, not to scare you; because many of you believe in Christianity and know from its teachings that your soul is lost. You do not have the fortitude of character to pass thru the "Pearly Gates." You flagellate yourself on a daily occurrence for your transgressions. I can only explain to you so much at this time and I will tell you this now; what has been told to you from just twenty centuries ago is not complete. Complete is sadly a generous understatement.

In Section Zero, souls are analyzed with a harsh exactness and a fortuitous understanding of how circumstances may not allow you to: "Turn the other cheek." Mercy and Forgiveness are present and are granted insofar as they are merited. For example; a beautiful angel that has guided me thru part of my change was Zelma. Her kindness and gentleness were a refuge for me when I was most afraid of what I was becoming. Who would restrict this saint from fulfilling her greatest glory because of the fact that during her time on Earth; she had had to murder a man that had drug her to the top floor of an abandoned building for the soul premise of raping and killing her. She had fought and pushed the man from the window: he plummeted to his death. She had been a young woman then, reared with the strictest Catholic principles; forty years went by and she passed from your universe with the self indoctrinated knowledge that she would be going to hell because she could never be cleansed of that immortal sin. The commandment that; "Thou shall not kill" doesn't advise you on those extreme circumstances, though, does it? Was it his fault or her sin?

People who retell their account of near-death experiences describe going through a spiraling tunnel: a passageway hurtling them ceaselessly towards a dazzling powerful light. The events of their life, zooming past in incredible speed. They recount feeling as though they were being presented with knowledge about not only their own life; but the universe as well. How will you feel when your life is reviewed, your soul scoured?" What feelings of joy, shame and pain will race by as if they'd occurred not more than five seconds ago? Even transgressed memories are awakened; you would know everything that has happened to you: from the traumatic pain of being born through the womb until the day of your death. Will dread and dismay accompany the tumult of feelings during your passage of what is called a tunnel? Just for your information, that isn't a tunnel. And that ain't no damn bright light!

During a human's living existence, your brain transmits waves that keep this world and others closed. Once these waves cease to emit, it means you're dead. Myriads of differing spheres, unlike anything on earth open for you. Of course, physical form is useless. I am referring to what you call your soul. Your immaterial essence. It gives off the force to open gateways. The creator made souls for one reason. It's the only light in the cosmos that repels against matter itself. Each universe is guided by their own law, just as one of your universe's laws is gravity. The commonality these universes share is in name alone, any similar distinction stops past that. Similar to people; you are all made the same but your physical attributes are uniquely your own. Once in Section Zero, you will then understand that hell is very real.

Once the truth of your existence on Earth has been laid bare, you will be remanded to one of two places. Nueden or Sotterus. For those of you whose belief does not permit entrance to Nueden; The Realm Where I Am Dwells, Sotteros exists. It is the realm of eternal perdition and affliction. The results of judgment can render you incapable of ascension to either of those places. For these souls, there is the Doorway of Any Realm. It allows you to be continuously recycled through the metaverses until you come to the unique awareness regarding the true nature of the universe. In these parallel worlds, our physical forms assume whatever shape suitable to sustain life in its new environment.

You can go to Nueden, Sotteros or Any Realm. Provided that your ticket isn't punched for the one way trip to the Devil's Playground that is. There is some truth to your Bible; for those of you who still don't want to comprehend. Some of the legends relayed within it were told to the authors by those who had direct knowledge of these places; by the previous possessors of the Celestial Stones. The Bible was written so that you could have something to believe in; to keep you on the right path and to keep control over your fears about death. At the time of its publication, your world was mad. The Bible was the sustenance of life. Plagues and wars. Poverty and famine were prominent concerns of everyday life. Upsurges and civil unrest were a ruler's imminent threat. Rome ruled; and what was the punishment for not believing. Think of The Crusades. For some time it was either believe or give up your life; and by the way: Your Damned! Whatever life you had, religion was your answer and like tits to babes, you suckled it and passed on its wisdom and solace to your offspring. Even today, in your time; what you call your bible is the greatest book ever sold on your planet.

Mistress Pat stood next to the stone and Devy materialized inside it." GOOD LORD, WHAT THE HELL!" The mistress screamed. "Shit, not again". Devy said. "Are you here to serve me?" "Yes Master, you and only you. You are the new owner of the Hubriser stone." "Where is my new slave Carmen?" She asked. "YOU MEAN THAT FANTASY BITCH WHO CALLS HERSELF CARMEN DREAMS?! SHE JUST USED US FOR PRACTICE! HER SPELLS ARE BEYOND BELIEF!" Devy yelled. "You have seen her? Where is she? Bring her to me." The Master ordered. "She's in your bedroom, waiting for your command my mistress." The red mist filled the stone and Devy faded away.

My readers, my soul was taken by the Hubriser Stone and absorbed into its outer reaches and transformed. The abomination I have become is the only problem. The Angel of Dreams always was the owner of the Spanton Spells. When the Replacer signs the scroll, they must fulfill this roll of power. Mistress Pat exerted her power in an unparallel fashion. She made her first wish be for a new Angel of Dreams. Even when the Stone of the Hubriser is signed for by its new Replacer; I will always be accursed to live the nightmare of knowing the truth about life. I will never have any rest, for me there is no respite. When my Mistress wished upon the stone and said. "I wish for a new Angel of Dreams." she changed the essential nature of this Seraphim's role in the metaverses. Prior to her wish, the Angels responsibilities followed the possessor of the Hubriser Stone. Now I am Immortal. The Immortal First Seraphim of Dreams. As long as there are people or beings to dream, I will exist. My mistress still has the title Angel of Dreams; but lost the ability to know the truth. My Masters will be many. The Heavens don't want me and Hell fears me. I will dwell indefinitely in time with the power of Spanton in me because of my mistress's inadvertent imprecation. By doing this she lost the Gift of Knowing yet she still possesses the power of the cosmos. Who I Believe to Be God knows she got the better deal. She was just saving her own ass; thinking of Carlos and Sonya. Under the circumstances, I kind of understand. But really, under the circumstances; I'd give anything to not have rung that goddamn doorbell! Knowing the truth about life is lonely and scary!

I know you must be wondering thus far, "Is what she telling me just some fantastic story spun together by some crazy nypmho?" Sorry to tell you ladies and gents, the shit ain't even started to hit the fan! The metaverses is a place you are ill equipped for at this time. You ask me how I know, have faith, I know! I live a new nightmare every night. At ten forty-four pm the door to my dreams opens until six forty four am. Mistress Pat is commanded to feed the portal for The Them! Since every universe has been created; it is commanded that every universe must feed it. Be it by using the power of persuasion, coercion, trickery or downright deceit, the portal must be fed. This is for the sole purpose of your evolution. Sometime things must be adjusted: even humans. The dreamer must be kept in my dreams past the eighth hour. Those lost by lust and fantasy, those who don't realize that the Eighth Hour has fell upon them, are doomed. Before Mistress Pat's communion with the Stone of the Hubriser, she had never been malicious or evil. She secretly delights in those who escape and she has intervened when it was demanded upon her. Those who fall prey, she keeps. Keeping them in a secret chamber not knowing what to do with them. She has monopolized the balance of the cosmos and The Them have taken notice. You humans are a communicating part of parallel universes. The Them roam the greater edges of what you can conceive of and they are the Creators and owner of your universe. You are but an experiment; descendants of terrestrial hitchhikers, who too had to succumb to The Truth. They track, your desires, wants, progress and they are who judge you upon your transcendence to Section Zero. If you are lucky then your soul will move on to Nueden. And my mistress hasn't given up one soul yet. The Them's vengeance, my master caused it upon herself because she wanted to do the right thing and try to save people's souls. Why can't your soul just go straight to heaven? Who gives these creatures the right to touch your souls? The Them bring into existence things you can't even think of. THEY ARE WHO ALLOCATE YOUR SOUL FOR EXPLORATION!

Mistress Pat reserves the lost for herself. On the premise that she is keeping them safe from The Them. Her dungeon is deep, and in its bowls lie the hordes of those who forgot where they were dreaming. Those who slept, who dreamt past the forsworn time and were consumed. The very state of their eternal being was the price. If my deepest desire was being entertained; would I also lose out to the mist? Would you my reader, would You? My Master has devised me as the plaything for very, very rich people. Heads of state, kings and queens parade through my mistress' halls for the chance of entering my slumber. And it is often those most powerful who have the most deepest and treacherously rooted of passions. At the eighth hour of my dreams, I hear these disgusting vermin's wails for Jesus salvation and I am appalled.

My mistress forgot that Bailey had warned her: She must keep feeding the portal with humans or The Them will come for the stone and her. I fear that it's too late. In spite of my mistress forgetfulness; she has a pretty good gig going on for herself here. It profits her greatly that I permit guest's to enter my dreams. She has been dealing with this curse for three weeks on Earth. People must know! You must stay close to the world's oceans! Get to the shore! After writing this scroll I won't be safe in my world. I am Immortal and torture can last a really, really long time. The compassion for you, who I once was is great. I cannot allow you to blindly weather the storm to come completely unknowing. Why do I have to be the one to go and completely piss off the powers that be?

Mistress Pat walked upstairs towards her bedroom. A gust of wind stirred throughout the mansion. The spirits were restless this night. The treacherous sound of whisperers plotting could be heard throughout the walls of her home. She opened the bedroom door and saw me lying in a coffin of what appeared to be just glass; It was six feet long and four feet wide with armored diamond Plexiglas that was one inch thick. All trimmed in the purest of gold. Mistress Pat watched while I slumbered. My dreams render me in an incapacitated state of bliss or stuck in the most whorish of nightmares. My rest cannot be disturbed; only my master can awaken me from my slumber. Friends, I have started to carry a small bead of hope. I will share it with you; please don't think of me as foolish. What if I could somehow manage to wake from my slumber. I could possibly go onto Nueden too, yes? I know it is just a mad hope. I am in my infancy as the Seraphim of Dreams and though I know everything; I am ignorant as to how to pull this all together for my own cause. There has never been an Angel of Dreams in my predicament and therefore all of the previous knowledge I am keen to is useless. The mistress gazed into my sleeping box. Dressed in nothing but a black bra and black panties with one red rose between my legs; I was a feast for her eyes. My hands were locked in the Golden Handcuffs, crossed in front of my vagina. I felt her approach and telepathically opened the kinetic door that barred any unwanted into my chamber. I anticipated seeing the look in my Mistress' eyes as she beheld me truly, for the very first time. She was my owner and as long as she possessed The Hubriser Stone, my most desire was to please her. I opened my eyes and asked; "HOW MAY I SERVE YOU MASTER, WHAT IS YOUR PLEASURE?" My masters' reply was," Wow this is awesome! So I see you learned pretty fast my slave." So delighted was I that she had noticed my change, that I floated! I floated right out of my glass bed; I sprouted my bright wings of light and came to kneel at the foot of my new Master!

"I was trained by the Four Celestial Stones of the Cosmos master." "Tell me what you saw and all you know! I must know; please tell me!" She pleaded. "Dear mistress, it hurts my heart to hear your supplications. In time, you will know all. You need not beg." Just as I have been seasoned by the Celestial Stones, so must you. My tempering was able to be accomplished because I was whisked away into the mist. Your brain cannot tolerate the levity of what you are to learn. It is part of my obligation that no ill will befalls you and if I tell you what you are anxious to know, you would go mad." "You weren't gone that long, I wouldn't put it at more than ten minutes, what happened?" She asked. "Please forgive me Master. I had to go away for seven weeks of training. The World of Spanton time is much faster than what exists here on Earth. This planet is moving at the fraction of a snail's pace; this is why the advancement of Earth's people is so gradual." I explained. "Seven weeks!" She yelled. "Yes Master, people could be in my dreams for weeks and it would only be eight hours here on Earth." "Wow that's amazing Carmen; my dearest, I'm sorry I had to do this to you but I had no choice." "For what I have become I cannot thank you enough my mistress." "Good; the first guests will be arranged to arrive tomorrow evening. Your services will be extended and the remuneration I will receive will be great! Paul!" My mistress summoned the butler. He scurried in from the hall into the library. Certainly he had never been more than ten feet away. "Yes Mistress." He said straightening his tie. If I had not been gazing besotted at my Mistress when she spoke those next words from her kissable mouth, I would have thought they were words that had escaped from the bowels of Sotterus. They were; "Prepare my dungeon!" "Yes Mistress Pat." "Oh and Paul." "Yes Mistress." "Pull up your zipper, what were you doing?" "Forgive me master." Flushed a deep, scarlet red, Paul rushed hastily from the room.

Mistress Pat looked deep into my eyes. "You are so beautiful my slave. Take off your bra and panties, now! I want you to service me." "Yes Master, whatever you demand." As she entered my chamber; I bid the door to close. She blew the Hell's Curse inside around us from her finger and I had my way with her flesh. I creamed myself; I savagely ripped every piece of cloth from her body: the last piece being her French silk panties. Then I savored her; cell by cell I ravished her. I fell upon her nipples with a hunger that stole her breath away. Gently biting those two mounds, I suckled from her while my hands explored. Her body guided me to her utmost fulfillment; my long fingers plunged in and out of her hot; melting butter. With the tenderness of a virgin exploring her husband's body for the first time; I sought to touch the fiber of her very womanhood. I grinded my soft mold into hers. If I wanted I could create myself the right equipment to give it to my mistress. And good! I caressed her slick juicy folds apart to reveal the sweet pearl within and I lapped: I lapped and I drank and she came and she came until spent and exhausted, she pulled from me. The cream of her deliciousness was spread across my face and I much like a kitten, licked every savory drop from my whiskers. What sort of perversion we've become in this mansion?

Done allowing me to fulfill her, we slept in the bed of glass until six forty-four am. The Door to my dreams is now closed. After I had blissfully fell asleep in my mistress's arms, I had dreamt. The madness that perpetuated itself is unforgettable. Twenty four years on Earth for me were useless, they taught me nothing. Scientists would like to make you think that you are the Masters of this Universe that Earth is spinning around in. Maybe it's man's ego that keeps them from accepting the stark naked truth. And that truth is that you're not even able to knock on the door of the next galaxy over. Your so called space ships can't make it to Mars and your hopes for reaching the known edges of your own existence are nonexistent. What really makes us laugh in Spanton is when you humans say. "We need evidence about life in outer space." How about just some damn common sense. Can you really be so stupid to believe you're the only ones. Your so stuck on your self! I'm sorry, forgive me. You are the monkeys on the missile waving your own hairy asses' goodbye. Do you really think that your the best we can do? You have no clue as to what is really going on around you. Our intellectual superiors have no doubt that you are a virus to the Earth. Just a Petri dish of specimens, all waiting your turn for examination. And until they are done with their "testing", that just the way they are going to keep it!

Scripture 8: The Dead Descend

Mistress Pat listened to my slow and rhythmic breathing. She herself was dazed and fatigued. The events of the last ten hours in her life had left her spent. "My wish came true." she said and she fell into the most blessed sleep a human can have: and she dreamt. She dreamt she was surrounded by a wall of glass. To her left and right was dense tropical foliage. The heavy perfumes of the blossoms were intoxicating. Under her feet, baby pink sand caressed her bare; red-painted toes. She was planted to that spot however and she could not turn around and see what was behind her: only in front. Somehow she knew the danger; if any, did not loom elsewhere. She just stood there looking out at the most oppressively dark and ominous sea. She watched it froth and boil as though heated from the depths of Hell; the water parted: What emerged out of that roiling cauldron was a malformation of nature. The beast had seven heads and ten horns and upon those horns were crowns. The seven heads each had ten mouths and out of those mouths, utter blasphemies were screamed! Mistress Pat screamed as though her immortal being had been stabbed. She arose out of my diamond chamber and knew what must be done.

The mistress summoned Paul and James to her office. She told them most of what had transpired over the past several hours and that I was now a permanent figure in her home. I was to be given whatever I needed. She also gave them a choice. Mistress Pat could not conceive of what would very soon befall her but she knew that she had a moral right to give them the choice to either stay with her or leave. If they stayed, they would be paid handsomely. More money than either man could spend in both of their lifetimes. But if they chose to leave, they must leave immediately with the oath to never return and to never speak of anything they had seen: both men stayed. Paul, genuinely caring for his Mistress; refused the sum of money and pledged to her his loyal service. James, a much more practical man, took the money. Mistress Pat was thankful both stayed not caring what personal choice helped them come to their individual decisions. She trusted them to a great degree and she would rather have those she already trusted in her employ than have to find a new driver. Paul was irreplaceable by her estimates and she was silently stunned by his refusal of the most money he would ever be offered in his life: maybe Paul loved his mistress more then she know. She hoped both had made the wisest choice and thought of the dream she had had and shivered.

My Mistress has decided that she would not allow any souls to go to The Them. She would sell my dreams to the highest bidder but she would not permit the desecration they would havoc. The souls of the succumbed would go to the dungeon. The Them be damned! Bailey had told her that she must collect souls but he didn't say one damned thing about giving them over. If a person wanted to pay handsomely to take their own life into their own hands, that was up to them. Mistress Pat alerted the elite that they could live their ultimate fantasy. Under one condition; they must pick a charity and donate to them two million dollars. To Mistress Pat, money was useless. She had more that she would ever spend in a lifetime. She wanted to be sure that any gains would go to help a starving family, a needy child. No matter how much she gave, more was needed and more like her to make a dent in the depravity most of the world lived in. While many of these same elite were too stingy to even drop a nickel in the cup of the homeless; these same sounded the most interested in throwing a hefty sum down the drain for eight hours of their own ecstasy. They would soon learn that every wish isn't meant to be granted.

The weeks that followed in the mansion were a blur. During the day; I served my Mistress happily; while at night, the paying customers came and maybe went. One of the first of those who had entered my dreams, battled The Mist and lost. His soul went to the underground prison but his body was left deader than a doornail in Mistress Pat's library. My Mistress had planned carefully, but she hadn't planned on being stuck with getting rid of dead bodies. It would have been kind of hard to call nine-one-one. I mean, what could she have said; "Yes, I'd like the coroner to come and pick up a body." No, I don't think so. So she had wished upon The Stone of the Hubriser and had wished to have the bodies disappear from her existence. I fear her wish wasn't exact enough however. You see, the stone requires precise clarification; just as in my dreams. She didn't say where she wanted those bodies to vanish to and what would follow my Masters omission, shook the world. She never questioned where they went just as long as they continued to go away.

Maybe by some reprehensible cosmic wit or divine intent, that first body landed in a cornfield in Grand Island, Nebraska. The farmer and his family were out harvesting their crop before the heavy frosts were to arrive and a man's body fell within ten feet of where they were plowing. Fell right out of the sky. They saw him come out of a hole in the air and then his body hit the ground; the body's arms and legs were twisted and broken and bones protruded everywhere. Blood splattered the field. The farmer's wife ran and called the police. A statement was taken from them and the local chief chalked it up to yokels who had probably been hitting the still too hard. The medical examiner did the autopsy and reported the cause of death as unknown. It was clear that the body had sustained severe trauma due to the blunt force of hitting the ground; he could not identify the cause of death. He was dead way before he landed: rigor mortis had set in. His prints came back in the database and the name that came back was Reginald Ware.

Ware was a cad turned widower- millionaire due to the accidental deaths of all three of his past wives. He was under extreme scrutiny for the death of the last woman who had committed accidental suicide by mixing her blood pressure medication and nitroglycerin. The fact that she was seventy and had been taking her meds successfully for ten years is what struck the light bulb for the Memphis Police Department. Well that and that her family outright accused him of their loved ones murder. Until then, they had just come and collected the bodies of his other two victims without so much as batting an eye. He was spending his ill-begotten gains earnestly when he got wind of Carmen Dreams. He knew his luck was running out and that the nosy detectives would be back: back and asking questions. So he wanted to go into my dreams and escape. He was warned by Mistress Pat about the time limit and the Mist. He ignored everything she said. He thought to himself. "This whore ain't nothing but a power drunk cunt and if I wasn't already running, I'd kill this bitch and take all her fucking dough." He was a real scumbag. My mistress was delighted when his soul was sent to her prison. She would have a very good time with him: Yes, a very good time indeed!

The second case got full media attention and over the two weeks that followed, bodies fell out of holes all over the globe. Runway Nine of the Sea-Tac Airport, within the walled enclaves of Vatican City, on the flight deck of the Russian naval ship Admiral Kuznetsov and on the Gaza Strip, bodies descended from the sky. Millionaire after millionaire found sometime a week or two after they "went missing". The media dubbed it the Descended Corpses Phenomena. There was yet another body found and when his home was investigated his wife was found tucked safely in her bed. But her decomposing body was estimated to have been there for at least a week. Everyone all over the world was looking up. Watching the sky to see where the next body would fall. Mistress Pat turned on the TV one day and was stunned. One body fell into the propellers of a cargo plane barreling down the runway for takeoff. The world was stunned beyond belief. Religious fanatics were out in full force proclaiming it to be a telling of the woes to come. She did not allow the Stone to fill in the blank again. None of what was going on could be connected to her; she didn't feel bad in the least bit that some of the most degrading people had met their ends. That's what happens when you battle with the Mist of Darkness!

Those patrons who wished to live their deepest fulfillment in my dreams made the most insane and impractical of wishes. One of them was a very kind and generous man. He had been married for twenty years to his childhood sweetheart; she had complained incessantly through the years that he was too docile in bed and always asked him to do things to her that he was to ashamed to even contemplate. He wasn't the "animal" she needed. He came to me and wished to mate with his wife in whatever primal manner he could. He wished to ravish her. He or she I should say, didn't get what they bargained for. So devoured was he in consuming her he morphed into a wolf. Yes; literally, he shape-shifted. Consume her is exactly what he did: Bite by bite, he ate his wife until nothing was left but her shiny four karat wedding ring. Tears fell from his wolfen gaze as he tore his wife to shreds. The gore and blood was everywhere. Shreds of her hung from the ceiling fan of their bedroom and her blood stained the walls. He stayed past the eighth hour in my dreams and now my Mistress has both of their souls.

The blood of many has been absorbed by the mansion; the mansion itself became some sort of encasement for the cosmos: but not all make thoughtless wishes. A little boy who had been adopted by a very wealthy man, longed to see his birth mother. She had died during his birth and he yearned to know what she looked like. His was a good life and he wanted for nothing but his adopted father never stopped harping on the fact that he was adopted. Therefore, this little boy would never be good enough and that is all he most desperately wanted to be. Good enough for his real mother. He ran away from home and I found him wandering out in my Masters gardens. His wish was to be loved and cared for by what would have been his beloved mother. I laid him upon the soft moss and rose petals and covered his face with my palms; he went into an innocent slumber and there he embraced his mother and had his tears assuaged and his fears allayed. He was plenty enough for her and she endowed in him that knowledge. So that it would last him for the rest of his life and he wouldn't walk through the world apprehensive because of his adopted father's shortcomings. When he awoke from his nap, I had James drive him home. The glow in this boy's face brought tears to my eyes.

Three weeks went by so swiftly that it makes me dizzy. It was November 30th when my car stopped. When Mistress Pat signed for The Stone of the Hubriser. I remember now getting out of my car and having my assent up the driveway be lit by the full moon above with lightening blazing in the sky. I had originally thought it could be an electrical storm since both my phone and my car stopped. Now I possess the knowledge of all and I know that wasn't a storm. Twenty one days to most but to me, an eternity. I live ahead of your time: or behind it. The space-time continuum is of no consequence to me. Picture all of the cars on a typical busy freeway during morning rush-hour. Those cars are all passing each other. Each going at a different rate of speed. Time is kind of like that in the cosmos. Everything that exists in the universe is going at its on speed and therefore has its own time. It's easy to imagine on a planetary level but imagine all that on a super galactic level. Really all you have to do is be able to bring the realms together within each other; then your mixing the speeds of time. Damn! I'm sorry; you can't do that. I wish last night could be undone. I wish my guest would had wished for anything other than what she had. What right, what nerve had she to utter the forbidden wish of Spanton? But wish she did, and I can't wish it undone. I must live forever in this ruined world while peril lies ahead. Prophecy is perpetuating itself as we speak. Life on Earth will soon meet with an abrupt end. Some will survive what is to come because when he returns he will leave your souls for The First Ones. You'll survive seeing all that you love is decimated. I have ensured my Mistress' survival. The curse of Remembrance will be emblazoned upon her and any others who last or be reborn. Things are coming to pass that cannot be changed. My nightmares are real. I exist in them as I do here and live out the outcome with those who have entered my sleep. You must stay close to the waters!

Mistress Pat's driver James was an intoxicating man to behold. His possessed abs that made you weep and an ass that made you bite your cheek to keep you from grabbing it. Six feet and one inch tall worth of meat in good hard condition. He was as handsome as he was built and his long wavy blond hair fell down to caress the nape of his neck. His emerald green eyes were quite a contrast to the tan of his bronzed skin and the undulating golden mass of silken mane. He knew that he had been blessed and when he walked it made you wonder if he could move that way in bed. Stripper turned driver, he was now a real playboy and lived in the opulence that my master provided. To him, he has the best job in the world and in his leisure time; he works extra hard for his tips. Whatever favors he does for my Mistress isn't really my concern but I would be lying if I said I was not jealous when she has him summoned to her. At any time of day he would come, as fodder for my Mistress. But after the first soul committed suicide in my dreams rather than let the Mist have them; the mansion has been frequented at night by tormented apparitions. Now, he will only come to the house before dusk and no further than the stairs leading to the entrance. Even though his master commands him, he didn't change his mind. I don't blame him really. At night those damned souls escape the dungeon and roam the mansion. As I remember; it's what you humans call haunted.

I know some of you survivors think I'm raving mad! I'm not telling this testimonial to scare you; but I would be afraid if I were you. I'm telling it to try and save your soul on that horrible last day of life as you know it! The day of forgiveness! December twentieth, two thousand twelve. Let me tell you about this Last Historical Holy Night.

Scripture 9: My Last Three Guest's

At ten o'clock last night three limos pulled up. James drove the first which contained Judy Clark. She was daddy's little rich girl and he had lavished her at birth with the best that money could buy. She had whined at the airport that the limo wasn't a hummer stretch and that it also didn't have any Bling H2O in it. Her blue eyes and ash blond hair accentuated her five-seven height and her Barbie dollish figure. Just turned twenty-one she was a party girl and after popping two ecstasy pills; she was steaming in her panties. She already knew what she wanted her wish to be. She would wish for a hot night of carnal sex with a man who was big. Just thinking about it made her cross and uncross her legs: she licked her lips in anticipation.

The second limo brought Rick Stanville to my masters' domain. A wealthy media mogul by his mid-thirties he was the golden boy of South Beach. It was only his money that attracted women and more often than not he hired out to receive the services he desired. He was an average looking guy. Only five-nine with an average body; his hair was a glossy black that he wore in a mushroom cut, complete with bangs. All that glossy black hair was glorified by the paleness of his gossamer skin. His mother had left them when he was so young he couldn't even remember her and if she was good or kind didn't matter to him. The fact that she had abandoned him with a raging alcoholic that beat him incessantly growing up was all he needed to know. He was always told during the beatings that it was for the glory of God or he had sinned against The Father. He was beating the evil out of Rick and when the nun's at school weren't instilling in him what the true meaning of a sacramental life to the Church meant, his father was sure to follow. Rick had grown into a man who needed to have his sexual appetite sated in a very strange nature. His close friends would call him an average guy who liked to have a good time. While behind private doors; his greatest desire was to be punished with the severity he deserved. His money, the house the car all deserved punishment. His very desire to be tortured and suffer deserved retribution. His wish would be to receive his ultimate punishment!

The last limo carried the diva herself, Amber Stone. Readers, I was so excited that she was coming and I was so going to love getting her autograph. I was listening to her new single "Unhuman" when the car died; Sorry got carried away, back to the main subject - Amber. She was a Latino goddess. Golden bronze skin was accentuated by her long brown curls. They trailed the length of her slender back and stopped at the round curve her bottom. A petite something; she was breathtaking to behold with the voice of an angel. And a body that could make a person's mouth water. A millionaire many times over, she's not looking for Mr. Right. She looking for The Truth. All her life she remembers seeing strange lights in the skies over her family's home in Santiago, Chile. She had told her mother of what she used to see and she would be admonished for it. Told to stick to her lessons so that she could be an accomplished young woman for a suitable man. Amber's mother thought that a man would be the only way to her real happiness because she had wasted all of the ability she had gifted to her daughter on her philandering husband. But Amber believed what she saw. She believed with all her heart that we were not alone. She wanted to see one of the "others" for herself. No it was more than that: she wanted to see the Creator of All.

The decision for me to write this scroll was made with great levity. My original intent was to publish my journal as an autobiography. However, the combined efforts of Rome, Israel and the government in North America ensured that would not be so. It had to be addressed as fiction or not be addressed at all. What you don't yet understand but I am certainly going to tell you; is that everything has already transpired. You are already dead in my time. It has all taken place in your galaxies future. You are like a DVD that has been rewound and set on slow-play. Just for Their own amusement. Your life, your own world's demise has already taken place. None of this was by Chance. You are not here by accident nor did you crawl out of the primordial ooze and evolve into upper class apes! Adam and Eve were a noble attempt to give a more religious and noble heritage to your background but even that falls short of the inherent actuality of man's just purpose on your Protector; solar system and galaxy. But all of your history, lore and religion has real roots that lead you back to the divine plan for you that was created from the beginning.

I am not alone in my quest to lift the veil from your eyes and there will be more Principalities of Enlightenment from Spanton whose writings will help awake your sleeping planet. We are of third hierarchy to I AM and we will face and endure with his courage what is to come. All of this will very soon be gone. It has been ordained in the divine Book of Spanton of The Parousia! THE RETURN OF SENZOVAL! PLEASE YOU MUST KNOW THAT IT IS NOT MY INTENT TO DISRESPECT ANYONES RELIGIOUS BELIEF! I have metamorphosed into something inconceivable in your plane of existence and come to acknowledge the ultimate reality of my being! I breath and exist at my current masters behest but my true owner has always been I AM. The experiences of all the prior possessors is at my disposal. How could anyone human make up such a fantastic story. Please let me uncover one other mystery for you. Have you ever felt déjà vu before? Like you had experienced an event; said something or been somewhere yet you know you never had. Well, It's not a feeling. You were there before. Time was simply turned back and you have no control over the momentum of this all. This happens because man was given free well. Sometimes you make the wrong move in your life that upsets the written story of life itself. When you meet a friend walking down the street, you might stop and talk or keep walking and wave. If you stop and talk you could of just saved or killed yourself or them: meaning if the person kept walking they could have been hit by a speeding car out of control crossing the street. Now if this happens and it was written for that person to die on this day or you: may I add. Both of you will feel déjà vu; and do it all over again until you get it right. This time one of you will die by that speeding car. Also your soul could have been there before and not your current body. Some souls are over a million years old. If The Them suddenly decided to pick up the remote so to speak; right now and fast forward the earth: you would all be fucked. You just live with it not knowing, not feeling a thing. You must come to believing what I tell you on your own. If nothing of what I have told you thus far is conceivable, plausible to within some degree; then you are but an ostrich with his or her head in the sand. Your ass a ready target for those monkey's on a missile I told you about earlier.

Paul went down to meet the guests in the driveway. It was going to be a very busy night for them and me as well. I was going to bring three people into my dreams this night. My mistress had been overwhelmed with requests from people seeking to act out their most carnal cravings. She had only been allowing one person to enter my dreams at a time; sometimes two if the spouse came to me as well. But never three separate people enacting three different desires. I haven't really been allowed to show off my skills to my Mistress and I truly wanted to impress her. Rick and Amber exited their limo first. Paul looked disgusted and shook his head sadly. He said to himself. "That damn James, can't he think with his brain for once and not that monster between his legs. I hope the Mistress catches him." Through the ajar window he could see James pounding Judy from behind. She was on her knees on the floor of the car with all that ash blond hair thrown over the seat. James must not have been given it to her hard enough because she grabbed his behind and made him plunge ever more furiously into her hole. He brought her in one long drive that made the limo rock back and forth from the intense force of it. Paul took the other guest to the mansion, when she pulled herself off his still hard manhood; swiveled around and started giving him what looked to be some pretty mean head. All the time, he was just shaking his head and wondered when was the last time he had a decent blowjob. Meanwhile, my mistress was in the library talking to The Great Devy.

The mist and the stone were one and its radiance bathed the library in an amber haze. How could sheer terror look so beautiful. Not Devy readers; just the haze. He is an ugly motherfucker! "Master we have a problem." Devy said. "Tell me my slave, damn hurry up and go away with that face!" Mistress Pat yelled. "The Them my master, they know that you have not been giving them their rightful souls." "GOOD LORD, WHAT SHOULD I DO!" "Tonight they are on a journey to your vicinity with the specific purpose of collecting the souls you owe them. The battle that is to be waged in Carmen's Dreams tonight will be legendary. This will be the epic battle where creatures of light and darkness will face off in final combat. The war that is foretold of in the pages of the human's Bible!" There was a gleam in Devy's hideous eyes that made my blood run cold. He was the Master of the Devil's Playground and when the battle starts, I know which side he will align himself. He is trapped as the servant of the Possessor of the Hubriser Stone. It was shown to me how Devy became to be trapped in his position and I do not want to be anywhere around when he meets back up with his true master; but I will be. His blood will rain down and scorch the earth!

When Rick and Amber converged together at the base of the stairwell, they stood awestruck. They were both money, mostly new; and this large imposing beast of a residence was nothing any of them had ever seen. My mistress had always prized her anonymity more than the spotlight and she placed extreme care in keeping her home private. The steep staircase leading up to the main house offered complete assurance that no nosy paparazzi could glimpse her from across the street. There were no residences directly across; behind or next door to the mansion and two huge gates further protected my mistress's secrecy. Amber stared up at the four pillars and shivered. They looked to her like the teeth of some huge imposing beast waiting to swallow her whole. She was awakened from this vision when Rick said. "This looks like it's going to be fun." Amber had met a lot of people; she had even had a few stalkers over the course of her career. Something about Rick didn't sit very well with her but she couldn't quite put a finger on it. She had just met the man but still there was this something. She had opined that he must be some stock trader or real estate mogul and thought to herself that she was just being silly. She didn't know anything about this guy and here she was judging him. She hated when the press did that to her, she had sworn to never do it to others. The butler interrupted those talking and James flirting with Judy as he grabbed her ass getting out of the limo when he said," Please follow me this way." Paul escorted the guests up the staircase and into my possessors' sitting room. Judy and James were still straightening their clothes when James asked her "Sweetie, what did you say your name was?". "MY NAME IS JUDY, DAMN! YOU FORGOT THAT FAST!" She yelled. "I'm sorry, I just have a lot on my mind" He said lying. "Lose my number until you can remember!" She stomped off to the mansion. "Wait Janet, shit, Jill I'm sorry." "It's Judy asshole!" She left James with a sarcastic grin on his face.

The front door was gaping open and Judy walked in. She could swear she heard the voice of a circus carney screaming. "Step Right In And Die With Us!" She looked backwards down the staircase and she had the most alarming thought to run back down those stairs; call her dad and get the fuck out of this place. What she did was open her brown and tan Louis bag; took out her Elgin pill case and popped one more Purple Buddha. Ecstasy was hers and she sashayed herself towards the door off the entry hall that had light coming from under it. A breeze stirred down the hall and it carried on it the sound of people suffering. Judy's stopped the clicking of her heels and looked around as if she would see where the voices were coming from. An icy chill ran up her spine and the front door slammed shut. She fastened her pace and knocked on the door where hopefully everyone else would be. Paul opened it and she entered. She told Paul, "You all might want to consider getting that front door fixed." Rubbing her arms as if chilled to the bone she added, " And I think you have something in your vents too or is that part of the spookiness factor here." She laughed but the look on her face was entirely serious. Paul simply told her. "I will do that Ms. Judy, please have a seat." He thought to himself. "This drugged up little whore has no idea."

It was now ten-thirty pm and Mistress Pat entered the room. She was attired in black; tight leather pants with a matching jacket. Going up the side of her legs, the pants were laced in a criss-cross fashion and starting at her ankle to her waist juicy pieces of her flesh peered out. Her succulent breasts were in clear view and the red high heel pumps dug into the lushness of the Persian rug. She had pulled her silken mane up in a severe ponytail and its snakelike coil slithered down her back to an abrupt stop above the round curve of her ass. The pronounced red streaks running through it made it look as though she had been kissed by the Devil. She was Rick's dream bitch and when he laid his eyes upon her, he started to salivate. His erection pressed itself tight against his pants and he shifted uncomfortably in his seat. He couldn't believe that the woman he had spent a lifetime dreaming of was standing here before him. Every detail in his imagination ripped from the pages of his mind and melded into this glorious she-demon who stood before him. He swallowed the acid that rose from his stomach when he thought about the kind of punishment she could deliver and a sweat broke out across his forehead. Those full red lips; her skin the color of coffee drunk on the richest of creams. The flowing raven richness of her hair and the way all that supple leather showed every delicious curve of her round ample ass. Rick had only been with white girls and Spanish chicks. Never a black woman. He had never even looked at one but if Mistress Pat could castigate him with the severity he deserved, he would worship her as a God.

"Good Evening guests. Welcome to my home. I trust Paul has made you all comfortable." Mistress Pat looked around the room and lingered her gaze on Judy. She had seen James and her from the security cameras and he would be dealt with later. She on the other hand would be handled shortly. "Ms. Clark's "delay" has left us insufficient time for cordials and introductions and we only have ten minutes to prepare for the evening to come." She smiled a most menacing smile and said directly to the blushing Judy. "I trust your delay was fortuitous." Directing her focus back to the group, she said "If you would all follow me please." My mistress led them to the elevator where Paul hit the button for the third floor. When all of them had gotten inside; a spirit manifested itself not more than ten feet from the doors. Amber, Rick and Judy stared out at the apparition as it seemingly stared back at them. It was the vision of a woman who was bloody and torn to shreds. Bits and pieces of her seemed to eternally drip down and plop in disgusting heaps on the floor. The ghost moved as if to come into the elevator and all three guests inside it started screaming. Just then the ghost changed into a wolf. The mistress bid the doors to close and the group made the horrible ascent to the third floor shaking in horror and asking the mistress of this haunted mansion. "What the fuck was that!" She told them "We have no time for explanations now. The portal to enter Carmen's Dreams will open before long. If you still wish to speak of such things, do so in the morning when you awake from the dreams of my slave!" The door to the elevator opened and they emerged in a beautifully appointed bedroom. She led them thru her sleeping area and into her dressing room where I slept encased in my bed of glass. I was having a horrible nightmare and I thrashed inside my encasement. As beautiful as Nefertiti, I lay gripped in a vision that was so horrible; I still can't believe it!

It was now ten-forty pm and the guests stood around my protective glass shield and waited for what was to occur next. They looked down on my tawny-gold; supernaturally beautiful body. I had been a knock-out before the change but since then, my beauty was unparalleled. None on earth, not even my idol Amber, could light a candle to me. I am The Seraphim of Dreams. I lay there embellished in nothing more than a black leather micro g-string that covered little else but my clitoris and soaking hole. My breasts were in a bra that matched the panties because all there was to it was the cups. My beautiful breasts were held firmly by twin leather studded cups that only served to keep my twins staring straight ahead. The tan perky nipples pointed out as if they knew all eyes were on them. The black rose that lay between my legs had more material to it and the black polish on my bare toes glistened as though they had been dipped in black blood. I could feel Rick's glaring and his drool hit the glass where my toes lay tantalizing him.

I dreamt I was standing in the Siberian wilderness. Surrounded by huge, ancient trees that were saplings when the dinosaurs had walked the earth. The sounds of living things doing what they have done since the beginning of time filled the night. I looked up into the cloudless, most beautiful night sky and was awestruck at its splendor. A breeze swept through that emptiness and I was overcome by the smell of fresh mown grass and spermatozoa. As I marveled at the ancient grandness of this place: I saw the Soulless Slaves descend from the sky. Armies of expendable waist; not even worth a soul, they roamed the forest side. They are what we Angels call the Walking Dead. I screamed and willed myself to awake from this wretched dream but I made no sound and the infantry passed through me as though I was not standing amidst the wilderness. Bulb-like heads and black almond shaped eyes searched the foreign landscape. I followed them in their pursuit, an unwilling witness to the spectacle displayed before me. We came to within the Tunguska River because I could hear it lapping at the shoreline in the distance. Before my eyes, the beings surrounded a freshly turned patch of earth and a brilliant blue lyre emerged from out of the dirt. It was the most exquisite instrument ever crafted. Legend tells that it was honed by the mighty hand of Zeus as a gift to his daughter, the Muse of Music and that it was made from the branches of the Wishing Tree in Spanton and inlaid with the rarest of lapis lazuli. It flushed a brilliant electric blue glow and bathed us all in a bluish haze. Then an explosion that rivaled Hiroshima one thousand times over shook the stillness. A great fist of heat rushed towards me and its fiery menace was mirrored in my hazel eyes! The Lyre of Eutarpa was destroyed.

I awoke to my mistress telling the guests. "I received all of your wishes and they will be granted in the World of Spanton. You may have a seat, Carmen is now ready to arise from her slumber." Mistress Pat took out the Armatura and opened it. The rays of colors lacking names shined with elaborate profusion! Rick stood up quickly from the armoire and backed away from the stone. He was trying to appear calm and in control but he wasn't doing a very good job. His hands were visibly shaking and beads of sweat were lining his upper lip. I sensed his fear and I knew that the Mist of Darkness smelled it too. Amber just sat there star-struck, staring at all the pretty colors. Judy was bouncing up and down clapping her hands like a little girl who knew it was Christmas morning. The doorway to my dreams manifested itself in front of the fireplace. Rick backed further away and a stricken look of panic now accompanied the sweat on lip and brow. It was now the anointed hour and the inter-dimensional gate to the other planes of existence via my dream-gate is now open!

They were all standing now as I willed my chamber door opened and allowed me passage. I levitated free of my encasement, long flowing hair swinging lazily. Drifting through them suspended by the air alone: I sprouted wings the color of new snow that sparkled with a glittery brilliance. They are my wings of flight and appear only at my behest. As their fluttering strokes disturbed the quiet in the room, they created a wonderful breeze that stirred everyone's hair. I landed among them just like a butterfly landing among the lilies. "HOW MAY I SERVE YOU MASTER,WHAT IS YOUR PLEASURE?' "Carmen, mon ensclave, these are the guests who you shall induce into your dreams tonight" "Your wish is my command master. Everyone, follow me over to the portal."

Like ducks in a row they lined up and followed me over to the mantle. Rick, Amber and Judy. I had done this all before but tonight I had this horrible sense of foreboding. As though tonight, with this group on the twentieth of December in the year twenty-twelve was about to preempt an onslaught of cataclysmic change. I looked at them all and asked. "So, are you all ready to go?" Judy screamed and the shrill ring of it resonated within my very core. As though her throat had uttered what my soul could not! "What is it Judy?" Amber asked. Judy, horror-stricken, was looking at where they had been sitting earlier. "LOOK!" she gasped. They all turned and looked then. Amber exclaimed, "Jesuscristo!" They saw their own bodies all laying back in the chairs: I was in my Diamond Bed asleep. "That looks like us Carmen. Are we, oh my God!" Rick stuttered. So as not to alarm them any further I intervened. "Yes, that is you. Your bodies have gone to sleep, with no harm in my master's home. No damage shall befall you there, unless you stay past the forbidden time. If this happens, your souls will be forfeited and I am sure you all have seen the news. Where your corpses will fall is anyone's guess." The relief on Rick's face that he wasn't dead would have been evident to a blind man. He did however watch all the major news channels and had seen the weird stories about bodies falling from the sky. To hear Carmen admit that she or her master was responsible for that chaos stunned him. He asked Carmen. "So you're saying that if I die living my wish, my body is just going to fall out of the sky in any godforsaken place! What type of crazy shit is that?" "Yes Rick." I said. "But isn't crazy being in this portal now, staring back at yourself lying asleep. Getting ready to go and live the fantasy of your dreams. You didn't think it would be simple as that did you?" I laughed at him in pity because he had no idea what tonight had in store for him; but at that moment, neither did I. "Wow! This shit is fucking crazy!" Judy said giggling. Still tripping on her never ending supply of drugs. "Please touch my wings so you can float. We must go to the Wishing Tree in The World of Spanton." They all touched my wings at the exact same moment. A vision of blood falling to the earth and thirty-three flaming mountains falling into the sea assaulted my mind. The sharp loud cries of the persecuted screamed inside my head and the innocence of children taken away. A menacing dread chilled me to the bone.

I accessed the part of my mind that allows me to telekinetically communicate with my master and said. "Master, may I speak to you." "Of course, my pet. Speak" In a torrent of emotions and words I showed her my visions and said "I fear that something horribly tragic will occur this night. I have foreseen the future, my mistress." "Carmen, they are aware of my break with universal law. They know of my outright refusal to feed the soul portal and they are coming for me" she told me. I would fight in the depths of hell to purge my mistress from its bowels, if necessary. It was my duty to protect her from all harm. "Who my master?" I implored her to tell me but I fear I already knew. "The Them." She said. "They're coming for the souls I have secreted away in my dungeon; those I keep to prevent them from being inflicted with pain by The Mist. Carmen, there must be a way that I can prevent these creatures from accomplishing their task." My master was sitting in her boudoir, staring at herself in a round oval mirror wondering how the hell she had allowed this madness to contemplate itself. She tossed her raven mane back from her shoulder with a defiant stance as though the decision she had made to defy The Them was final. I said to her. "Master, I keep having pernicious visions about the end of days for the humans of earth. Is there anything we can do to help them?" My mistress could hear the desperation in my voice. If there was any way I could fend off the evil to come, I would. The finality in my Master's voice was heartbreaking. She told me. "I'm sorry Carmen, but it's written in the scroll of Spanton. What is to come has been in motion since the beginning of life on this planet. It may be that I have helped to accelerate the natural course of things by bringing The Them's awareness upon me; but I am not the cause or the effect of the rules at play here on this Earth. I have read some of the Scroll until I could not read anymore and in its pages, the future of us all was laid bare." I gleamed from her defeated tone and the sound of tears in her throat that any hope I had was futile. She told me further that. "Nothing can change the earth's fate! He's Coming Back!" I already knew the truth but I needed to hear it from someone else to believe it. This has all happen before and going to happen again. It's like you're a movie; they can watch the earth for four billion years and rewind. Just like you do your favorite movie and watch it again: later on I'll explain about the illusion of Time.

Now it's time to lead my guests through the portal and towards the Great Tree of All knowledge that has lived forever in the center of Spanton's realm. "What's wrong Carmen" my mistress have asked. I saw her there, my seductive enchantress sitting in the mirror and all of a sudden I was overwhelmed by a keen sense of loss and I feared that nothing would ever be the same again. I told my seductive enchantress. "I am filled with fear my beloved possessor." "What are you afraid of mon cherie?" She was still trying to sweet talk me even though she knew the shit was about to hit the fan. "I fear my mistress, that I may never come to you again." A fierce gleam ignited then within her and I saw that she would fight for me as ardently as I would fight for her. She told me." I'll do whatever I can to help you my dear, you use all the power you have at your disposal and get your sexy ass back here!" Mistress Pat knew what I was talking about. We both saw the same thing in our minds but dared not to speak it. After I escorted our guest to the realm of dreams. My Mistress took action. "Devy show yourself now!" Devy responded in haste." Yes my Master." "I saw it Devy; I saw the vision, is this madness true?" "Yes my Mistress, it's coming." I didn't want to speak its name nor did my Mistress. The Master of Nueden has set free what your bible call The Thief of the Night. Yes readers, I'm talking about the Rapture. Nueden knows it as The Gofogen. Mistress Pat became frighten." My BABIES! Devy save my children, bring them to me!" "Yes my master." "No wait Devy!" "Yes master." "I want you to send someone else, you go to my kids looking like that and you will scare the shit out of them." 'Yes my lord, but I suggest you go yourself master. My army will wait for your next command." "That's a good idea Devy; but how exactly am I going to make it from here to my mother's house in the short time we have left." Hanging in mid-air, a plain silver medallion in the shape of a eagle was brought forth. This legendary medallion from Nab'ee can transport anyone to anywhere they want to be on earth. It moved magically through the air and hung itself neatly around Mistress Pat's neck. From there, Mistress Pat passed from existence.

Sonya and Carlos were playing with the play station in their grandmother's living room. Chubb Chubb Carlos puppy,a cute little Australian Terrier,was jumping at the television. It was ten fifty-nine pm and Carlos wasn't feeling well. "Carlos what's wrong, you don't look to good?" Sonya asked. Chubb Chubb started licking Carlos's face. "I feel funny Sonya, I feel sick; like I'm far away from myself." "What does that mean Carlos, make sense." Just then a hole open in the floor right in front of them; and out came the mistress. "MOMMY!" Carlos yelled. Mistress Pat did not say a word. She just grabbed her children, dropped a note for her mother and went back from which she came. Sonya managed to grab Chubb Chubb. Her Mother came out of her bedroom and called for the children but got no answer. She picked up the letter and read it yelling out "WHAT DOES THIS MEAN,CHILDREN WHERE ARE YOU?!" When the mistress got her children back home she pushed them threw the portal to safety with a note explaining for them to wait until further notice. Chubb Chubb started barking at the mistress. "Go watch over my kids Chubb Chubb." He jumped in the portal. It was now eleven pm in Spanaway,Washington.

Scripture 10: The Wonderful World Of Spanton

The world of Spanton is enchantment at its best. The deep blue skies are where angels soar free. Unashamed and unafraid to be seen because there is only public acceptance. It's bright blue sun bathes the world in a beautiful blue glow and the three moons that orbit her cast the realm in a twilight so bright that at night, you would think it's still day. Their troposphere experiences almost no climatic changes and if it rains, it's only a wet mist to ensure water for the thriving species of tropical plants and trees. It is like a semi-dry rainforest oasis. Well, minus the poisonous snake like creatures and anything else trying to kill you in the forest of Deadlife. Here the trees can walk the world of Spanton at the eighth hour on my dreams and search for late souls. Well the good news is the material needs of Spanton's inhabitants are met without utterance and if they want water, all they have to do is wish for it to appear. This is because the Spantonites are primordial beings who are the source of the creation of the universe and Our "I AM" to them is called Hiranyagharbha. All is provided to them by the unchanging, infinite, immanent and transcendent reality which is the divine ground between all matter, energy, space, time and being. All of this astonishing beauty and unrequited need is off-set by the very ground beneath their feet. The athenosphere for them was formed of transparent dimension stone and as you travel around Spantons majestic paradise, you see the Kingdom of Corrupted Archangels beneath. The Creators made it this way for a reminder; a reminder of what a lack of morals, manners or actions could lead to. The fiery world that burned below the ground served as just that. A constant inspiration for the residents not to wander from the path of True Enlightenment. They Did Not Believe In Him! This could be anyone of them. And it wasn't some quiet display. The echoes of the evil dark angels beating under the clear ground rang across the world like some ancient horn that had been bellowing since the ages of times. Unholy ones begging to be set free from the pain of being stripped of their former selves and voided down into the Darkness. The Darkness incessantly weighed in upon them and the Cherubim's of Distress enacted unending revenge. But the people of Spanton just went on about their lives while the reprobates received their sufferance in plain sight. There was a harmonious congruity that enveloped this world and somehow both the worlds, above and below, were in perfect balance.

"Damn! This place is too fucking cool Carmen!" Judy said. "Uh Carmen, when do we get our wish sweetheart? I mean this is nice and all, but I didn't pay for a cosmic field trip." Rick asked. He was consumed with visions of Mistress Pat punishing him. Her leather whips biting into his skin and the welts of momentous pleasure she would lavish upon him were calling. The sooner he could experience her wrath the better. "We are headed there, to the Great Wishing Tree of Spanton." I told them; pointing towards the center of Spanton's core. "WWWEEE I can't believe I'm fucking flying, how cool is this shit!" Judy screams out tripping. "Sorry to tell you my love, but I'm the one who's flying." "Your just a floater." I had to explain. "Judy so crazy." Amber said; enjoying the ride herself. What their gazes beheld was a tree that was otherworldly, beyond your precepts of reality. It's ancient roots spanned as deep through the transparent core as the towering mass above it spanned upward. It is the Tree of Consciousness. "Once the tree was on planet earth." I went on to explain to them "The story of Adam and Eve bears truth. The Tree of Knowledge of Good and Evil had always been meant to flourish among the earth. But a young boy Aleph and a little girl Kheba, beings from Nueden, were placed on earth back in your beginning. They lived for many years on earth and grew up together. They were subjects meant to have a happy life and live in total bliss but broke with their obedience to Hiranyagharbha and desecrated the tree. Kheba and Aleph were told they could eat whatever they wanted from the tree; but were to never ever eat from the forest of Deadlife: which was also on your planet before being removed. Eleven years passed and when one unfortunate day they was playing near the Deadlife forest when cherries rolled out of the woods." "So what's wrong with cherries Carmen?" Rick asked. "Nothing is wrong, it's just they never saw a cherry before; because the cherries only grow on the very top of the tree. Darkness knew this fact and used it against them. Kheba saw the fruit, picked it up and put it to her mouth. The man yelled "STOP" and grabbed the cherry and it burst in his hand. The juice squirted into the woman's mouth and in his eyes. I AM was angry with them and they were cursed by him and the tree was brought to Spanton. Here it will forever reside. "Are you trying to tell us that this is the tree from the Garden of Eden?" Rick asked. "No I'm not saying that." Because the chances of you believing what is evident to your eyes and ears is to remarkable. I tell you what I know to be true. This tree was the very first tree on earth." "IMPOSSIBLE!" Judy yelled. IMPOSSIBLE is you ever flying Judy." Continuing I told them. "The tree is said to date back when your planet started to cool off. It was planted by the creator." " The Cherubim's of Morality surround and protect the tree and their sole obligation is to ensure the wishing tree's continuation of life; this is because it bears every known fruit, vegetable and seeds to man and the juices from its bark can cure any ailment; it is the sustenance of life."

All my passengers could only float closer toward their destination, dumbfounded at what grandeur they were being allowed to glimpse. Amber appreciated it even more than Rick with all his religious upbringing. She had always believed that there was more to what the Bible had been compiled down to. This was all just affirmation of that and she would cherish it for the rest of her life: I also told them. "The tree blooms only one seed every five hundred years. Only during the syzygy. When Spanton and all three of its moons come into exact gravitational alignment with its distinctive blue sun. When the occultation happens; a seed is birthed from a pod that hangs off a spiraling vine and legend say that it is the source of all plant life. The seed propagated emits a shiny brilliance and it will be taken by the Creators to another realm and planted so that life in another universe can share the gift. As we approach, we must be careful because there is a hole of dark energy that roams around the external layers of the trees surface: Your eyes are unable to discern it presence but I feel it's toxic pull and if we fly to close, we will be sucked in." I navigated my guest down a safe distance from Cherubim's of Morality among the moss fields created by the shadows and dampness caused by the tree's massive boughs.

"It is very important that you all remember to leave my dreams before the eighth hour! The Mist of Darkness' evil presence is stronger than ever on this night." I just had to give them that last warning. "I will do just that Carmen." Amber said. There was a fierce look of determination in her face and I looked around and saw Rick and Judy staring desperately lost; yet hopeful at the same time. An overwhelming sense of sorrow overcame me and I feared none of them might be seen alive again. Little did I realize, a chain of events foretold by prophets since the dawn of time had been ignited within the world of Earth. Captivated by my dream state; I was in Spanton guiding three spoiled souls on how to live yet another fantasy when the world they knew would be completely changed by six forty-four in the morning. Helpless as to what must be, I continued the wishing ritual. "You must all eat from the womb of the wishing tree. Pick from it what you will and bite." Standing under the damp stillness, they reached up towards the closet limbs near them and plucked something. "Make your wish Rick, I see you have a banana." I directed him. He took a bite and said "I've been a very; very bad boy and wish to be punished: and a laugh erupted from his throat that hinted at the deranged state of his mind. Judy started giggling and the look of disgust that Amber leveled at her was classic. "Your wish is my command: and just like that, Rick faded away! "Wow, how cool is that! Do me next, look I got a potato!" Judy pleaded. "Just like your head." Amber said. "Ok Judy, make your wish." Judy took a bite and said. "Please, all I wish for is a hot night with a big man, you know what I mean girl!" "Your wish is my command." Judy too disappeared into the beyond yelling. "HOW KOOL!" Surrounded by the Cherubim's of Morality with the Kingdom of Corrupted Archangels underfoot I turned to my last guest and said. "Amber, make your wish; I see you have the Legendary Red Apple." Amber looked at the apple and took a bite. "I wish to see The Creator of all things and learn the truth about life here on Earth." The thin, polished finish of the ground beneath us rumbled and I gasped. Foolish wishes, noble dreams and harmful needs had been pursued through the Stone of the Hubriser for countless millenniums and no one had ever made such a wish before. Imploring her with my eyes to change her mind I asked. "Are you sure that's what you want Amber?" Just then thunder clap over our heads; it's forbidden for me to question a wish. "Yes, show me" she said. "Amber, please be careful." Amber also faded away saying. "See you in the afterlife Carmen." Amber had an odd feeling that she might not be coming back. It was her that I feared for the most. Now I see it's not my Mistress fault why

The Them are coming; this all must come to pass in order for Amber's wish to come true. This is truly bewildering.

Back in Spanaway, James was watching CSNN in Carlos' guest house. He turned up the volume and listened to what some cute black reporter from the Bronx was saying. Below her on the screen, news bulletins were streaming: updating viewers about the great phenomenon happening around the planet. People were reporting seeing a giant dark shadow come out of a silver fog in the skies over their cities. "It's now two thirty-five am in the Bronx and the next door neighbor at Thirteen fifty-nine Park Avenue said they heard screaming and called the police Matt at around ten minutes after two am; but what they found out was shear horror. When the police arrived, ten students, ages six to eight years old from Public School fifty-five in the Bronx was having a sleep over with the third grade math teacher Mrs.Reda Lewis; her home is located at Thirteen fifty-seven Park Avenue. Sandra Hall and Tonya Milton was there as chaperones. Sandra is the mother of Tiffany a beautiful eight year old with dreams of becoming president one day. Tonya wanted to help; but could not find a baby sitter and had to bring her six year old stepson Tommy. The children was playing their last game of hide and seek before bedtime. It appears that your planet earth made plans for some sort of holiday for December twenty first, two thousand twelve. School was closed and government offices was also. It was to be the biggest Earth party ever produced in your planet's history. Over two billion people around the world plan to call out from work and party in the streets. People was happy singing Christmas songs about Jesus. If what your scientist say is true; and if that do become your Day of Doom: people wanted to die happy. A very strange species you are; a very unusual kind of matter indeed: very interesting.

"Three, two, one--ready or not here I come." Tiffany ran through the house looking for her classmates. Little Tommy wasn't feeling good so his mother Tonya put him in bed to rest. Tiffany walk up to the closet in the hallway and swung the door open very fast and yells. "Got you!" "How come I always get caught first?" Markie said and ran to the caught box to wait for the others. "Because you hide in the stupid places." Tiffany said. The parents start to laugh: Tiffany walks up slow to the couch; she can see feet." Got you!" She yells. "I didn't have enough time to find a good spot." Kristina said and stomp off to the caught box. Sandra looks at her watch. "Hurry up Tiffany so you'll can get ready for bed. "It won't take long ma; come out, come out where ever you are?" Tiffany start to walk in the kitchen; the light was off. "Come out, come out where ever you are?" She disappear into the darkness. Tonya and Sandra are watching the news about the great fog around the world. "This isn't natural Tonya." "Your right Sandra, I'm getting kind of scared myself." Mrs.Lewis look at her watch. Then she looked out the window; she can see a very large dark shadow passing over her home. It made no sound. It came right out of the silver fog. People stop dancing in the street to witness the wonder. "Alright kids everybody come out game over." she said. "Children you hear me, game over!" She said much louder. Sandra see Kristina and Markie in the caught box. "Look, those two are already knocked out, now we got to carry them and put them to bed." Sandra calls her daughter. "Tiffany come on honey time for bed." No answer. She get up and walk to the kitchen; she turned on the light. "Tiffany why are you laying on the floor like that?" Tonya screams to the top of her lungs. "My God, I think Markie and Kristina are dead; they're not breathing." Mrs.Lewis screams; runs and look for the other kids. Sandra is getting worried about her own daughter. Tiffany baby, you o.k. honey." She bend down and Tiffany head was bleeding from the fall caused by her untimely death. "My baby, my baby!" Sandra yells. Mrs.Lewis screams through the house out of control crying. "Their all dead, my God what is this!?" Tonya runs out the bedroom holding her dead stepson Tommy. She looks around at all the dead children; she faint with him in her arms.

James can't take his eyes of the television, he can't believe what he's hearing. The news woman continues. "The police have the teacher and two female parents in holding and they are under intense questioning as we speak. We'll wait to release the names of the dead children until their parents are informed of this tragic news." Right at that moment a father comes busting out of his house two homes down from Mrs.Lewis's home; crying his two sons are dead right in front of the news camera. James sat stunned with his mouth open. Someone walked on the set of CSNN, during live television and handed Matt a sheet of paper. Whatever he read turned his skin a sickly pale color and he interrupted her. "Constance, hold on a moment. Umm, everyone this just in, the President of the United States has called a press conference. It would appear at this time that the parents of those mysteriously deceased children of the Bronx are not alone in their grief. The press conference is starting now; I will be with you throughout the course of these events, let us go immediately to the White House!

James looked on, transfixed as the rest of the world when Christina Deanvilt; President of the Unites States, took the podium." Good morning, everybody. Please be seated. I will skip all pretense of formality here and get straight to the urgent matter before us. At two o'clock this morning at Washington D.c., governments across the world, received calls from the Center for Disease Control. They alerted us that hospitals across the world were having deliveries of only stillborn children. These babies were experiencing no trauma during the delivery and the fact that they died directly after being born is what made hospitals alert the CDC. Shortly thereafter the hospitals reported that all of the newborn infants in the neonatal units had died, as well; also many pregnant women are calling nine-one-one saying their baby have stop moving inside them. Also, a sobering amount of miscarriages are being reported." James gasped as everyone else in the room there in Washington,D.C. did. The room full of reporters who had been stunned to silence assaulted President Deanvilt with questions during the pause she took to catch her breath. Dressed in a somber grey dress shirt and slacks, she raised her hands to silence the barrage. "Believing this was the spread of a disease, they quarantined neonatal departments where over the course of minutes that followed, all the children died starting from the youngest to the oldest born." Tears were streaming down most over everyone's faces; but President Deanvilt's face was strangely blank as though she was in no way connected to what was going on. "At this time, the CDC has reported that this is no disease nor a terrorist act of biological or chemical warfare. The children that we have been able to test so far for diseases or any other abnormalities were found to be healthy and no cause of death was able to be determined." James is in tears.

"Reports are flooding in from around the globe now. As I mentioned earlier the mortality spread from the youngest to oldest and at this hour we only have reports of children from the ages of zero to eight years of age have been affected. At this rate we are looking at near total extinction of the world's youth population under the ages of eleven by noon today." To some it sounded like the president knew more then what she was telling. Someone vomited in the background and James imagined that it must be some poor mom or dad stuck covering the press conference while their child was probably dead or dying. You could hear lots of murmuring and cell phones ringing in the background. "That is approximately twenty three percent of the earth's people or nearly one billion youths. If this plague will spread beyond that; we don't know. What we do know is that the Old City in Jerusalem is where the first deaths were confirmed. The Bikur Cholim Hospital in Jerusalem should be credited with that discovery and the world is monitoring them closely for how this event will unfold. It is there that the World Health Organization and combined governments shall focus our efforts to contain this catastrophe." The reporters were beside themselves and the slack look on their faces spoke the horror of what their brains hadn't yet comprehended. If it's happening all over the world and in our own country; what's so special about Jerusalem? Some thought to themselves. "The fears that you all have at this hour must be intolerable if you are a parent with a small child right now. I don't have children and to all you who grieve you have my utmost sympathy."

"I will meet with other world leaders in an emergency session of the United Nations. Leaders from every nation have simply no answers to give their people America. Just as I; I would like to tell you all to have faith but faith will not restore the dead innocents to their parents. So I can only tell you to pray to Who You Believe To Be God that we can find the cause of such insurmountable agony and stop it. I am aware that the heads of all churches will also be meeting with the Vatican later this afternoon. Hopefully, they will provide some comfort to you all. That is all." President Deanvilt stepped away from the podium and strode off. The secret service men assigned to her protection immediately fanned out around her; blocking any would be assassins from having a direct target. As the first female president of the U.S. who was succeeding the first black president, her life had been put in imminent danger more than five times since the November sixth election. That's not counting the three attempts during her run for office. Nonetheless, she walked away with her back ram-rod straight and her nose in the air as though she dared a son-of-a-bitch to try it. She had to take office early because the former president took his wife and kids and left the White House before his time; without a word to anyone. No one know their whereabouts. The only thing the secret service found left behind by the former president was a note, and it read: MAY GOD FORGIVE US ALL! Do you think he know some top secret that you don't know and ran for his life? Why look at you; your still just sitting there reading the Scriptures of Spanton while the clock is ticking. If you knew what I know; you would be calling all your loved ones and telling them you love them. Start with your children first. Trust Me!

Matt intervened then, back on cue to be with America through the worst disaster that had every struck the Earth. "Well, there you have it ladies and gentleman. President Deanvilt will be meeting shortly in an emergency meeting of the United Nations." "Umm, it is clear at this time that what has caused this tragedy is not a chemical warfare, the president has said." James pressed the remote and cut the television off. He couldn't believe what he had just fucking heard. His mind refused to wrap around it; he wasn't alarmed for himself. Hell, weird shit had been in the making ever since he had picked up that Kirk Bailey character from the airport. Him and his strange wind with The Them and shit. "Yep." He thought. "Strange shit indeed." Beneath James' playboy visage and even though he was an only child without any family, his heart broke for the families that had just been destroyed. He broke down in an uncontrollable huddle and cried his heart out. Him along with all the other heartbroken people across the world. It would be said later that the lamenting and keening could be heard all the way to the International Space Station. For the first time in earth's history, death had a voice of its own; and it was heard from across the oceans.

Mistress Pat was still in the bedroom, staring intently at the Stone of the Hubriser. As she watched, the universe appeared and not very far from the miniature Milky Way, she saw a fleet of flying objects approaching the Sextans A galaxy. Only four million light years away; she watched the beings steady approach. She knew without a doubt, that they were fixed on Earth, more importantly: she was their ultimate destination. Just then, a face came into view. A face unlike any she could ever imagine! It's skin was a pale grey and in its oblong bulbous shaped head; were two huge imposing eyes. The black depths of them seemed to look right through you! It's mouth was a small slit and as she looked deeper into its eyes; the extraterrestrial entered her mind. Inside, it sifted through the recesses of her, pulling every experience she had ever had. Things she was too young to even remember: like when she was two years old. Now she know the name of the man who molested her as a child; and she cried out in agony when the childbirth's of her babies was relived by the being controlling her mind. She screamed out, "Carlos and Sonya!" As if in response to her scream a dragon like voice spilled into her head, "WHERE ARE OUR SOULS!" it demanded. A fear that made her heart ice over resonated within her. "No God! Please no!" she screamed. "COME UP HITHER AND I WILL SHEW THEE THINGS WHICH MUST BE HERE AFTER!" , the dragon voice commanded. Mistress Pat closed the armatura and ran out of the room!

Meanwhile, in my dreams; Rick was walking threw a slimy green hued mist. He could barely see three feet in front of him, so he walked with his arms outstretched to make sure he didn't bump into anything. He was starting to wonder when the party was going to get started so he yelled out. "Hello, I've been naughty." Just for fun. Out of the greenish puss colored mist, three nuns arose around him. The outer robes and vestments of the three were soaking in blood and as it ran from their veils, Rick had no choice but to take notice of their faces. They were ruined masses of flesh and eyes and lips, the noses were sunken malformations. All of them wore grotesque masques of tendons; bones and sockets. It was like they had been decaying for centuries and then frozen at some absurd climax of rot. Rivulets of blood ran and was absorbed by their hideous faces as Rick stood motionless and said. "Hey, this is not what I had in mind!" The nuns bared rulers in their right hands and as they slapped them against their left hands in unison, he knew it wasn't their faces and the blood soaked clothes that was the real problem. It was their eyes! They were the color of liquid flame encircled in a ring of dark black. Their brilliant blaze was lit from the depths of Hell and as he stared into the blazing emptiness, their instruments of punishment raised high in the air and in one instance, he heard the sailing of them. In the next, he heard the sudden blows to his body as they struck him with vicious force. They flogged him relentlessly and as the instruments of torture raised and lowered, blood stained both the bloody Mary's hands and their rulers. "DON'T TALK IN CLASS RICK, SIT IN YOUR SEAT!" They screamed. Rick tried to run from them and with every step he took, the ground cracked with earsplitting destructiveness; it started to rain green pus that felt like acid to the skin. Rick thought the ground was trying to open up and swallow him whole; he can see bright green pus boiling in the cracks below his feet. The slithery serpentine voice of a dragon roared "YOU'VE BEEN BAD!" Rick kept running , yelling "Carmen this isn't what I had in mind you bitch!" A hand shot out of the pus beneath his feet and pulled Rick's leg. He spilled to the ground and looked back; fearing the pursuit of the anti-stratosphere. What he saw was his dead father spilling from up out of the dank earth in a gelatinous heap of putrefaction. Besides the rotting mess, he was just as he remembered him. All business in a dress shirt; slacks, belt with black shoes. As it broke free of the ground's grasp, it screamed. "GO STAND IN THE CORNER BOY, YOU KNOW WHAT THE FUCK YOU DID!" And just like that, Rick was back in his old apartment over the liquor store. The nuns were no longer pursuing him but he prayed with everything inside of him not to be where he thought he was. Mortified, he looked around the dusty beat up studio that he and his father had shared for fifteen years and it looked like he had just left it that morning instead of twenty years ago. He looked over to his father's armchair, afraid for dear life that his dad would be there with a beer in his hand watching the Knick's game, just like when he was a child. And he was. Rick scrambled into the kitchen to huddle as he used to; squeezed into his protective shelter between the stove and the fridge and braced himself for the blows that would very soon rain down on his head. His father rose from the chair and stalked towards him, beer still in hand. He pulled his whipping lash from around his waist, and the real beating began. Around the studio apartment that reeked of stale booze and Rick's blood, his father chased him. Yelling at the top of his lungs because he didn't give a fuck if the world knew he was beating his son to a bloody pulp, "DON'T YOU RUN FROM ME BOY, YOU KNOW WHAT THE FUCK YOU DID!"

Judy was in a night club, dancing. It was the hottest and naughtiest club she had ever been too, and she had been to quite a few. Weed, pills and plenty of liquor were free flowing. It was filled with beautiful people and as one of them, she fit right in. She was also pleased to learn that shirts were not required and pants were also optional. Gorgeous young men and women pumped and gyrated to the most insane discothèque she had ever heard and in the massive swarm of people, she danced along to the beat of the music. Her heart beating in time to it when in mid hip swing, two men came up to her and started to dance. The first was exotic, Persian maybe; dressed in nothing but some very; very tight leather pants and as Judy stared this exotic piece of cock up and down: she stopped at the bulging section between his thighs and caught her breath. Dancing even more sensually than before, while seducing him with her eyes; she placed her palm over his crotch and squeezed. Judy thought that she must have gotten the one dancing in behind her going because he turned her fiercely towards him. The momentum of it caused her to bump into a chest so hard it looked as though it had been cut from stone. He was a brown Adonis without a stitch of clothing on; but a tiny g-string and she didn't need to put her hand on his crotch to know he was packing. One step back and one glance downward and she saw all eleven inches of him swollen and erect, pressed against his stomach like a cobra ready to strike. Her shadow god bent down and whispered in her ear. "Would you like to go to the back and have some private fun with me and my mate?" His Aussie accent sent chills down her body and her throat went so dry that all she could do was nod her head; vigorously. They were going down a dark hall in the back of the club Judy knew because she could still hear the rhythmic tempo music of S.K.C.J.'s techno. The Aussie was leading the way with the Persian behind her rubbing her ass when suddenly she started to feel hot. Sweat broke out all over her body and Judy looked at the back of the Aussie; it's sculpted mass was trickling beads of sweat. She raised her hand as if to fan herself when the wall nearest them crashed down. Before Judy's eyes, a yellow hand the size and thickness of the L.A. telephone book shot through the abyss. It seized the Aussie's head and squeezed. So close was Judy that blood sprayed in her face and she could hear the crunching of the man's skull as it collapsed; also the crushing of more tender things. The hand squeezed and then began to make a grinding motion, the pulverized remains of the man's head oozed down his neck. Brain fragments and skull shards clumped together in a way that should never be; ran down his back making dark bloody streaks. The yellowed hand of dripping, gory mess pushed it's victim to the side. Judy had been in an immobile state of shock; too afraid to scream, move or even piss herself. But when that yellow hand attached to a yellow arm the width of a tree trunk started moving, in search of its next demolition, she screamed. She screamed and ran for her life and she hoped the fucking Persian did the same. She ran back the way the Aussie had led them down the hall, out of the club and into the dark night of a strange world. As Judy ran, bloody images ran through her alcohol and drug induced brain. She looked back and the big man was after her. Bile and vomit rose to her throat and her lungs were aching from her desperate attempt to escape whatever death the giant had in store for her. This wasn't what she had wished for! She had wished for a hot night with a big man,not some twelve foot tall; Nine hundred pound behemoth with a murderous impulse! What the hell had Carmen gotten her into. Tears streaming, she willed herself to run faster but couldn't; she seemed to be going interminably slow and the big man too fast. Suddenly she saw two torch red suns begin to rise over the mountains in the distance. With its steady ascent over the ridges, the darkness turned to day and the temperature climbed. As dramatic as the beautiful duos appearance was, it their sudden descent to where they had been that was the most stunning illusion. Judy ran over to hide behind a tree, hoping that she would be able to hide from the gargantuan. But just as soon as she had ducked down, he was upon her. He grabbed Judy by her hair and drug her from the bushes. Judy kicked and screamed; begged and pleaded but the towering beast paid no attention. "Where are you taking me?" she screamed. His long strides never ceased, but. "Down to where I dwell!" was the reply. The First Hour; the Wishing Hour: Has now passed in my dreams.

Scripture 11: Witness the Spanton Spells

Amber was walking down a long dirt road. Nothing existed for her but a light far ahead in the distance. A shiny golden mist enveloped her and as she breathed out; her breath stirred it in circles before her. She didn't know how long she had been walking but the light didn't seem to be getting any closer: it didn't seem to get any further either. It was just there, taunting her to hurry up and get there already. She had been walking since she left me at the wishing tree and not only was she tired; her feet were hurting and she was fuming. It had crept into Ambers mind as she walked ceaselessly onward, that she had paid two million to be slipped a roofie. She prayed that some sick fucks weren't doing some sick twisted shit to her body right now. How could she have been so stupid to believe something so crazy. Suddenly a wind stirred the mist around her and she looked up. Beyond the mist, she saw me. The glittering brilliance of my white wings of light were beautiful to behold and Amber watched as I seamlessly floated to the ground. Amber clapped her hands and sarcastically said. "Bravo!" She walked around me and continued her journey down the dusty track. "Amber wait!" Amber swirled around and stalked back to where I was standing. "Carmen, what the hell is this; this isn't what I wished for!" "This is your wish Amber. Before the eighth hour, you will see The Them." "The Them? Who the hell are The Them? I wished to see The Creator and learn the truth about life! Walking down some dusty road isn't my idea of the truth!" Amber screamed. "And why are you here anyway Carmen, why are you in my fantasy?" "Amber, I need your help." "My help? What could you want from me?" "All of this has been foretold of in the scroll. Amber, you asked to know the truth and now The Them are coming" "I knew it! I knew we came from aliens! I just want to see one, that's all." "O you will Amber, you will" "What do you need me to do Carmen?"

"I will need your help to fight The Them, they come to wreak havoc upon the earth. We must defeat them and the only way that can be done is to find the last three Stones of the Cosmos. There are four in all and Mistress Pat has one." I told her. Amber stared at me and a look of disbelief crossed her face and she looked ahead. In front of her, the long dirty stretch of road awaited. The light waiting at the end. She knew she couldn't afford to disbelieve. She was here in the World of Spanton; in my dreams and I saw the acceptance dawn on her face. The acceptance as she realized that everything I had just told her was true. I didn't try to hide the remorse on my face. Remorse that it could not be anyone other than her who could help me undertake this giant task. "Oh my God, what the hell have you gotten me into!" she yelled. "What do they want?" "They come for the lost souls my mistress is coveting away in her dungeon." I told her. "Fucking then, tell that power crazy bitch to give the souls back or whatever!" she shouted. "Amber, there's more to it than that, the Scroll of Spanton tells of the day The Them return; it says that day will be the end of life on earth! It is the return of his Son and the planet earth will be judged!" "It sounds like you're talking about REV..." "Don't! Do not speak that word Amber. I'm not sure what all of this means, first we must go to the valley of the Spantonites to learn where to find the stones."

Mistress Pat was looking out of the window in her bedroom. In the skies over Spanaway, dark ominous cumulus clouds had settled in. So deep was their mass, that they blotted out the moon's glow and plunged the city into an eternal night. It's heavy presence just hunkered there above the city as though the very sky it existed in was no longer safe. Something was coming and even the Silver Fog knew it was running out of time. Mistress Pat shivered as the wails of the disembodied souls resonated from within the walls. The giant mass in the sky began to roil as though it was being stirred from within and as she looked out on her grounds; her beautiful grounds, the grass was a dark bloody lake. The trees were leaking blood like it was sap and it ran down the trunks in bright red streaks. As though afraid, the dark clouds parted; it made way for the Gofogen. The sky cleared and Washington State was left with a breathtaking view of the night sky. The looming clouds mysterious presence and departure was replaced by the stillness of the night. It was though no breathing thing dared exhale for fear The Gofogen might hear them. Even the insects knew that danger was coming; so did the restless spirits that lurked the halls of the mansion. Master of her domain, Mistress Pat ran back to the stone to summon her dark slaves. She cautioned before she opened it because she always had to brace herself for what came next. Those horrible demon eyes with lips charred to a black ruin haunted Mistress Pat. She might never stop wishing to not see Devy's monstrous ruin of a face. Summoning a deeper strength than fear, she opened the armatura and a rainbow of colors from a galaxy far away radiated prismatically from the stone. "Devy, Master of The Mist of Darkness! Come to me!" she summoned. The red mist began to fill the stone and as Devy's' boiled raw face appeared, his deep wraith-like voice answered her. "Yes my master, tell me what you desire!" "For Christ's sake Devy, can't you cover that fucking face!" Mistress Pat screamed. "I was punished by I'AM to burn in hell forever and be subject of the Stone of the Hubriser. I sleep in a bed of molten lava and walls of fire build my mansion: I apologize my mistress if this offends you." He sneered the last part and for some reason Mistress Pat was truly glad Devy's ass was in the stone and not standing there before her. Shocked she asked "So what the hell did you do to deserve that sentence?" A shadow crossed the black abyss of Devy's eyes and in them she saw Devy standing on a field. Tens of thousands of people were dead around his feet. He wore a toga and he was young and beautiful except for the blood soaked ruins of his dress. He had slaughtered a very long time ago and a slaughterer is what she would need to combat The Them. "Devy, an epic battle is about to be fought. The Them want war and you will help me give it to them." "I and my Nephilim of Strife are at your service, my lord!"

Paul huddled in the corner, staring at the shadows of dead lost souls hovering at his bedroom door. He didn't know what to do. He was devoted to Mistress Pat but this was bullshit. He understood her reasons for not giving the souls over to The Them; but this was madness. The voices of the long departed slithered under the door whispering "Stay and die like us Paul!" Shivers ran down his spine and he screamed! Cold lifeless fingers played down his spine and he bolted for the door. Benign spirits laid in wait for him and he felt them tugging at him; trying to keep him within the mansion. He ran to Mistress Pat's bedroom and saw her staring into the stone talking to Devy. He did something he would never do. He interrupted his master while she was speaking. "Mistress Pat, I am sorry, but I must leave!" Mistress Pat started to interrupt but he was quick to cut her off again. "NO! I am sorry my Mistress, but I must flee this wicked place that you have helped to create and I pray you save yourself!" He didn't wait for her reply or her acquiescence, he ran from her bedroom and fled for his life! Mistress Pat was stunned but she had seen the look in Paul's eyes. Hell, she couldn't really blame him for wanting to leave but she needed him, damn it. "Paul, don't leave!" she yelled after him; but Paul was gone. She ran from the bedroom, leaving Devy and everything else behind. Paul had made it to the front door and she watched as he opened it and started to leave. The clacking of her heels was ingrained in his soul and he turned back to see her rushing down the stairs after him. That was his mistake. Had he continued, not looked back to steal that last glance of his Mistress, he would have been free. Free to leave and maybe have some kind of life. The second he looked back the door was yanked from his grasped and slammed shut in his face! A voice that would make your being shivered screamed through the mansion. "HELL AWAITS PAUL!" When Paul turned from the door, the next thing he saw was Rick Stanville's head filled with a black lifeless hunger that promised of consuming him. Rick's eyes glaring out of a green fog: waiting and watching. "THE GUEST ARE ALREADY DEAD!" Paul yelled. Rick screamed and jumped like a banshee in Paul's face! Rick's eyes turned to deep red fire in the fog. Paul almost fainted and he backed up and ran head long through the plate glass window that lined each of the front doors. Mistress Pat watched as he rolled and sprang to his feet, screaming the whole time. It occurred to her then that she might not know as much as she thought she did about her beloved Paul.

James was sitting out in the driveway listening to the radio. "The mayor wants people to stay in their homes until the police learn more about the bleeding of the trees and the Silver Fog." He looked out the passenger window and saw Paul sprinting down the driveway. James clicked the door locks to secure the car. Paul banged on the sedan and kept running. James rolled down the window just a bit, just enough to ask, "Paul, where you going?" "THE HELL AWAY FROM HERE!" he screamed as he flew past the car, past the gates and out onto the night. The bloody trees had so saturated the ground that tiny streams had begun to run into the street. Paul slips on the blood sap and screams. "WHAT THE FUCK!" The trees started to lean over the limo and James shrank down in his seat, trying to make his self smaller. Blood started dripping on the windshield and James started the car. Turning on wipers, blood smeared across the windshield and he peeled out of the driveway. He turned in the same direction Paul had turned, the most direct way out of Spanaway. He floored the gas pedal on the limo. Going over ninety miles an hour, he passed Paul; Leaving him to choke on the exhaust and debris he had created as he zoomed past. The dark foreboding cloud had once again returned to the mansion and there it hovered. From space, it was the only cloud over the state of Washington.

Mistress Pat had ran back to the stone. "Devy that damn black cloud is back! Destroy this phantom of darkness!" "Yes Master!" Devy summoned The Dark Angel Allana. From the Kingdom of Corrupted Archangels Allana busted forth out of the ground in front of the mansion. It was as though a comet had landed not from above the earth, but below it; so great was the blast of Allana's arrival. She was an obscene beauty. Her skin was the color of the moon and it shone from within a dusty glittering gold. Her lips were that of an overripe tomato dangling from the vine; on the very verge over ripe. Skin and lips were the only thing that made you think she had anything close to a human once ended there. In her head sat seven eyes. All seven were the color of the universe combined and they stared everywhere and nowhere at once. The eyes were adorned by a set of horns. Horns covered with the blackest of raven's wings. She was armored in a lattice metal imbedded with the images of every she had slaughtered and she stood their casting her moony glow over the grounds. To encase her brilliance was set of thick, black feathery wings that spanned over twelve meters. They fluctuated with every breath that she took and the earth breathed in with her as though it knew true darkness was about to arrive. She was savage beauty Allana, one of the Underground Dark Angels. Her armor bared her breasts which were covered in a luxurious black fur; the same silky looking fur that ran between her legs. Imposing in her majesty was Shadows of Raven's Death Spell behind her. Thousands of silken black ravens enveloped her, waiting for her to command them. The mist broke itself apart and then reattached. The wind from their wings; the ravens blew the cumulus high into the sky. Cars stopped in front of the mansion and people got out of their cars in disbelief, some even called the police. The dark cloud departed the mansion and swooped over the motor vehicles on the road. Police sirens could be heard in the background and the thick black ravens flew over the black cloud and surrounded it. Their beating wings darkened the skies and the entire time, Dark Angel Allana just stood there in her shimmering, metal brilliance! The flock of black assassins could not restrain the darkness sent by The Them. Allana's pale moon glow skin deepened and a horde of large pterodactyls came out of the hole from hell; wind is what she needed to defeat the black invader. The moon was completely blocked out over the mansion. Giant pterodactyls poured from the mouth of earth Allana had created and still the evil mass could not be stopped. Mistress Pat yelled, barely heard over the strum of the beating wings outside and asked, "Devy what's wrong!" "Their dark magic is just as strong as ours my lord. Summon the fantasy bitch Carmen Dreams." "That is the second time you have called her a bitch Devy. I wish you do not let me hear you call her one again!" "Yes my lord,your wish is my command." The dark ravens and pterodactyls of the underworld surrounds the invader and spun within its core of evil. The Dark Mist of Evil transformed it's shape and size; it poured out The Eye of the Black Storm. Black dust blast threw Spanaway,Washington:darkness was everywhere.

James was hauling ass down the road, it was dark outside and his headlights barely cast a glow into the silent darkness. He clenched and unclenched the steering wheel as thoughts of Mistress Pat raced through his head. He was worried about her and he wasn't sure if his cowardice would allow him to just leave her behind. He pressed the brakes and pulled over to the side of the road. He needed to just sit and think for a minute. He turned on the radio and stopped on a man screaming in the microphone, hysterical. "Just reported that the bodies of monks and nuns are being found dead all over the world; with no known cause of death. Much like the mysterious deaths of the children across the globe not more than two hours ago. The C.I.A. has ruled out terrorism." His lungs had run out of air, the reporter took a deep, gasping breath and resumed his screaming broadcast, desperate to get the news out to the people. "The C.D.C. is advising everyone to avoid drinking the water. Any fresh water is not to be consumed and only bottled water is certain to be free from any foreign chemicals. If you have limited access to bottled water, the C.D.C. recommends you boil the water first before using it for consumption. James couldn't believe what he was hearing. Mouth gaped open, staring at the radio, he startled when Paul caught up to the limo; frantically beating on the window. James unlocked the door and yelled for Paul to get in. Paul jumped inside and James told him. "I'm afraid for Mistress Pat, I want to go back and make sure we get her away from there!" Paul turned on James like a man who had seen too much and said. "She can take care of herself James! She is the reason for the contemptuous madness tonight and the havoc that is being reeked across the globe! Look around, everything changed after you picked up that Bailey guy that day and bought him here. You can't even enter the mansion now James! Don't be blind man, look around you!" And that is what James did, he looked around him and everywhere; there was screaming. Mothers screaming for their babies; husbands screaming for their families: everywhere people were screaming in the eye of The Black Storm! The world was in chaos and James could not deny that it had all started that day with Kirk Bailey at the airport. The streets had grown crowded with cars of people who were rushing to the store to get bottled water. Thousands of people started to leave Washington state. The world was in panic mode and as James and Paul sat there in the limo, parked on the side of the road; they saw a plane of fire descend from the sky. It was engulfed in flames, doing a perfect swan dive. The side of it read Children of God. All the major news channels would cover it, 'Chariot of God's Holy Burns'. Some smart onlooker had thought enough to tape the spectacle and it's fiery descent would be broadcast over and over. A plane full of clergy from Rome, on the way to meet with the U.N.and the president.

In my dreams, Rick was being beaten with thorn lined switches and each vicious strike of them left his backside lined with thorn shaped holes. He was bound at his wrists and ankles and the dirty shirt stuffed in his mouth served to muffle his screams. His dead father stopped the beating long enough to roughly yank Rick's pants down to his ankles. He continued the beating on Rick's ass and when one of the thorns plucked his testicles a guttural moan erupted from his throat and he passed out. A splash of ice cold puss and a hard slap in the face made Rick come to; and as he did he saw his father's left ear begin to slide off his face. Embalming fluid leaked from the gaping hole left by the ear's departure and spittle sprayed in Rick's face as father yelled. "Didn't I tell you to be home by ten o'clock boy! Didn't do your school work did you boy!" The nuns came out of nowhere and began to whip Rick's bound hands with their rulers. His hands began to bleed and the voice of a dragon raged. "YOOOU BEEN BAAAD!"

Judy came to lying next to the giant in his bed. She hadn't remembered passing out but she had and as she looked down at her body; she was naked and her breasts and abdomen were covered with huge bite marks. As her eyes scanned lower, she saw her clitoris hanging in bloody pieces. He had tried to eat her pussy off. She laughed to herself, in shock; because she thought it was funny how it didn't hurt. He had his way with her and as she slid off the bed, gathering herself in an attempt to run, the room started to spin. She was suddenly very tired and hot. It felt like it had to be over one hundred ten degrees. She reached for the doorknob that she hoped led to her freedom and tried to turn. It seared her hand and when she was finally able to pull away; a third degree burn was left. She looked back and the giant was tasting her with his eyes; laughing to himself. The heat started to boil the paint on the walls and he held out his hand to her, much like a husband would his virgin bride on her wedding night and said. "Come to me Judy! Come get more of your wish!" And the evil giant laughed so sinisterly that Judy fell to the floor and started to cry. "Carmen, Carmen!" Deep wracking sobs came from Judy's throat. "This isn't what I wanted, this isn't what I wanted!"

Mistress Pat took Devy's advice and summoned my help. "Carmen, Seraphim of Dreams, aid me in my fight against the Mist Of Darkness!" I closed my eyes and I could see the mansion. The Dark Mist was trying to enter in from any crevice it could find. My master needed help and fast; so I summoned the Angel of Cosmic Winds. Tranise flew out the stone and her light pass through the bedroom window leaving it undamaged; out of the mansion and into battle with the Mist. The oppressing evil cloud that was spy for The Them. The Dark Mist feared the Angel of Wind. She waved her light and a tornado with category seven winds materialized out of nothingness. The Dark Angel Allana and her team of ravens and pterodactyls went back from which they came; they also fear the Angel of Cosmic Winds. Police cars and other vehicles were lifted off of the ground. People who weren't holding something were tumbling down the street; looking for something to grasp onto. The dark cloud transformed into a black shadow beast with the head of a dragonfly. It's wing span reached over a block long and people tried to run for cover from fear of the great black shadow. The police ignorantly started to fire their weapons but the dragonfly beast was unaffected. Had they known what was to soon come; they probably would have turned the guns on themselves.

A state trooper stuck in the mass of abandoned cars on the road after the shadow beast's appearance observed everything in awe. He radioed back to his base because he knew they needed help and fast! "Command, this is State Trooper Jordan, come back!" The trooper tried to fight back the panic he heard in his voice. With the squawk of the radio base responded. "Go ahead Jordan." It could've been Keisha or Keara from the sound of the voice but he wasn't sure, it didn't matter really. He had gotten back in his car for safety and was praying that they would get the National Guard here right away. This was something that they just didn't prepare him for in trooper school. The fight between the dark menacing mist and the radiant energy of light raged on. Before his very eyes, the mist transformed itself into a giant dragonfly. Large multifaceted eyes burned a brilliant reddish glow and huge extendable jaws snapped at the Spell of Tranise! Six smoke possessed legs poked and jab at the radiant energy and suddenly it was as if Tranise had had enough! Tranise wrapped it spiraling tendrils around the apparition and blew. The dragonfly was blown apart and the evil mist raced away into the night sky! Then the radiant energy turned its attention on the bullets being flung at it. The trooper knew he was helpless to do anything but hide in his cruiser like a shameful coward. "Base, don't think I'm crazy but there was a giant dragonfly cloud ,umm fighting with what appears to look like an ghost made of light bulbs! The shit is going down around the twelfth mile marker on Mountain Highway! At the Brewster place, it's that huge mansion out in the sticks! We need the Armed Forces in here, now!" The operator responded. "I know where you're talking about trooper, several calls have poured in from that area. Back up is on the way, just hang in there trooper: Help is on the way!" Trooper Jordan was sure it was Keisha Brown now, her sweet little girl voice came through clear and crisp amidst the blast of gunshots. "We have officers and civilians injured Keisha and we need ambulances right away!" All around him, bullets were flying into the air: trying to take aim at the last foreign invader; not even making a dent. Angel of Wind Tranise just hung there in the air unphased. Made of the purist red, yellow, green and amber light; she brought her Power of Natures' Winds to a jolt category eight and repelled the insects made of lead the humans were flinging at her. The jolt of air pushed everything back over five hundred feet. She looked upon them, with pity in her eyes. She had been summoned to help them battle The Mist and her job was done. She whirled through the night and air hurled herself at the mansion. Trooper Jordan thought that she was going to make the mansion explode so he ducked down further but she or the mansion didn't explode. There was just a flash of brilliant light into the walls of the mansion and just like that it was gone. By the time, Police Chief Reeses Clay had arrived on the scene and he sat in his car and observed the radiant light disappear into the mansion. As he got out of the car, he gazed up into the clearest night sky he had ever seen, he said to himself. "Whatever the fuck is going on down here is coming from that damn mansion!' Twenty police cars had arrived to nothing but a crystal clear sky and devastation around them. Trees were flattened, cars were upturned. People were bleeding with their face covered in black dust and one woman was screaming for her dead husband. But through it all, the mansion just stood up there on its sloping hill; brilliantly and magnificently unscathed.

Scripture 12: The Quest for The Peruser

Secretary of Defense Robert Harden was the epitome of WASP breeding. Tall and broad shouldered, he worked out to keep his fifty year old body in top condition. He wore his dark brown hair shaved to within an inch of his brain, classic military and it somehow served to accentuate the startling green of his eyes. The liquid emerald of them isn't what made them startling. It was their stark emptiness: as though nothing could survive in that sea of molten ivy. But somehow the emptiness compelled you and you couldn't help but stare at him and wonder if anyone truly lived at mind-1-0 Harding. Sometimes, you just couldn't tell. He was a intelligent man, weathered through WestPoint and two wars and he had earned his position not only on the battlefield but at home during the 9-11 attacks. His wife was the military and the citizens of America his children. President Deanvilt was his God and it was at her behest that he had been sent to NASA'S Deep Space Network to collect a report of highly classified information: information that the government could not afford to leak to the media at any cost and it was for this reason that she had requested him, to do the job.

Harden had been met at the door of facility by a team of his own men. President Deanvilt had ordered that the astronomers credited with the discovery be sequestered away in a safe room until he could ensure they were not a threat to national security. She didn't want them "unintentionally" leaking their findings all over CSNN later that evening. Her presidency couldn't afford some mindless babbling of space nuts baking to death out in the Mojave. Anyone else working there was to also be detained until no concern of threat was evident. Any phone calls from the complex were to be traced and any leaks were to be handled appropriately. His team of elite forces had arrived hours before and the complex was on lockdown. He was ushered to where the waiting astronomers were and after collecting the packet of information ordered that they and the three other employees working that day be killed. It was to be made to look like an incident of group hysteria triggered a mass suicide. There is a group of only three humans that work for NWL. (New World Law.) You will never ever hear of this government but in this scroll. They are the only humans on earth who know of The Book of Spanton. Their job is to keep it a secret from the planet. When they are called that mean it's the end of days. Your world leaders keep many secrets from the public: believe it or not, it's for your own good.

Your planet will be in chaos if the public knew the truth. The only reason I tell the truth now is because the time has come!

As he walked from the air-conditioned sanctuary of the complex in the Mojave Desert, the dry heat assaulted him. He tried to concentrate through the blazing sauna but thoughts of President Deanvilt raced through his mind. She had been explicit in her command that there be no leaks to the media, no prying eyes. Prying, she had stressed. He knew the president could only be referring to his aid, Ross. He thought back on the event that had transpired upon them landing here and hoped to hell that he wouldn't have to fuck the kid up. Because he would. When he had asked Ross to wait in the Black Hawk transporting them, he had been given a curious and almost defiant look. Then after Harden had exited, the kid had tried to as well and Harden had strong armed him and settled him right back down in his seat. Then Ross had said something about him using undue force and Harden had blacked out on the kid. He punched Ross straight in the temple; the kid passed out and Harden went on to handle his country's affairs. Ross was lucky he wasn't dead.

He hadn't had a chance to look at the photos yet but the anticipation within him was mounting. He would try to steal a peak in the lavatory of the helicopter once onboard. Right now, it was urgent that he get back to Washington D.C. and deliver the contents of the package back to President Deanvilt. He walked across the sandy ground and bent down trained seconds before the rotating blades of the chopper could have taken a slice out of his head. He got into the waiting helicopter. The door was closed and they lifted off into the air. As he fit himself with the noise reducing headphones that allowed him to stay speak directly to the pilot he said. "To the White House, immediately!" "Yes sir." The pilot responded. When Ross came back to himself, he was in his bed; at his apartment. For the life of him, he couldn't remember how he had gotten there.

When Harden had arrived at the White House, President Deanvilt dismissed her Secret Servicemen and escorted him to a private antechamber under the floors of the Oval Office. "Show me the photos!" she said and he spread them out before her. Image after Image was lain before her. Of what appeared to be a huge, shadow colored plasma. A haunted, laughter-like cackle erupted from the President's throat and chills raced down Harden's spleen. He looked around the room while he tried his hardest not to pull his weapon. Only he and President Deanvilt were in the room. No hyena could be in this room, with them. Just as he thought that, the icy fingers raced down his spine again. Harden watched and listened as the President brayed and hawed like some side show act in the fucking circus. Whatever kept him from pulling the trigger, he didn't know. In fact he didn't know anything at all and he joined in on the laugh.

Christina must have zoned out because when she came back to herself, Harden was telling her. "The astronomers hadn't been able to tell exactly how dense this "plasma" field was but they knew it was huge when it passed by Jupiter and completely blocked out the storm called the Great Red spot from the telescopes view. When the object was further away, they thought it could be a rogue debris field; but as it progressed thru the cosmos, it was evident madam

President that they are on a direct course with Earth." "How long do we have before they arrive?" She asked. "Two, maybe three hours at the most." "Prepare the Armed Services for battle, Secretary Harden. Schedule a press conference for twenty minutes from now." And just like that, President Deanvilt got up and walked out of the antechamber. It was like she had known what was coming all along.

If part of the world still wasn't aware of what had transpired in Spanaway, Washington; they would be shortly. Police cars and fire trucks surrounded the mansion and a third helicopter marked, FBI was landing. Investigators were everywhere; combing through the debris left behind: hoping to find a clue of what had caused the damage. A news truck from the local station had arrived shortly after the chaos had subsided but they hadn't gotten their early enough. Many of the witnesses had already left, if they hadn't been carried away by the small fleet of ambulances that had been dispatched and Barbara O'Neil, the reporter, was having a difficult time getting any of the officers or agents to give her a statement of what had happened here earlier. If she couldn't get an eye-witness interview, then she had to get something. The truck for EBS news hit the brakes in front on the mansion and slid right into a tree; the blood sap was everywhere in the streets.

Carlton Callahan, the news anchor back at the station would begin airing live coverage in less than five minutes and Barbara knew that pretty soon, all the major news stations would be rolling into town. She was the first reporter on location for this breaking event and it was up to her get the scoop. So she had sneaked herself and Roger, her camera man past the taped off perimeter and they were stealthily making their way to the front door of the mansion. She was whispering back to Roger. "Get a shot of EBS news in the tree will you Roger; what a great blooper: and what is this red slippery wetness on the ground." "Freeze! FBI!" was barked at them from behind and Barbara and Roger froze making fun of the agent. Hadn't been the first time they had gotten caught snooping around, wasn't going to be the last.

"I'm Captain Ken Rollens of the F.B.I and where the hell do you think you're going?" In her head set, the producer was telling her that they would be cutting to her in five, four, three, two, Roger had been Barbara's camera guy for five years now and she only had to give him one look and he knew what to do. Barbara put her microphone to her mouth and began her interview. Roger flipped the light switch on the camera on and gave her the cue to go. "Carlton, I'm here with Captain Ken Rollens of the FBI. Captain Rollens, are you the head investigator of the occurrence here?" She poked the mic into Ken's face and Roger caught the comical look of confusion on camera. It was as though Ken just hadn't been ready to be put on the spot so completely. He was a trained interrogator however and he recovered quickly. "Yes, I am the head investigator here. I," It didn't matter what he was going to say next. That was all Barbara had needed to hear. Her next question was, "Can you tell us what happened?"

People were sitting in their homes watching in disbelief. Carlton, the local's favorite anchor, broke in and said. "This just in: we have uploaded live video of the celestial struggle that occurred only a few short moments ago. A passing motorist who witnessed the event sent this video in to the station from his cell. We will be back with Barbara O'Neil, our eyes on the ground: after the video. Please stay with us as we keep you updated." The video started and the battle between the Angel of Cosmic Wind Tranise and The Mist of Darkness was broadcast for all the world to see. Other videos like it had already landed on You Tube and My Space. The live feed button on the camera turned from red to green, letting Roger know that they were no longer streaming.

Ken glared at Barbara like she had grown eight extra heads in the few short minutes that had elapsed. "Special Agent Driscoll!" Rollens yelled and a huge linebacker in a grey suit lumbered over. "These two somehow managed to get past the perimeter. Detain them until I can make sure that it does not get breached again." He told Agent Driscoll. Barbara tried to interrupt but Ken wasn't trying to hear any of it. He strode away from them and if looks could kill, Barbara would be being held for stabbing Captain Ken Rollens in the back instead of impeding a federal investigation.

The commercial break was being put on hold and Carlton was back; presenting the information to the public. "In Pierce County, Washington; moments ago strange events took place. Viewers of this magnificent event swear to seeing ghosts and angels. Calls and emails are streaming in from many who believe that this is the epic battle between supernatural beings and that the end of times is upon us. We have all been affected by the plague like extinction of our children and now this. For those of you who may have just tuned in; we will be airing the video regularly because it is absolutely remarkable. If there was any doubt to the validity of supernatural beings, angels if you will; there can be none now. I have seen the video with my own eyes. Saw what appeared to be a womanly; otherworldly being of magnificent size and comprised of pure light battling an animated black cumulus cloud in the shape of a dragonfly. Is this a monumental hoax or mass hysteria, you may be asking yourself. What do all this mean? Yea, though I walk through the valley of the shadow of death, I will fear no evil: For thou art with me." He started to freak out: the news station cut off the sound.

The second hour in my dreams had now passed. The Hour of Awareness; it was now twelve forty-six am in Spanaway. Amber and I were in the Valley of Spanton. "It is here that we must find The Peruser." I told her. As we walked the streets, the rank smell of stale beer and nuts came from an alley. We turned that way and nearly stumbled over a drunken Spantonite passed out behind a trash bin. I learned no matter what world you go to; someone is always getting high. I nudged the drunk with my foot to get his attention and asked him. "Can you tell me where we can find The Peruser?" The stench of something that smell like cheap pine-sol came out with his answer. "He is two furlongs down; about four hundred two meters that way." He pointed. "Thank you sir." I replied and we continued on the way he had pointed. Amber looked back over her shoulder and noticed that the intoxicated man has disappeared." Carmen, why do I feel like theirs getting ready to be a royal showdown." Amber and the other guests in my dreams were oblivious as to what was going on back on earth. Here in Spanton, things were going as they had for countless millennia and undoubtedly, would go on four countless millennia more. "Carmen, maybe I shouldn't have made such a wish." "We can't do anything about it now Amber, you told the wishing tree what you want and trust me my friend you'll get your wish." We kept walking until we saw a hut surrounded by trees. "This must be where the Peruser dwells Amber. Stand back, behind me,just in case." I knocked on the door and heard an weary ancient voice respond. "Who enter my space of privacy?"

"Hello sir, my name is Carmen. I am the Seraphim of Dreams." The door open slowly; just enough for a dirty dwarf face to jut out from behind the door. Amber was standing just behind but to the right of me and she could only stare gape mouthed at what she saw before her. Black smears of grime and grease covered every inch of the filthy face that was sticking out of the door. She couldn't tell if the little man was black or green, beige or tan; so nasty was the dwarf face. A shaft of light poured out from above and below the head and it only served to illuminate the flecks of meat and other objects attached to the beard and moustache was mangy and matted; and the longer Amber stood there and gawked, the more a pungent odor started assaulting her senses. She thought to herself that of course he would have to be as foul as a dead rat and she prayed that we wouldn't have to go into the small square hut; and be confined with the pungent funk that was radiating out into open air.

"The Seraphim of Dreams you say. How do I know that what you say is true, show me any Spanton Spell and prove to me who you are." His black beady eyes sparkled with disbelief and I chuckled under my breath. "What do you think Amber? " I looked back at her and she was shielding her nose and mouth; trying to keep from breathing as much of the stench as she could. "Looks like your reading my mind sister." I did what the dwarf asked and gave him exactly what he needed. If this was The Peruser, we desperately needed his help. He needed me to prove that I was who I said I was. But I couldn't, nor Amber from the looks of it; stand the smell any longer. I bent down and scooped a handful of dirt from the ground. "Are you The Peruser?" I asked him. "I am who you seek." was his reply. "Come and stand before me." The short man finally came out from behind the door and Amber gasped when he came into full view. He was no taller than four feet; thin of stature and naked except for a loincloth. Every inch of him, including that little patch of cloth covering his twig and berries was covered in filth. I stopped him at arm's length because I don't think my stomach would have tolerated him being any closer. I waved my dirt filled hand over the little man's head and spoke the Rites of Purification; a powerful spell for cleansing. As the dirt sifted through my fingers, the scents of clove; sandalwood and honeycomb caught in the night breeze and the man and his single piece of clothing were made to be sparkling clean. The Peruser was completely bald except for midnight black eyebrows; moustache and matching beard that trailed the full length of his four foot frame. Freed now from the clinging debris and filth that had caused them to be so matted in the first place, the beard swayed in the breeze. His loincloth was made from leather and was a remarkable orangey-red hue. The Peruser looked down on himself and tears started to fall from his eyes." This is truly a wish come true Seraphim of Dreams. Ye have my thanks Carmen, what can I do for you?"

"Please my friend, I need the locations of the three remaining Celestial Stones." A look of fear appeared in the dwarfs eyes and as he looked between Amber and I: I knew he could aid us in our quest. His raspy voice said. "It's written in the scroll of Spanton that it would be a Peruser, a browser of all things; that would help bring the prophecy of Revelations to pass." The dwarf sat down on the ground, holding his head in his hands. "Why did it have to be me." he cried. "My fair Dream Angel, all I know is where you can find one of the stones. I know not of the others. I apologize for you; but we are all powerless to stop what is to come, you must play the part that was written for you just as Amber must: as well as myself." " Which of the Stones do you have knowledge of Peruser?"

"I know where you can find the Stone of Perfection." He grated. Amber looked to me and asked. "Stone of Perfection?" "Yes Amber, but it's not a stone like you think. It is a small planet, savaged by lightning strikes that allows the owner of the stone to summon Profective; a Golden Towering Angel of Perfection. He will create perfection in anything that his master orders." I explained. "Where can we find it little friend?" "You must go to the city of Rachelle at the end of Spanton and ask to meet with the leader of the city, Cyforah. She is the possessor of one of the stones you seek. She may also be able to tell you where the third and fourth stone's can be located." "Thank you my friend." I told the aged man." No, thank you my beloved Wish Angel. I've never looked and smelled so fine in all me life. I think that I'll search for a mate this evening." "Best of luck." Amber told him and with a big grin on his face he walk away with a bop in his step; he walked like he felt eight feet tall. Amber and I look at each other and laughed; when we looked back at him he was gone.

Scripture 13: Seal Off Washington State

Rick was still caught in his horrible nightmare. He was running down a dark, foggy road and his hands and buttocks were bleeding. He had managed to break free of the hook in the ceiling he had been tethered too and was now running for his life. His dead father was screaming behind him. "You can't run boy, I can smell the sin in your blood!" Rick saw a barn on his right and ran towards it, hoping he would find a place that he could hide. The trees over the barn bent down and tried to grab him. "That's right! There's nowhere you can hide: I'm going to get you boy." His father yelled. He ran away from the barn and on into the foggy night. Terrified for his very soul Rick screamed. "Carmen, you bitch! Wake the fuck up now!" The sky darkened and pus drops began falling from the sky. This wasn't an ordinary pus and as the drops splattered on the ground they sizzled. Tiny drops of pain seared his head, neck and arms and it was as though every drop was a burnt match striking his body. The agony was too much to bare in addition to all of the damage his father have inflicted and Rick decided to risk the tree's grasp; even that he might get caught by his demented father's souls to escape the dark rain's torment. The trees clawed at him but he was able to make it past and as he slammed the barn door closed, he looked down at his arms. Acid burns lined them and he could feel the searing heat on his head. Rick was in so much pain that his father chasing him didn't matter anymore. Nothing mattered at all except for the pain and that was his last thought before he blacked out. As far as the Hubriser Stone was concerned, he was getting his wish of affliction.

Judy was sitting in a corner crying. She didn't try to run for the door, she didn't have the strength. When she had tried to make a run for it before, she had burned her hand on the doorknob. Now, she just sat there feeling like she had been torn from the inside out. Blood was running down her leg because it had soaked through the panties that had, somehow, been put back on her. Held captive by her nightmarish fantasy, she felt the edges of shock began to blur her vision. She averted her eyes from the bloody smears and wet pieces that covered the sheets on the bed and instead tried to focus on not making the whimpering sound that kept escaping from her throat. It hurt so badly on the inside of her stomach and she wrapped her arms further around her, as she tried to remember what he had done to her. When had she passed out.

After her attempt to escape had failed, he had slapped her repeatedly and made her promise to never try and run away from him again. He had even told her that she had been given to him as a testament to his godhead and after that, he had stripped naked before her. She remembered watching, as his massive penis uncoiled itself. She had turned away from him when he began stroking himself, to get the blood flowing and that's when he had grabbed her and tried to stuff it's thick mass into her mouth. It was then that she had blacked out because she remembered not being able to breathe: then nothingness.

Now he was standing over her scowling and she shrunk in on herself, not wanting to look up and see the monster's hideous face. "You and me will marry soon Judy. We will make love everyday!" He started laughing then and Judy could only cry more hysterically. "I can't take anymore." She hiccupped and sobbed but he heard none of it. He gripped her by her hair and drug her back to the bed. He wrapped his hand around her neck and lifted her from the floor and threw her to the bed. He picked up the pink bloody pieces of shredded uterus on the bed and began smearing them over Judy's body. Under his breath, she heard him chanting. "So pretty, so pre-tty." She begged him for mercy but blood lust had deafened him. When his hellish penis hardened, fear caused her stomach to spasm in one huge cramp. She felt and heard a huge wet plopping sound escape her vagina and she raised her head up off of the mattress down to see what the fuck that had been. There lay her uterus, it's tattered remains out for all to see. "Perfect." The demented giant said and picked it up. He began rubbing it all over his penis and testicles and the temperature in the room spiked to over a hundred-twenty degrees. "Just let me die already lord." Was the last thing she said before blessed shock came and took her into the dark abyss.

Captain Rollens had had the security increased around the perimeter of the mansion and the reporter and her cameraman escorted out by Driscoll. He had bigger fish to catch than some nosy reporter looking for a scoop. They could set up like everybody else. Outside his perimeter. From the reports gathered so far by his team, he thought it a miracle that there had been only one death in this bizarre chaos. That had been an unfortunate man who had been hit by a falling tree as he and his wife ran for shelter. She had been carried away by paramedics still asking for him.

Something just kept bugging Ken, though. Nothing he had seen and heard so far about the battle in the sky could account for the huge fucking hole in the ground. Forensics had combed every inch of the scene so far and other than the physical damage, no proof of either of those beings could be found. They had been able to tell them that an abnormal amount of bird shit was found and Ken had nearly lost it. "Bird shit didn't make that hole in the ground so why in the hell do it matter. No mist I had ever seen had been able to morph into a dragonfly, either."

Chief Clay walked up to Ken at just that moment. "So Captain Rollens, what have you and your men been able to find out." The chief asked him. Ken looked at Clay and couldn't believe this man was the police chief of a town in north America. Chief Clay was only about five-five; with a rounded gut and balding head of gray hair. How dare this hick cop ask him what he had "found out." Ken had better things to do than explain himself to this nitwit but he would play nice as long as the sheriff kept giving him information. "Well Chief Clay, as the Special Investigator the bureau assigned to this case: I should be asking you that. What have you found out." he smirked.

Ken would never know it but masked behind the good old' boy face that Chief Clay wore at work, was a mind of keen intelligence. Police work had been born into him for five generations and he knew the likes of Ken Rollens. Ken wanted to show that he was the big cock; the head man in charge of this investigation and Reese knew it. He also knew that Ken probably thought he was his own grandpa. So who gave a fuck. Didn't Rollens understand that none of them could afford to have a pissing match? It was incredulous to Clay that out of all had happened, Rollens could stay caught up on nonsense: Clay wanted answers. Technically, he was right but it still burned Reeses' ass to have this guy calling the shots. Priorities; priorities the voice in Chief Clay's head warned him. Obviously the bureau didn't take what had happened in his county seriously: he did. That the FBI would send this guy to do a man's work wasn't his problem. He would leave his personal feelings out of it until the time was right. "No one has been seen leaving the mansion. Patricia Brewster is the owner of this estate and as we have it, she's an upstanding member of the community; never any problems here before and right now: we don't have a reason to suspect she's involved."

"Speak for yourself Chief Clay." Rollens snapped at him. "What do you mean by right now." Rollens started raising his voice. "I suggest you do not withhold information from me or I will see to it that you go back to pushing brooms or whatever you did before the real sheriff died. "Why what's happening in there right now Chief." Rollens asked him with a quizzical look on his face. Ken was surprised it was so easy to get all this information from the chief but attributed to incompetence. He was treating the chief like a suspect and he didn't give a damn. As long as he got useful information to report back to his superiors.

"Well, yeah. Right now, she and her staff haven't answered the door nor have we been able to reach anyone on the telephone." Ken said looking away. "It's past one o'clock in the morning. Don't you think it's kind of odd that no one's answering the door. Not even answering the phone? Hell, she couldn't be running errands at this time of night so we have to assume she's either in there or that she and her family are involve." Rollens said feeling sure of himself. Clay looks at Ken and say. "Well how about innocent until proven guilty and all that. I know she has two children and it is possible that they are in there as well." "It could be a hostage situation." Ken said quickly. "We just don't know enough right now. What we need to do is..," but Investigator Rollens cut him off.

"I think I know what this situation needs Chief Clay. Make sure your men keep the reporters and curious bystanders back and I will take it from here." And just like that, Investigator Rollens strode off; Smart cell at his ear: Getting ready to turn a bad situation to worse.

The SWAT team had observed motion behind windows throughout the house and the squawk on the radio alerted Chief Clay. The ray beams of the line spot lights pin pointed on the mistress home. They were trying to get a visual but nothing yet. "Keep me updated Jeff." Chief Clay said into the radio. "Wilhelm, come back."

Wilhelm here Chief." a deep base like voice crackled through the radio. Chief Clay had recruited Wilhelm as a teenager for the department and groomed him to be one of the best the department had on staff. Wilhelm was an example of what a mixed up teen could become if someone gave a fuck. This kid had turned out okay and Reese found it hard to believe that twenty years had gone by since he'd first met Wilhelm. A troubled, snot-nosed; sixteen year old kid. He was brought in after getting caught trying to steal yet another car and Wilhelm had had enough. He had gave the kid a permanent home, a good ass-kicking or two and the kid turned it around. It made Reese proud that his adopted son had wanted to follow after him and join the force. He had been tough as nails on the kid after joining but he had proven himself on his own terms and Reese respected Wilhelm for the being the man he had raised him to be.

"Tell me what your team has." Reese couldn't help but smile. He never stopped feeling that same sense of pride when he was on duty with his son. Clay had never married and Wilhelm coming into his life had been a godsend not only for Wilhelm but Reese too. No one knew, not even his son; that the night before Reese had met Wilhelm, Chief Reese Clay of the Spanaway Police Department had tried to commit suicide. There he sat, with his service pistol in his mouth; finger on the trigger, seconds away from blowing his brains out: when he heard a voice say. "Have Faith Son. I made no man to be alone and your purpose is yet to be fulfilled." Reese, sad and naked in his bathtub; took his firearm out of his mouth and he felt the arms of something surround him, then squeeze: No, not squeeze. Embrace him. He felt pouring into him the knowledge that he was greatly loved by one mightier than he and Reese flung himself flat, face down on the floor of his bathroom; as naked as the day he was born and thanked his God for his love. He had always been a good man but he was a stronger man after that.

"We'll be tapped into the security system in less than a minute and should be able to get a visual inside of the house. We'll only be able to see where there are cameras but it's a start for now." "We've got to get closer than the FBI will allow us if we hope to catch anything real on the directional mic's."

"Real?" "What do you mean real?" Reese pressed his son. Every little bit of information that could help make sense of all this was extremely important. Nothing could be overlooked.

"Well, right now all we're getting is some strange static that sounds like hundreds of people praying to die. It's gotta be something playing on one of the televisions in the house, right." Wilhelm said.

"Maybe not, son. Maybe not. You and your team keep on it and update me in five."

Chief Clay had been able to come up with a set of plans to the house and he was studying them now. What the hell was going on in that house. Investigator Rollens picked just that moment to come and snatch the map of the Brewster's estate out of Chief Clay's hand and looked at it like it was used toilet tissue. "Thank you Chief. I thought I asked your team to provide me with these blueprints over an hour ago."

Chief Clay fought a strong urge to punch the teeth out of Investigators Rollens face and nearly lost. He settled for stuffing both his hands (better safe than sorry) in his pants pockets and said. "Yep, you are right about that." He gave Ken his good old boy smile but something about that smile didn't reach to his eyes. Rollens took two steps back and that satisfied Reese a great deal.

Unnerved by the smile but encouraged by Clay's silence, Rollens continued. "Of course I'm right. You see Reese, as the local sheriff of this hick town: I didn't think you would have the people or equipment necessary to handle this operation. So I called in an elite team who could get the job done." When he had phoned back to Virginia, the Hostage Rescue Team or HRT for short was dispatched. Chopper blades sounded in the air and both Chief Clay and Investigator Rollens looked up. Three transport helicopters hovered stationary in midair, blades slicing into the night while black clad figures slid down ropes hanging from the belly of the three; giant metal beasts. Five feet from the ground they leapt from the rope, dropped to the ground and were gone. Clay and Rollens couldn't help but look at each other and then back again at the sight before them. Reese tried really hard to watch the next one land and then follow the skulking form to its hiding place but they were like smoke. Once their feet hit the ground, they were gone. Guess Investigator Rollens hadn't been kidding when he had said "elite". One giant hulk of a man dropped last. He was all business and apparently the one in charge because he didn't disappear. He just stood there and surveyed the damage. He was making hand signals to his invisible comrades and as the shadows started to move, so did hulk.

Investigator Rollens ran up to the man but was met with a highly classified assault weapon in his face. "Who the hell are you?" Hulk asked him. Chief Clay wasn't a rookie so he just hung back and enjoyed the show.

"I'm Special Investigator Rollens. You must be Special Agent in Charge Drinkwater. I'm the one that called the bureau and alerted them to the situation here so I'll be in charge and you can just follow my lead. Over there, is Chief Clay of the local PD. He's not much help; probably won't get much else from him." He slapped hulk on the back then: like they had been buddies back in high school.

Special Agent Drinkwater looked at Rollens like a roach on the wall. One that needed to be squished, badly. He shrugged the man's hand off of him, violently: and said. "Look here, Investigator Rollens. I answer directly to Assistant Director Heim who answers directly to Director Mueller. You might have heard of him kid. He's over the entire FBI. My team and I are here because you reported that civilians may be being held by the hostile forces seen earlier. This mission has the potential to be seriously dangerous because we have no idea what we're up against. I won't waste your time on a pissing contest here; so I'll just tell you now: my dick is way bigger than yours. So whatever you were doing before we got here, I suggest you continue!"

Rollens watched the back of Special Agent Drinkwater as he stalked away from him and wondered what the hell was bothering that guy.

Willie Drinkwater was big. Not big like in fat big but in huge, linebacker whose all muscle big. He was a Native American and proud of it. He wore his thick, black hair long but tied back from his face; rubber bands keeping the dense mass at bay. The fact that he led the most elite task force in bureau history was a testament to his leadership and tactical skill. He had met many a Rollens before and would again. New agents would always want to throw their weight around and seasoned vets would always get to come along and knock them back down a notch. That isn't what was chewing at his intestines like some malevolent piranha. No. It was the shit he had seen on the television. Headquarters hadn't been able to give them any more information that he had seen on TV. In short, they were stumped. When HQ was shit out of ideas, he and his team was on their own. He needed more information than Rollens had been able to provide and fast. He walked over to where Chief Clay was standing.

"Chief Clay, I'm Special Agent in Charge Willie Drinkwater." The men shook hands and as Drinkwater looked at Clay, he knew the man was smarter than he let on. Beneath that ready smile lurked a brilliant cop and Drinkwater was glad that someone with experience had been on the scene with Rollens. "Chief, what do we have here?"

"Well, we haven't been able to determine if anyone is in the house. Our mics can't pick up a damn thing because of some strange feedback coming in." " That Rollens of yours, he's been up to the house three times but, no answer. My SWAT team is ready to enter the house with force but we'll let you and your team take point."

Investigator Rollens had decided to pursue the threat in his own fashion and had mobilized himself and his two man team in front of the doors of the mansion with a blow horn. "Please come out with your hands up!"

Mistress Pat had knew about everything that was going on outside off the mansion. Her beautiful home was about to be invaded by the police and she knew she had to act. She ran down to her dungeon an unlocked the doors to let out the souls she had saved. She was going to need all the help she could get. When she opened the doors, the souls burst forth; still screaming from the pain and horror they had experienced in Carmen's Dreams! They swept through the mansion, through unseen crevices in the mansion walls and outside over the roof top: But no further. They couldn't leave from the vicinity around the house: tethered by an invisible leash. Bound by the power of the Hubriser Stone.

Rollens saw the spirits materialize outside of the walls of the mansion. So did everyone else standing outside of the mansion. News crews from every station were sending live feed of the event back to their networks. Bullhorn in tow, Rollens hauled ass with Driscoll right on his ass.

The phone in the mansion was ringing incessantly. The shrill, annoying ring of it was echoing among the wails of the dead and it was driving Pat insane. Pat thought it was the authorities again, trying to get in. Wanting to find out what was happening, if she knew anything. The voicemail picked up on the fourth ring and when her mother's voice came across the line and said, "Patricia, it's Mom." She picked up. "Yes, Ma. I can't talk now, please; I don't know what's going on with me." Pat could hardly get a word in because her mother was assaulting her with a barrage of questions that she just couldn't answer. "Patricia, your place is all over the news. I am so glad your father is not alive to see this mess." That did it for Pat and she started crying "Ma, I can't talk to you right now, I'll call you back." "What have you done Patricia, where are Carlos and Sonya?" The scorn in her mother's voice was thick. If her mother knew that she had sent her children into a portal; a portal to another world: to save them from the Rapture. "Bye, Ma. I love you!" Pat hung up the phone and cried.

Outside, cell phones began ringing. The tactical members were working so their phones started to vibrate.. Then another, and another. Rollens phone was ringing but he ignored it. He was intent on giving "Special Agent" Drink, as he had dubbed him, a piece of his mind. How dare he and his men ignore his attempt to enter the mansion. They should have been there to have his back and he was going to tell him so. Rollens, not Drink, was in charge. He spotted the third man in his team: Agent Johns, running towards him at break neck speed. Agent J.Johns skidded to a stop in front of Rollens, crying like a baby. "Ken, I'm sorry. I can't do this. I have to go, my son. Oh god, my boy is dead." Agent Johns wailed. He was overcome by grief and he threw himself on Rollens' shoulder, hanging on for dear life. "He was only twelve years, Billy, only twelve." He cried. Snot ran from his nose and onto Ken's suit. He pushed the grieving man away from him and told him to go. Just then, Ken's phone rang. He prayed that it wouldn't be his wife when he looked at the number. With trembling hands, he looked at the number. It was his wife. He slipped the phone back in his jacket pocket. If he didn't answer the phone, there might be a chance that his ten year old boy, his only son, his only child, might still be alive. Alive and at home with his mother.

With the information the NASA scientists had compiled, Secretary Harden had been able to plot the landing area of the space fleet. "Mrs. President, we believe that if the course of these beings remain undeterred, they will land in Spanaway, Washington." President Deanvilt was livid. "You dumb fuck! Do you really think I need you to tell me where they are going! Do you look at the news, Secretary Harden!? Do you! Why, why are they going to Spanaway Robert!? That is what you can tell me! What the hell is going on in Spanaway, Washington Robert?" President Deanvilt didn't know it, but as she became more enraged, her pupils were lost. In their stead, were two; deep black holes that promised death. Secretary Harden was entranced and could only reply. "Yes, Madam President." "That's better Robert, in the meantime, seal off Washington State. No one is allowed in or out." "Yes my master."

Within a half hour, the U.S. Army had sealed off any point allowing entrance to the state. The third largest ferry system in the world had been suspended until further notice and no planes were allowed to land or take off from any of the sixteen airports sprinkled throughout the state. All state routes leading in or out were also blocked. Phone grids were backed up from the millions of families trying to get in contact with their loved ones. The press was on it like hotcakes. Death had come like a Thief In The Night and stolen away more innocent lives: now the U.S. Government was quarantining the entire state of Washington. News helicopter flew perilously close to the no fly zone that had been enacted and the pictures they were sending back were riveting. Thousands of motorists were clogging the major arteries out of the state and the roads were gridlocked. Mobs of people had abandoned their vehicles, if they even had one; and were at the borders: trying to get across. The armed sentinels were having none of it. They pushed the growing mass back and hoped to hell, things didn't get much worse. They had been authorized to use force if necessary, and pretty soon it was going to be necessary. Other countries around the world started to make threats toward the State of Washington. If the United States couldn't control this problem a nuclear missile could. The world started to believe that Washington State is causing this madness to happen across the globe.

Scripture Fourteen: The Legendary Diamond Shield Of Atlantis

Humans around the world were in shock. Every channel on television showed images of dazed, crying men and women; bodies of dead children piled up high as ten feet in some countries seen on the news. People of every ethnicity were praying, calling out to their respective "God's." The World Health Organization had still been trying to get a count on the number of deaths so far and with the recent "outbreak", they were estimating the toll to be well near two billion youth's deceased. Some countries went as far as burning piles of children at a time; to keep the harmful development at bay. Mother's and fathers of teenagers were holding fast to them. Teens were clutching back because they could feel the peril. Youthful rebellion was over, death was coming again: soon. They could feel it. The arms they had been fighting were the arms they ran to now. The sense of normalcy that had been, less than twenty four hours ago, had been stripped away. Their wouldn't be any school this week; or next month: whatever had been was gone. Now they just wanted to go to sleep and wake up. For those who had had younger brothers and sisters, their fear was multiplied tenfold. Imagine playing a game of basketball out back with your little brother and see him make a jump shot and then crumple to the ground. Gone. Brushing your sisters hair, listening to her talk about the boy she liked at school. Next, her lifeless body slumping out of the chair. They would be next if the "epidemic" continued. They could see the helplessness and fear in the eyes of their parents. The End of Times prophets were out on their street corners in full effect; preaching that it was the work of the all mighty. "WE MUST REPENT." They yelled. Houses of worship were full of people seeking answers. When would it all end? What was happening? Could they be saved? Answers the clergyman desperately wanted to give them, but couldn't. Hell, they had no clue themselves. It was apparent that nothing could stop this invader from heaven. The silver Fog slithered around looking for innocent souls. Crowds of people in Africa tried to out run the dark shadow of the Gofogen. Busting out of the silver fog it passed through the guilty leaving them unharmed. Some people in Paris had taken their children to air tight chambers wearing gas masks. This will not stop The Thief Of The Night. It materialized in the middle of the chamber in mid-air. Parents held tight to their children and begged god for forgiveness. The Gofogen passed through them and took their souls. It pass though the walls of the chamber and left behind dead children in the arms of their parents.

Mistress Pat had refused to respond to the FBI. Some asshole was still out their telling her to come out with her hands up. She had let the souls loose because she had hoped it would scare them into backing off. "We will enter the house with force in five minutes if you don't respond. We will shoot if forced." The voice bellowed again out of the bullhorn.

"The hell you will!" Mistress Pat exclaimed and went to the stone. She called upon the Great Devy and like clockwork, he was there in the stone. "Yes Master, What is your desire?"

"Devy, the FBI is here. They are threatening to bust threw the door if I don't answer it. What can be done?" she asked him.

"Mistress, have you forgotten? You are the owner of the cosmos, whatever you have need of; just wish for it and it will be."

Mistress Pat walked to a window and looked out at the small army surrounding her house. She had seen the three people in black drop from the chopper marked N.W.L. and she knew they would mean business. She knew she couldn't ignore them for much longer and she damn sure wasn't going outside to "talk" to them. And she hadn't forgotten not one goddamn bit about The Them heading her way! Protection is what she needed. Protection from a threat as old as time. From the window, she told Devy. "I wish for my home to be protected against any weapon known."

"Your wish is my command my Mistress." Devy's demented black eyes rolled back into their boiled red sockets and he began to call upon The Legendary Diamond Shield Of Atlantis. Speaking a language that human ears had never heard uttered, a transparent impervious shield made with diamonds from the universe E'ly, like a huge dome: it began to appear around the mansion.

Pat watched while the substance began to materialize around the edges of the police blockage. The police and crowd pushed back from it and they too watched as the substance hardened in to a transparent shield; upward and over the mansion until the entire place was completely surrounded. With seemingly no way in, or no way out. The mistress walked over to the shield and put her hand to it; it went right through. She was thinking to herself that no way in hell was a giant soap bubble with rainbow lights going to protect them from the threat headed their way and she walked back over to the stone. Pat sometimes forgot who she was dealing with. "Uhh, Devy, I don't have time for your bullshit! What the fuck is that? What the fuck! You think the fucking Them is going to attack us with a Q-tip. Bastard, fucking explain: now!" She raged. She was furious, Devy wanted to play fucking games while the world was coming to a end. Motherfucker!

Devy was thinking that it was a great damn thing that she could only see his face in the Hubriser Stone. He had a huge erection right now, caused from how she had degraded him. He did sometimes forgot how ill educated humans really were and sighed to himself. Now he would educate his Mistress, he smiled then, smugly; back at his master, saying. "Mistress, you may have read in your texts; school books you call them: that Atlantis was a mythical place. An island somewhere in the sea that was destroyed by cataclysmic events over ninety-six hundred years before Christ but that isn't the case. Plato's account of Atlantis wasn't far from the truth however. Atlantis was never destroyed, it was reborn. The Atlantian's were a powerful people, not only in war but in technology. Long ago they had been visited by The E'lyians from the universe E'ly. This is what caused the thriving advances of their civilization. The E'lyians are who brought the Diamond Shield into existence. Given to the Atlantian's as a gift of peace; they used it as their escape to another world; a world where their society could flourish undeterred by man's thirst for bloodshed. Their out was the oceanic world below your very feet. Your silly human race as they call themselves today will never see into the world at your ocean's floor; because you are to consumed with division and personal wealth. The Atlantian's knew that they needed to be able to live inside of the waters lapping at their shores. They respected what makes up over seventy-five percent of the world you all inhabit and it is in the greatest depths of the ocean trenches that they reside. Below there is another world, controlled by the Atlantian's. Some of what you call u.f.o.'s, aren't always from another realm: some of these crafts come from the deep right here on your planet. The shield chooses who or what may pass through its matter. The Diamond Shield is impermeable and no harm will come to you under its protection Mistress Pat."

Devy went on to explain. "When The Them first arrived on your planet, you were but Neanderthals. Scrounging for berries, running naked; through your wilderness. Your race had to be orientated, a process that first begun over four and half million years B.C at the Earth's equator. When they came, they gifted your species with the Missing Link. The Link that would take you humans from simple-minded survivalist to intellectual beings; able to reach unimaginable heights if you hadn't had to be left on your own. The Link was never of your planet which is why your scientists can't find it. They could if they could reach the outer realms of space but your people refuse to listen. Several attempts by Spanton's messengers have been made to teach your people the truth. Atlantis was one of the civilizations to profit from these messengers. Maybe this is a return of the old times. Devy had a wishful look in his eyes then and he looked at Mistress Pat as though he wasn't seeing her but civilizations long since past. "Mistress, why is it so easy for the human race to blindly ignore the truth if it is laid before them bare?"

Mistress Pat could only stare into the stone, slack-jawed and happy as hell that she was on the inside of the Diamond Shield. "Devy, I don't understand half of the shit you just told me but thank you for your help. Umm, exactly how old are you any damn way?"

Investigator Rollens and Agent Driscoll were trapped. They hadn't been able to escape before the dome covered the estate and Rollens was telling Agent Driscoll that it was now a hostage situation. He said that rescue would be there for them soon. He still hadn't answered the call from his wife. As though staving off talking to her would delay the inevitability that his son was among the tragic deaths. The apparitions were hovering above them both, taunting them telling them that they would soon join the host of souls already lost to the madness. They laughed and laughed and swirled around them until Ken ordered Driscoll to open fire over the evil things. The police on the outside of the shield took the gunplay for an attack against them and had had enough of the show. The waiting was over. They had to act: now. "FIRE!" was ordered and a barrage of gunfire rocked the night. The mansion had already become the greatest side show on earth, now the real fireworks were getting started. All around the globe, people watched as Mistress Pat's mansion was assaulted. Through the blaze of bullets, the networks covered it all. Never missing one news worthy scene. The shield stood unscathed. It didn't really repel the bullets, it more so absorbed them. The police could see and hear them hit the glass but the bullets just seemed to evaporate into whatever material made up the shield. Then the Diamond Shield turn the tables and shot their same bullets back at them. Warning them to leave the mansion. Everyone hit the ground.

Pat had witnessed it all and she knew she had to deal with the two agents who had gotten themselves caught on the wrong side of the fence: so to speak. Mistress Pat walked outside her front door, stood directly in front of the two men and said. "You two have a choice. Either you can let me escort you the hell off my property or I can lend you a hand into another life. Either way, you have to leave here; which will it be?"

Standing there on the opposite side of the law, near the scariest bitch either of them had ever met, under the strangest shit that had ever been witnessed on the planet; Driscoll and Rollens replied in unison. "Off." Mistress Pat thrust her arms forward and sent the two men flying into the night air. Through The Diamond Shield with two audible pops and just like that, they were landing among their fellow policemen. Scared shitless, pride shattered, but otherwise unharmed. Mistress Pat looks at her hands and started to believe in her power. "That felt fucking good." She said. Amazing colors shoot inside the shield of diamond like energy ready to explode. It was the greatest light show ever displayed on planet earth.

The news hounds started assaulting the two men with questions. They were the only ones who had spoken to anyone inside of the house. They had been inside of the shield and the media wanted to know about it. Agent Driscoll, with a look from Rollens was quick to fade quietly into the background. Rollens would handle the media. He brushed the dirt from his suit jacket, straightened his tie and smiled for the camera's. "Can you tell us what's going on up there? What did she say? Were your lives in danger?" Questions, questions and as he stood before the media regaling them of the events that had just transpired the police work continued on without him.

Unaware of what was going on around him, two black unmarked cars pulled in front of the blockade. Four men got out of the cars dressed in dark two piece suites and dark sunglasses. "Who's running this operation?" a loud voice yelled over the ruckus. Rollens raised his hand and ran over to the man, hand outstretched, ready to be acknowledged as the one running the show.

"I am, Special Investigator Rollens of the FBI. Who are you?" Ken looked the man up and down and added, "Must be CIA from the suit." He laughed then and looked around expecting everyone to join in. No one seemed to get the joke, even Driscoll. It's a cold lonely road to stardom, Ken amused to himself.

"Agent Rollens, I'm John Darnville with the CIA." " The media circus you have going is over. "You can stay and hang around if you like, but we have control over this now." Darnville motioned for one of the suits behind him to come over. "Mark, I want this media out of here thirty minutes ago. Civilians go to. The debriefing room should have been set-up already. Get on it." The man went about his duties without question. To Rollens he said. "The CIA has learned that we are dealing with a very wealthy woman who is into some oddities. That is all I can tell you at this time and I think it is a really good idea if you excuse yourself and see to your personal affairs. Grief has obviously overcome you, agent." He had said that last word as though it was a dirty thing and then walked away, towards the command center. Leaving Ken standing with a trail of tears on his face. He was ready to pick up the phone and call home.

Scripture 15: Assassination of the President

In Washington, President Deanvilt's news conference had begun. "People of the United States and across the world, I know what you must be seeing on the news, experiencing in your very homes, is unfathomable. Though I am not a parent, I grieve for the loss of the innocent as much as anyone. You have my condolences. I am urging you to stay in your home until we learn where we stand. There are false prophets who are teaching that this is the end of days. It is not true. This is a time of New World Order where all countries will join together and fight a common enemy. Let religion comfort in your grief but make no mistake. The terror that has fallen upon our planet is a threat from above. Yes, I repeat from above. Satellites have detected a fleet of unknown craft approaching earth. The exact number of craft at this time remains unknown. I urge you not to trust anything that comes from above. These beings are crafty and have been known throughout humanity to confuse and cloud the truth. Yes, your governments have known about it and to protect you, the truth was hidden. But now is the time for truth. Now is not the time for passiveness. It is the time for decisive leadership. Forgive your leaders for not disclosing a fundamental fact of life to you. They still haven't wanted to tell you but I made them see the necessity in allowing you, the world public, to be free from ignorance. We believe the events over Spanaway are to be blamed for why these beings are coming here and this is why I ordered the quarantine of Washington State. I have banded together the tribes of all nation and we are forming an army of unimaginable size and we will defeat this threat. At my next conference I will explain about the NWL: The New Worlds' Law. Thank you." Her staff stood around her, expressionless, simply nodding their heads. The media tried asking questions but none were answered. Flash bulbs were going off in the chaos and the next thing you saw was a hand with a gun pointed at President Deanvilt's head from point blank range. Everything and everyone seemed to stop. The next thing heard was a gunshot. Not a second had passed by. The Secret Service dove for the president but it was too late. Every camera caught a bullet blasting through the front of President Deanvilt's forehead and out the back. The brain splatter was on everyone surrounding her and as the lifeless body fell to the ground: the cry of. "The President of the United States has been shot!" rang out. The President was rushed from the media room by emergency paramedics and into a waiting medical-chopper. She was flown to John Hopkins in Maryland. "The man who shot the President was a sixty year old Priest from Jerusalem: no more info at this time."

The world went crazy. People ran to the stores and also broke into stores that was closed, trying to stock up on food; water and other supplies. Homes was broken into,police left their jobs to be with their own. Riots were taking place all over and any resemblance of world order was lost. People were killing each other over the last case of bottled water. Suddenly the stuff was more expensive than gold and if you didn't already have some at home, chances are you weren't going to get any. A bottled water plant in lower Virginia had been invaded by masked men. The vigilantes hadn't only taking as much water as they could; but raped the female employees and left the men for dead after beating them into unconsciousness.

In response to the shooting of the President, three stealth jets and three hypersonic bombers were flying in and around the airways over Baltimore and Washington. The country was in a cataclysmic state of terror. John Hopkins had been more than ready for her arrival but it was too late. Christina Deanvilt, forty-fifth and first female president of the United States of America was pronounced dead. The trauma staff said that she was moribund upon arriving; no hope of survival was possible. The bullet had struck her from point blank range. Her body had been taken to the morgue, where it was waiting to be flown to Andrews Air Force base for autopsy. Vice President Jeffrey Hillard was scheduled to take the oath of office. White House Press Secretary Andrew David would be giving a press conference in less than two minutes, to announce Deanvilt's death and Hillard succession. America's grief had just been triple folded and the world grieved with them.

Russian President Alexsandre Lomykin, used the Moscow-Washington Hotline to call President Hillard. In addition to conveying his and his countries deepest sympathies over the loss of President Deanvilt, there was a more urgent matter at hand. It was the fleet of flying objects heading to America and surprisingly, President Lomykin wanted to know if he could offer his assistance. His scientists observed the fleet less than fifty miles from the earth's aurora. It wouldn't be long before they got to where they made it to their final destination. What was the country, the world going to do. President Hillard had no answers. He hadn't even been aware of the u.f.o.'s coming until less than a half hour ago.

Jalmari Virtanen, a flight engineer on the International Space Station woke from a fitful sleep. He had been having a too vivid nightmare of floating, without a tether, in outer space. Suspended over the earth by some invisible string, he watched as the blue oceans turned red. The deep, crimson red of fresh blood, began its insidious spread from the northwest corner of the U.S. and then continued on until no trace of blue water could be found. The fear of floating out in space with no harness strangely isn't what had horrified him. Somehow the floating was safe and he knew; knew, that as long as he was there in space, he was safe from whatever had turned the oceans to blood. Then the bodies started falling. Hundreds of bodies falling from the heavens and plummeting into the earth's atmosphere. They weren't bodies he had ever seen before though. They were grey, humanoid beings. Sunken; almond shaped eyes stared out of egg-shaped heads. Hundreds, thousands of them falling to earth. He was staring into the empty, black, eye cavity of one of the beings when suddenly; he felt something grab his leg and then: he was falling too. Falling, carried faster by the being hanging from his leg and then he messed up. He looked down and what he had seen, freed him from the awful dream. He had looked down seen the devil, holding on to his leg. The devil looked up at him, smiled; and when it did so, he saw himself screaming in the pit of its belly. That had woke him up alright. Inside the Destiny Laboratory, his private quarters for the duration of the mission, he unfastened himself from a rack and floated over to the window. He thought it would help shake the last visages of the dream from him. Calm him down some but what he saw from the window shook him more than the nightmare had. Not hundreds of bodies falling. Hundreds upon hundreds of silver craft approaching earth; at break neck speed. "Dear God, save us all." He didn't wake his fellow astronauts; still sleeping. Oblivious to the tyranny headed their planet's way. He knew he should wake them up, the Captain, especially, but not yet. First, he called Prime Minister Mechelin of Finland and told of him the coming threat. Jalmari had been born in Finland and the love he had for his country, was immense. Having no family, it had been his small village of Kaskinen that had loved him, paid for his schooling. All fifteen hundred of the residents had seen him off at the airport. They sent him messages daily so that he knew he wasn't alone and he would let them know that they weren't alone now. From outer space he was watching over them. Prime Minister Mechelin asked no questions, just listened, told him thank you and hung up the phone. Stunned by Mechelin's brusqueness, he hung up as well and stopped delaying the inevitable. He woke everyone on the station and told them all to look out the window.

The United States Geoglogical Survey reported several magintude four-point-zero earthquakes in the Yellowstone National Park. They also reported that the quakes were increasing in frequency and intensity. Tremors could be felt for hundreds of miles around. Long fissures broke the terrain of the park apart, exposing chaotic fields of geothermal vents. Vents, inactive for six hundred thousand years were now busting through the surface. Ejecting forth an evil, pyro-plastic debris from the very bowels of the earth: your time is running out!

Unbelievable: all of this and you still sit there in your tiny space of matter reading the Scriptures of Spanton: what a brave species you are. Some of you already burned this scroll calling it the devil's work; and we know who you are: while others embraced the truth. Whatever you choose to do; believe me: I'm impressed. All you have to do is believe in him!

My Mistress was in distress. She ran to the stone and wished to see Kirk Bailey. The asshole that had brought all of this trouble upon her. The man who had brought the fucking Hubriser Stone to her doorstep. With the Gift of Knowing, she touched the stone and thought Bailey. She saw there had been a plane crash near the island of Montserrat. The pilot had died but Bailey lived, barely. Why had The Them allowed that bastard to live! As I watched my master stare into the stone, I saw a revelation of truth come over her. The Them hadn't allowed Bailey to live. Some other beings had, but who the hell were they. The harder she stared into the stone, the more difficult it became for her to see them. It was as though something kept clouding her mental vision. So she stopped trying to see them. The information that was being relayed to her was more important anyway.

The stone showed her fifteen hundred years before the birth of Christ. It showed her the native Mayan people, the Jaguar civilization of pre-Spanish South America. They were a proud and technically advanced people and she saw them gazing into their Meso calendar. Then she saw a man unlike any she had ever seen before. He moved as though he was fluid and in her mind she heard the name Chilam Bilam spoken. She saw the Mayan people bow before him. Mistress Pat saw Chilam telling the Jaguarian's something dreadful and watched as he pointed to the south. She couldn't hear what was being said and doubted greatly that if she could hear, she would even be able to understand the ancient language that must have been spoken by these awesome people. It was Chilam that she kept focus on. She had never seen anyone like him. He wore a suit of eel skin and it fit him just as such. His hair was the color of ocean water being churned up before a storm. Inhumanly tall with long thin finger and long web feet, she couldn't help but wonder where this man had come from. She saw Chilam leading the Jaguarian elders to the ocean and the fear on their faces was evident. They bowed to him after that and she wondered again, what was being said, what was taken place. The next thing she saw was most of the Mayan's coming down from the highlands to meet together at the water's edge. Thousands of men, women and children stood at the shore with a look of dazed confusion on their faces. The mother's clutched their infants and pregnant bellies, grasping their husbands, looking to them for assurance but there was none to be had. They had brought nothing with them and obviously they wouldn't be going home. Then she saw Chilam emerge from out of the ocean. The Jaguarian's fell to their knees and worshipped. There were some to afraid however and they ran back to where they had come from and did not return. Those who stayed and bowed at Chilam's feet were motioned to rise and follow him. Into the ocean they went, one after another. Over two hundred thousand Mayan people she guessed had vanished into the ocean's abyss. Mistress Pat thought it was craziness she was seeing through the stone, but she knew it was real. What she was witnessing was Mayan's salvation. No one ever knew what had caused the abrupt end of such a great civilization but they had seen their own demise with the help of the great one known as Chilam. He had came and told them of the Spanish conquistadors and their thirst for blood and warned that those who stayed behind, would be enslaved for one thousand years to come. It was either follow him into the ocean's dark abyss for salvation or perish. Chilam had come from the Atlantian's civilization and they knew of the great Jaguar people. The Atlantian's needed to add new blood or else their culture would die. The Jaguar people had been selected because they embodied most of the principles that the Atlantian's did. So the Mayan's didn't die out. Of course those who stayed behind did but the majority of those people who were led to a greater destiny by a civilization greater than them. They had received an invitation and they took it. They knew of war and strife, hunger and famine and they trusted Chilam to keep them safe. They were taught secrets you could never understand and will never be able to until you can withstand the pressure of the ocean's trenches. They come and go as they please and not all of the ufo craft you see are from outer space. They come from your world's oceans. The Mayans rule the sky;not you!

My master was astounded. She felt as though her head was about to explode because of the epiphany that had just been shown to her. The stone continued to show her Bailey's plight. After Bailey's plane had crashed, he had been pulled from the water and taken into Nab'ee, located deep below the Puerto Rico Trench. Our scientists have estimated the trench to be almost thirty thousand feet deep but how wrong they are. It goes much deeper than that. Into Nab'ee Kirk Bailey was taken and after they had scanned his brain for knowledge of the Hubriser Stone, they left him on a raft floating in the English Channel, not far from where the Seine River empties. He hadn't floated for very long when a private plane flew by and called help for him. Once rescued and well enough to travel, Bailey had moved himself into the Sainte Trinity church in Paris, France. He had barricaded himself inside of a private room at the top of the church and covered every square inch of the walls and floors with pages from the bible. Kirk was going to do whatever he could to keep the evil at bay. There he was sitting now,rocking back and forth,quoting scripture."That won't keep you safe, motherfucker! Devy, bring him to me!" Mistress Pat watched as Devy burst into the room that Kirk had tried to make holy before she could finish her words. With eyes of fire, the beast of hell looked around and saw the words of God. He laughed at the former Angel of Dreams, but when unseen flames started to consume him from within, he knew he couldn't stay. Devy grabbed Kirk with a huge clawed red hand and threw him through the portal.

The giant red hand burst out of the portal in front of Mistress Pat holding Bailey by the feet dangling from his fist. Kirk cried and screamed and even tried to bite Devy, but Devy held Kirk tight by his ankles. He wasn't going anywhere unless Devy or rather the master, consented. Mistress Pat started kicking him in and up; around his ass and was yelling at him, "What the hell did you give me Bailey! Get me out of this hell." she screamed. Devy drop him on his head.

Kirk was dazed. "I can't Mistress Pat." He whimpered. "This must all come to pass. For the rest of my life I'll see the souls that go through the portal, I can hear what they wish for. Last night one of your guest made The Forbidden Wish. One of your guest wished to see the Creator of All. It's forbidden Mistress Pat. When I heard this I ran to a church to hide behind God. He's our only hope." Kirk said with eyes wide from fear.

"Who is God Bailey," Pat asked. "He's coming my mistress, you'll find out." "Well it's Amber's wish, why is all this shit happening to me," she asked. "Forbidden wishes can leak into the outer world. You can't control anyone's wish. They must have free will," he said. "How do I get out of this hell that you put me in asshole?"

"You must find someone to sign the Scroll of Spanton. Then they'll live the nightmare." He explained. "Mistress Pat, I told you to give your guest souls to The Them. You did not, and now they're coming to collect. Please send me back to the church in Paris." "You say all I have to do is find The Replacer." She contemplated. "Yes, but you can't until after six forty-four am, all this must come to pass, The Forbidden Wish has already been made!"

Scripture 16: The Seraphim Of Distraction

The Peruser had told Amber and I that we must go to the city of Rachelle in Spanton and meet with the leader there, Cyforah. We left for the city shortly after and were almost there, but something was filling me with an immense dread. With the knowing that leaves me certain of the earth's fulfillment, I know that Julie will be able to help us in our quest, and it was her I could not stop thinking about on the way to the city.

Julie Covington was my dearest and only childhood friend. Laughing to myself, I think back on all of the crazy shit we did together as young girls and after my cousin Kim, I couldn't have asked for a better friend. She came into my life right after Kim had disappeared. Strangely as a transfer student although now I realize, I never knew where the hell she had been transferred from. From the first day we met, we had been like two peas from the same pod and I like to think that she was sent to me when I needed a friend the most. Through middle school and high school we were inseparable and when she told me she would be eloping with Stoney, her boyfriend all through high school; I had been happy for her. Since then, they had move to Seattle and avidly working on having some kids of their own. Under the current circumstances, I don't believe it's wrong of me to say I am happy that they hadn't been successful. To say that I'm happy I wasn't a godmother to Julie's children. Well, I am happy she has no children because I know her grief would be triple fold if they had been successful. I would never want to hear my dear friend cry her soul out and not be able to do something about it.

My family, my friend, those that meant so much to me are lost. I could save them if I choose. Yet, how can I make that decision for them. All of this has been so bazaar, too unreal to me and I can imagine talking to my father and mother, uncle and aunt would be even more bazaar. They couldn't, they wouldn't be able to understand. How could I choose to help my own family escape into the dark of night when the rest of humanity will be left at the mercy of those who call themselves Gods. So I leave them all to perish. The best I can do is be sure that it happens quickly for them. I must be blunt with myself if I have to live with the destiny of the world. I cannot afford to look through rose colored glasses. Yet, I know I can go back in time and be with them.

Julie isn't meant to perish. The feelings that are coming over me, the knowing that I have because I am the Seraphim of Dreams is telling me that Julie wasn't just sent to me on a whim.

She possessed something all along. Something I would need to fight the battle about to be waged. She has the spirit of Larishta hidden deep inside her. Larishta is a beautiful spirit that was honored before time by Nueden and Sotteros. It is able to travel through to other realms and share it's beautiful gift of distraction. When Julie was born, Larishta entered her body to hide and learn. I needed the Spell of Distraction that Larishta possessed and which my dearest friend Julie now owned. With all hell breaking loose on earth; Julie not hearing from me in weeks, I didn't think I would have the time to convince her of what had been lying dormant in her all these years. It would be like I was telling her that she had a benign cancer that had been sitting in her, waiting; inactive and now it had come malignant. Nope, I didn't think she was going to believe me at all. The choice was hers. She could either believe or die with the rest of the planet. As for me, I needed that spell; so I had to go back in time and i entered Julie's dream three days before the madness: while she and Stoney was sleeping. In the midst of the chaos I entered her dreams and I saw her there in a dark room calling out. Calling out for me. I felt so heartbroken for her there. I hadn't talked to her since my disappearance and it was obvious that she had missed me, just as much as I had missed her. I walked out of the darkness and like a shining beacon, I was there before her. She ran to me and we hugged and I barely didn't want to let her go but duty for both of us called. I explained what lay within her and that I needed the spirit to fight the Soulless Slaves.

Unfortunately, the only way I could release Larishta would be to release Julie's soul and take it to Spanton. "You mean, you're going to kill me Carmen." Tears welled in both of our eyes and I told her the truth. "Not kill you my beloved friend; but, Yes: I would have to put you to rest to release the spirit of Larishta; your body is useless for what you about to become. Spinning it in a way that any publicist would be proud, I managed to convince her that who; or what she would become would be far greater than what she could ever be if left to die here on the planet with everyone else. Julie wasn't having it. "Uh-uh bitch! You are telling me, that I have a fucking ghost inside me! What crazy drugs have you gone and got yourself hooked on." God, I loved this woman but I didn't have time to play pull-the-wool-over-Julie's-eyes so I did the only thing I could. I pulled her to me in a second embrace, this time an embrace of the lips and I kissed her with all of the passion a friendship can hold over the course of a lifetime. The truth poured from my mind, through my lips and into her heart. After I was done showing her; I released her and we both stumbled back. We looked at each other and kissed once again: but this time it was personal. When we finished expressing our deep feeling for each other Julie said. "Now, it all makes sense," she stammered. "Makes sense, how," I asked her.

"Well, I've always felt kind of strange. Like someone or something was trying to talk to me but I just didn't have the right equipment to listen. Only my father knew how I felt and I told him of a dream I had where God told me he needed me and that I must wait for him to call upon me." Chill bumps ran up my spine with what Julie had said and as I looked at her, I knew why we had been so close. The Creator had plans for us both from the very beginning. Both of us would perform his miracles against evil. Julie continued on, trapped in the memories of long ago. "My father, God bless his soul, he knew. He knew far more than I did and I remember him coming into my room on Christmas morning. He told me I was in a trance and shook me out of it and asked me where I had been. I thought it was kind of strange for him to ask me where I had been, but you know how religious papa was Carmen. He believed all along in miracles and the unseen and I think at some level, he knew what was inside of me, even though I didn't. I told him I had been with seven angels with seven trumpets and I was asking them if they could play a song for me. Papa had turned ghostly pale and performed the sign of the cross over us both. He told me then that I would be having more visions; visions of Revelation he said and he told me how blessed I was. I wish Papa was here now Carmen. I hugged her again because I could tell how much that memory had cost her. Julie's father had died not long after they had moved to our neighborhood and just as she had helped me grieve the loss of Kim, so did I with her father. To grieving little girls with the weight of the universe on their shoulders. Who the hell knew!

"Can I ask one favor, Carmen." "Anything girl, just say it." "Don't let Stoney wake up and find me dead, it would break his heart and I could never do that to him, okay. Just let him wake up and let me be gone." It's all ready done my friend and just like that Julie Covington was no more. With a wave of my hand, she was gone and she was on her way with me back to The World of Spanton. I felt sorry for Stoney, her husband, who would wake up and find her missing. But Julie's fate was far greater than the love either of them had for one another. It wasn't fair but what has already been written in the Book of Spanton that Larishta would rise against the beast. Larishta had been dormant in Julie since birth and now it demanded release. It's best I did it this way, I didn't want the power of the cosmos to choose Julie death for her. She's my best friend and I wanted this as painless as possible for her. I watched as she traveled back with me through the portal and saw Julie become an Angel of Spanton. They let the spirit out and the illumination of spectacular light that Julie became before my eyes made me wet between my thong. I left her in the Hall of Seraphims in Spanton with a promise that we will meet again.

Scripture 17: The Stone of Perfection

Everything is swiftly coming to pass. The next few hours, will require all of the powers that the cosmos can give me. I dread knowing the secret of life. The secret that I AM was so insistent on protecting. Amber and I were now approaching the land of Rashelle where the Queen of Perfection rules. The land there is perfect in every aspect, from the level of salt in the ocean to the level of acid in the dirt. Even the homes of its inhabitants were designed to line up precisely with the transit of the stars in the sky. Solid gold pyramids dominate the land and make it obvious where the Egyptians and ancient Mayans derived there technological expertise from. The knowledge from this ancient city is evident throughout your planet. Amber and I had landed amongst the palm fronds of a huge oasis teaming with life. Fish never seen before leapt out of the water and seemingly straight into the nets of the fisherman at the oasis's edge. We walked out from the cover the fronds had provided and were immediately met by a young man with fine silver mesh nets slung over his shoulder. He wore one of the nets over his own head and as he walked up to us he said, "Hello, may I sell you a mosca net?"

"Mosca net, what's that," Amber looked quizzically up at the young man. As soon as she had asked the question, she found out the answer. A flying object the size of a quarter buzzed up to Amber's neck and it bit her square in the jugular vein. "Ouch," she screamed and slapped at her neck. So quick was the thing that it had bitten her and flown away before she had even been able to swat at it. It looked like a strange breed of mosquitoes and biting fly and being larger than a quarter didn't stop it from being one of the quickest insects we had ever laid eyes on.

"That's a mosca," the young man said. "Please, give us two." Amber cried. "Excuse me my young friend, but would you be able to point the way to Queen Cyforah." I asked him. Strangely, the young man stared back at me and said. "My lady, please tell me what your name is because someone as beautiful as you must have a name just as legendary." In spite of myself, I couldn't help but blush and I told the young man my name. Amber was busy putting her net over her head and was only managing to get tangled up. When he heard me say. I'm Carmen, the Seraphim of Dreams." The boy screamed out loud. "As foretold in The Wonderful Scroll of Spanton; a seller would meet the Dream Angel and aid her in her quest! How honored my mother and father must be that their son was that seller! Please, you must let me take you to the Queen myself. You would honor me greatly in allowing me to escort you and your handmaid."

"Oh, she isn't my maid." I told the young man but he looked like I could have told him she was gold and he would have believed it. We walked through the woods on the dirt path to Rachelle. Just then the sky got dark and the sound of death came from above. We was being attacked by a swarm of moscas. "RUN!" The seller screamed. We ran through the woods and i use my wings of light for a protective shield. Just then a whole open in the sky and out shoots the Planet Perfection. It absorb the swarm and vanished.

Past the oasis and through the crowded streets, we followed the seller until we had come to a huge gate under heavy guard. Since my birth as the Seraphim of Dreams I had been too many realms in Spanton but never to the land of Rashelle and I had never met their Queen Cyforah but her cosmic spells were well-known throughout all the realms.

The guards at the gate approached us and said, "Stay where you are. What is your purpose for being here?" Undaunted I replied. "Please, I must talk to Queen Cyforah. I am Carmen Dreams and I believe she may be expecting me." A look of terror came over the face of the guards and they fell to the ground bowing at me and Amber's feet. The young seller jumped back surprised. He had probably never seen this side of the guards before and was rightfully, a bit scared. In unison they chanted. "Carmen Dreams, The Seraphim of Dreams: the Queen awaits you. Please follow us this way." One of the guards waived his arm and the gates opened. The seller stopped just past the gates and said. "Thank you Miss Dreams. It has been my eternal pleasure to await this day and help you on your journey." I told the seller thank you and just like that he was gone; right before my eyes he just vanished. Like someone put him here and took him away. The guards led the way up the golden palace steps into a huge golden pyramid that would put the Pyramid at Giza to shame. Even with its grandness back on earth, it didn't come close to the real splendor an active pyramid held. It was surreal. Her palace, for lack of a better word, was simply perfect. So perfect in its creation, that it was built directly under the portal to Nueden. The guard stopped us all ten feet short of the throne and requested a closer audience with the queen. Under constant guard, the Planet Perfection protects the queen from anyone and anything. Getting close to the queen without her permission first, will cost you dearly: with your life. The sound of thundered resounded with the walls of the golden pyramid and as Amber and I stood there, we were awed by the sheer enormity of what lay behind the bronze doors leading into the queen's chamber. The queen bid us to enter and as we did, I could see thunder bolts shooting straight at the queen. "Queen Cyforah." I shouted and started to run to her. To try and protect her from the massive bolts being thrown in her direction; but the guard grabbed my arm. He told us that she was ok and that is The Stone of Perfection that was shooting the thunder bolts, zapping the mosca bugs around her. The queen must really hate them and once I had looked upon her fully, I could see why. She was lovely in an odd way that I had never seen before. Her skin was honed to a shiny brilliance so that you could see your reflection. Literally she was a walking mirror. Naked except for the long, black hair that trailed down and pooled around her feet, she rose from her throne and came to stand before us. Hovering constantly by her side was the Stone of Perfection.

"I know why you have come here Dream Angel and I am pleased I can be of help." I stared into her mirrored brilliance and saw I stared back at myself. She could be anyone and everyone with that skin of hers and I felt almost light headed if I stared at her to long. She wasn't made to look upon, only to rule and I wondered to myself what curse or blessing had been laid upon her long ago to give her the power she possessed. Instinctively, I knew I could trust Queen Cyforah. I chanced at glance at Amber to see if the queen was having the same effect on her as she was me and saw that she was looking at her own feet. Afraid to look up and inching ever closer to me as the planet hovered closer to her. Ready to strike if need be. "Don't worry about my protector, it's really all bite and no bark." The queen laughed at her own joke and I found myself joining in. "Whatever you say, Queen." Amber said. Standing fully behind me now.

"Queen, I know you are aware of why we have come here. We need your help in fighting the Soulless Slaves." "You are right, Carmen. I do know why you are here and I see that The Them's minions will reach the earth shortly." The queen glanced up and looked at her protector and smiled. "Perfection and I haven't been there since Michel died." "Michel," Amber asked. "Yes, Michel. He was a very dear friend of mine and I keep him buried here in Rashelle to protect his grave from robbers. The dead get no rest when they were great on your planet." The queen frown at that thought and I could see a ripple course along her body as though the thought of grave robbers sickened even her. "He would have been honored to be here and aid you with your quest, but since he cannot be, let us honor him with a visit: Follow me." Through to more huge bronze doors were led, deeper into the catacombs of the pyramid until we came to a room awash in light from the Nova fly. What appears and look like fire flies on earth. The Nova flies give off a hundred times more light. It give off the illusion of a hundred watt bulb flying in mid air. She led us to a glass coffin and I heard Amber whisper under her breath. "You've got to be fucking kidding me. "Michel De Nostradamus." "Yes Amber." The queen replied. "Michel became the keeper of the Hubriser stone in the year fifteen-fifty-four and he was able to use it for great good. Or he tried to at least. He helped the sick people of that time and created his quatrains, some of the greatest prophecies ever gifted to man." I was stunned. I had something in common with Nostradamus. I was an Angel of Dreams just like he had been. "Plague and famine were ripe in his time and just like now, he had to feed the portal. He would take the sick people to his home to die and he would send them threw the portal so The Them could take their souls. Because of the fear of the plague, the families never wanted the bodies back and he was able to dispose of them without any problems. He was a great man who knew that if he didn't feed the portal, the madness to follow would be unbearable. No matter who had possessed the stone Hubriser throughout history, no one had chose to break with celestial law: except for Mistress Pat." As soon as Queen Cyforah finished, the Planet Perfection zoomed around her like an excited pet. Amber stepped back, she couldn't help it; but that damn planet frightened her. The fact that it had a mind of its own and could attack without Queen Cyforah's bidding was a major part of her fear. "Oh, don't mind my protector Amber, Perfection just loves a good fight." She began laughing. "Well a fight is exactly what it shall have." Amber yelled. Ever vigilant on keeping the rotating orb in her sights. Little did she know that back on her own planet, pandemonium had already set in.

Scripture 18: Death Is All Around

The Third hour, The Hour of Hope had just begun in my dreams. Hope was a futile though for the parents of children up to the ages of twelve because now the plague had come and taken most all of them. But strangely enough some children were in fact still alive. Small sects of children were popping up. Parents had taken their babies, taken and hidden them away in mosques, churches, basements; anywhere they could be safe. Religious zealots were spouting that these children were the beloved children of God and it was his mercy that had spared them. I grieved for the children left alive most of all. The reason they were alive was not because they were more beloved, but because they were the most corrupted of all the children on the planet. Your bible and other books of the religious significance all mention something about their being an age of accountability. The children that had been taken had still been innocent, unaccountable yet for wrong. The children left living would have to live through what came next just as the adults would have to. The grief that the world had suffered thus far was about to be multiplied a thousand times over. Fighter pilots purveying the skies all across the globe were reporting strange anomalies. Ghosts of babies and children floating high up over the silver fog.

The churches were crowed with people searching for reason but none was available to be had. The Vatican Palace doors were open and the priests were there in full force offering mass for their patrons in turmoil. People who had never before seen the inside of church now lined their walls, hoping for communion, reassurance; even salvation. How could any of those be provided. Some ministers were even telling their followers that soon they would need to lead themselves because they would no longer be there. Surely the righteous would not be left to live through what would surely come to pass. How little did they truly now. The churches had grown so corrupt over the years that only a very few would be saved. What no one expected and whom the world often forgot about until they saw them was the thousands of nuns and monks who had devoted their entire lives to God and everything else they had left to the world. Unlike most priests and imams, deacons and ministers; who drove the big flashy cars to church every Sunday or whatever day of worship was there pick; the sisters and brothers in Christ lived daily lives of fidelity: obedience and stability. Everyone who has ever come unto them has been received as Christ himself would be received. Like a Thief In The Night: death came and stole the breath from all of the nuns and monks around the world as they lay in their beds or went about their daily work. They had not been as alarmed as the rest of the world and since they had no televisions to listen to, most of them had gone to sleep at their regular hour. The world would shake to it's very timbers in the morning when all realized that the truly faithful, the long devoted of Christ had been taken away from them and no one even knew who they were. That is the true way to Christendom. Only those filled with truly holy belief were taken. Not those filled with pretentious holy beliefs. They were left to continue to mislead the masses.

Death spread faster then. Animals fell dead were they stood. Zoos around the world felled silent. Birds dropped out of the air in mid flap. The news was reported that the plague that had struck people was now spreading to livestock and animals and right before their owners very eyes, domesticated cats and dogs fell dead around the globe. Famine or Plague, the headlines would read in the morning paper. If there was going to be a morning paper. No one knew anything and the fear on everyone's faces was just as palpable as a handshake. Sheer terror gripped the world over and there was nothing anyone seemed to be able to do about it. The food in the can became paramount. People was losing their lives over can goods. As though it was going to help, some of the reporters went on air wearing gas masks. "This may very well be our last day on this planet. It is obvious that the unseen forces at work are attempting to destroy the human races by all means necessary. If your neighbors are asleep, wake them up. Warn them of what is going on. No one should be left to wake up to the chaos that will surely be in the morning. I pray with you all." The newsman said but it sounded hollow even to him. NASA had sent yet another report to the White House but no one was there to get it. They were reporting strange weather patterns never seen before forming over the world's oceans: also missive beams of light shinning deep under the sea.

For Judy, the nightmare raged on as well. She was in so much pain and the giant bastard was even more infatuated with her. "Judy my dear, when you get better we will go on a vacation. I know of a very romantic place outside of Spanton called Tholicia. It is full of love and only true lovers are allowed in their city." Judy looked at the damned fool like he had lost his mind. "Judy, you do love me like I love you, don't you." he asked. Judy screamed and the sheer force of it caused her insides to roll. She began vomiting on herself and didn't give a damn. "Dear God, Please wake me up out of this nightmare! Whatever I did or didn't do, dear Lord I am so very sorry, just please save me!" The giant grabbed Judy off of the floor and shook her. She pounded on his huge chest and begged him to let her down. She was dripping in her own blood from head to toe and as she slapped his chest, she see the bloody trail her hands were leaving. That only made the beast laugh, so she spit in his face. Wiping the spittle from his eye, he drew his fingers into his mouth and licked every savory bit from his fingertips. Repulsed, Judy looked away and she thought that finally she was going to get her second wish. She was finally dying. She thought so because she could see a swirl of amazing colors transform right before her eyes. Spinning and twirling at an unimaginable rate, a bolt of lightning struck from within the spinning portal and hit the giant in the back of his head. The giant was fazed but not very much and the giant tried to lash out but there was nothing there to hit. From the portal, a brilliant orb appeared and it zoomed around the fool faster than the speed of light. The Planet of Perfection was taking action. Amazing red, blue, green and yellow spun faster and faster until it all became one beautiful blur. The celestial stone shot red and blue laser beams at the giant's legs and finally, he fell to the ground: carrying Judy with him. He must have been in great pain because he unwrapped the hand that held Judy and she ran free. Dazed but not dead, the giant looked up in front of him and he could see a pair of legs. He would know those legs from anywhere. He seemed to be endlessly, staring up at them instead of driving between them and he reached out as though he would stroke them. The Planet wasn't having it though and another lightning bolt struck his outstretched palm. The smell of burning giant meat filled the room. The giant yelled out in torment but he made no move to get up off the ground. He had been here before and he knew what would be coming next. Looking past the gorgeous legs, he found the face of Queen Cyforah staring back at him. Looking upon her; he can see the sorry look in his own face. She was pissed and he had no idea why. He hadn't gone against her wishes, why the hell was she here interrupting in his love life. His beautiful queen with the near invisible wings of light. She was beautiful to behold but a terror to cross. "My Queen, I was just having a little fun with my new love, that's all," He said nervously. With her voice of melodic scourge, the queen replied. "Rapere, didn't I ban you from Spanton?" "Yes my queen, but The Mist came for me!" The colossus trembled with fear before Queen Cyforah. "I tried to escape but was caught and then I found myself in this woman's fantasy. I could not go against the wish my queen." "I understand, we are all helpless against The Wish. I will need you in service, Rapere. For your unknown wrongs against this human, swear your oath."   "I will serve the Angel of Perfection and do my Queen's bidding," he said. "Very good then, it shall be done." Just then the Planet Perfection opened a portal within itself, and the giant: Rapere was absorbed. Judy didn't know or care where he had gone and as soon as the last of him was sucked through, she fainted.

Rick was back in his old elementary school. In his favorite class, math, with Sister Kathy Elizabeth Stewart. The class was filled with his school friends of long ago and even four students that he knew for a fact had died, were there. They all watched while Rick's father whipped him in front of them. Rick was tied from the ceiling with his hands pointing straight up. "Why you be talking in class boy?!" Rick's father yelled. His father flung his arm back, readying the whip to cut skin from Rick's back when his hand flew off at the wrist. Completely detached, the hand and whip went flying and struck a little girl in the face. The little girl focused evil eyes of unknown light at Rick, like it had been his fault that his dead fucking father's hand had fallen off. The girl got up, opened her desk and took out a steak knife. She walked over to Rick's father, handed him the knife and said, "Do it!" The dead man held the knife up to his face and started cutting his own cheek. Green fluid dripped down his chin while he looked at Rick with malevolent intent. He cut the rope so his arms will be down: but his wrist was still tied. His father smiled and said. "Take the knife boy; Oh; I'll tell you what you did." Rick took the blade from the last remaining hand his father had hoping that he could cut this demon of hell into pieces. Rick swing the knife straight forward, aiming directly for his father's heart but something stopped his arm in mid air. Possessed by an unseen force, his arm started to move slowly down towards his midsection, towards where his penis lay safely tucked away. "Cut it off, Cut it off, Cut it off, " the children started to chant. He took the knife and sliced through his pants and underwear, leaving his member exposed for everyone to see.

"No! No! Please God help me," Rick screamed. With no control, he grabbed himself, placed the knife at its base and braced himself for what was coming next. His hand was going to cut away his problem. "Cut it off boy, dammit; don't you know what you did?" Then his father gave him a evil grin. " O' you know what the fuck you did!" His father said devilishly.. Just then, the black board changed shape and a giant dark hole appeared. A lightning bolt struck the knife, knocking it from Rick's grasp and blessedly away from his penis. Out the portal, the Planet Perfection came and zoomed around the classroom and absorbed every oozing green inch of Rick's father's dead flesh. The planet shot a bolt at the ropes still binding his wrist and Rick was free. At the sight of the queen; the classroom of ghosts saw their own reflection and melted in fear. They became liquid flesh all over the floor. Rick fell to the floor crying and cursing Carmen and her damned dreams. "Carmen, you fucking bitch! How could you do this to me." Rick screamed in pain. Every inch of his body was covered in lashes and the tatters that remained of his clothes were a testament to the abuse he had suffered: and the smell of pee, shit and puss was pretty bad. "Nonsense, Rick. You were the fool. You played with the power of the cosmos, unknowing. Do not blame Carmen for that," Queen Cyforah said. "I am very sorry for what happened to you but the stone gave you what it believed you wanted, it was you who was not precise," I told Rick. I was very sorry for him though. Looking at him brought tears to my eyes but we had no time for sorrow. Amber and Judy were there with me along with Queen Cyforah: and my guest had seen the last of the brutal punishment. Tears were running down Amber's face and Judy was still reeling from her own ordeal of pain. Rick just simply wanted to kill me. "Perfection, take us to the location of the Lamp of Jinni right away," Queen Cyforah commanded. A hole ten feet around appeared there before them all. A demented wail shook the classroom where we all stood and everyone turned and saw Judy curled in a tight ball on the floor, crying her heart out. "I'm not going down there, I'm not going down there. You're all fucking crazy, are you out of your fucking minds!"

I couldn't really blame her after what she had been through; but I didn't have time to hold her hand through this. "O.k. this is the deal guys. I'm not going to hold anything back because you will find out soon enough on your own." The sadness that I had been trying to hide for their sake could now be shown. With a ragged sigh, I continued, "The world is swiftly coming to an end. The world we all knew when you first entered my dreams last night is lost. If you wake up from this, earth may still be there but man will not." They looked at each other like I had lost my mind and Queen Cyforah just stood there looking bemused at us all. "What kind of madness is this Carmen! I paid two million dollars for this." Rick screamed. An audible hum was emitting from the Planet of Perfection and I warned Rick to take it down a notch. "Carmen, your scaring me; what about my family?" Judy cried. "Tell them Carmen, we do not have time for this; tell them so we can move on." Cyforah ordered. "Tell us what?" Amber asked. "I'm sure you have all heard of The Revelation; The Return of Jesus Christ."

Scripture 19: Jesus and the Stone of Mirabilia

In the Book of Spanton, nowhere is it written regarding the existence of time. Earth's attempt at measuring time in this universe has been found highly amusing by more intelligent beings in the cosmos. The greatest scholars that homo-sapiens have produced have been unable to define time, it's concept consistently eludes them. Once I became the Seraphim of Dreams, I learned that time in itself is a mere illusion. When physical dimensions no longer exist for you, the idea of "earth" time loses its meaning. How would you like to go to work at nine, close your eyes and when you open them, it's already five. You see, it's not really about time at all. It's about the speed in which you travel through your own reality that prohibits you from moving with freewill throughout the cosmos: the speed that you travel through space and matter; that determines "time."

When I travel through the metaverses, I create a magnitude of speed equal to that of three times the speed of light. Matter ceases to exist and I am in a state of being that all I need to do is use my brain waves to control the flow of matter around me. The universe for me becomes like a touch screen computer; everything is at my reach at a touch of my hand. Please don't call me crazy again my reader; I know who you are. If I need to slow down once I am getting close to my destination, I do so. If I need to speed up because I want to go a billion more light years away into another universe, I will it to be so. I am not a physicist, I don't really understand how I am able to do what I can do myself but it never ceases to amaze me. Mind over matter, that's all it truly is. You wouldn't understand any way. One hundred eighty six thousand miles a second is the speed of light. Three times that is probably hard for you to comprehend but for me it exists as one of the celestial laws. A second for you happens in the blink of an eye but for me, I could get pregnant, have the baby and been to have sent them off to college and still have time left over to get my nails done. Einstein almost had it right, he was at least thinking in the right frame of mind with regards to the relativity of time but he was just a few puzzle pieces short of completing the puzzle. I'm sorry to say that E=mc2 is part of an inherited knowledge that higher beings pass on through birth from one generation to the next. In addition to the vast amount of knowledge that they have accumulated thus far. Their children don't spend time in classrooms, learning the information that the adults already know. The unknown knowledge is what they seek and being born with all the former knowledge of the universe leaves them lots of time to figure it out. This is why other civilizations look so harshly upon earth, your own animals on your planet have the ability to pass on inherited information but humans do not. It's quite sad really because it is humans own ignorance that leaves them ignorant. You just can't seem to get out of the way of your own development path.

The Great Book of Spanton knows the future because it has been there. It was here from the beginning and it has witnessed what you consider to be the beginning of the universe itself, the Big Bang. Just so you know it didn't make a sound: there was no bang. However, what you call the Big Bang really wasn't the beginning but an end. An end of unused matter from other realms. Unholy matter that was dumped by other universes which became your own. It is not my attention to upset anyone but I must explain as much as I can so that the same misassumptions aren't made again. So that the next seed are giving a better chance at surviving in the chaos that was created for them. Everything surrounding you, even the matter that makes up a human being is unclean. Your Bible told the truth about that, the sin that everything created and everyone born was birthed from unclean matter. That is why The Creator sent Sensoval to cleanse the impurities from you all. When The Them realized that the black waste was starting to coalesce and could communicate, yes communicate, they took interest. Your scientists would have you believe that there was a giant bang and boom; and religion say God said let there be light and the world was. That's just not realistic and it is quite egotistical on mans' part. The black matter could communicate with itself and it pulled together to form the world you all inhabit now. It took billions of years for this to happen; but you can if you want to believe it took seven days: Earth time. Sometimes I think they keep the human race around for our amusement. All of what you are able to observe and beyond was by intelligent design. There may have been a bang so to speak, but you had better believe that even that was caused to happen. Everything in itself must be step by step. The one thing about humans that I learned is you just accept it for what it is. That's because you are programmed that way; intentionally.

Thirteen billion years. That's how long ago your scientists believe the universe to have originated. That's a pretty good guess. I have direct cognizance of a five billion years before that. I know not only of your universes origins but the entire cosmos so you can see why I might know a bit more than you could ever anticipate. Out of the billion of planetary systems that exist in your universe, each one of those that has intelligent life was sent a messenger. A messenger that is to deliver to the beings inhabiting of that world, a wealth of knowledge. Your planet was given who you call Jesus Christ. He existed first in spirit alone, housed in the heart of The Creator. Then he was given form and became the First Seraphim, sent from Nueden to enlighten your planet. He was the only one of his kind because he was an extension of I AM himself. Yes, Mary's baby was planted inside her body by the seed of I AM himself in her dreams. This is how carefully loved and cared for your planet was. Jesus was sent to teach you all the laws of the way and warn you to never deter from it. Great was his hopes for Earth's inhabitants. Unfortunately, Senzoval's' mission always ends up the same in every universe I Am has sent him to and your ancestors cannot be blamed for the demise he met. It was already written in The Scroll of Spanton what was to be. The keeper of Sensoval must die so that his blood can spill upon the planet. It is an act that has been going on since Nueden existed and it was written as celestial law before your universe was ever created.

The body of Jesus Christ was merely a shell for The First Divine Seraphim: Senzoval. Jesus was the first Artificially Inseminated human on your planet. I Am took Joseph Semen while he slept; to give his son Senzoval a human form: but Jesus' soul is from the seed of I AM. Jesus Christ was the first owner of the Stone of Mirabilia over two thousand years ago. The stone was given to him directly from heaven by the Cherubim Lanare as a gift from his father, I AM. He was just twenty five years old but the miracles that he became able to perform are legendary to this day. The night before his earthly body met its demise was foretold by him and he told his wife that she was to hide the celestial stone after his death. He was adamant with her that no one be allowed to ever find it. Jesus told her that he would be going home to his father and made her promise that she would take the stone far away. When she asked him where she should go, he told her that the stone would show her the way. That it would show her things that hadn't even happen yet and when he saw the look of fright in her eyes, he told her never to fear. Great was his love for his beloved wife and great was Mary's love for her cherished husband. He told her that it would be there last night together and when she asked how he knew that, he told her that the stone has shown him his horrendous, impending death. She wept at his feet and as her tears cleaned the dirt from them, she begged him to run away with her. He was stern but caring when he told her that he must go on and be with his almighty father in the stars above and that she must not make it any harder than it already was. Yes, Jesus was married and his wife was Mary of Magdala. I cannot omit the truth here for man's sake because it is convenient. I'm not taking any glory from this great man; he also washed away my sins before I became the Seraphim of Dreams. Some of the important truths about your Lord and Savior was taken out of the original scrolls to make him seem more divine to his followers and other religions. What Jesus became after his death was never real and it is sad how quickly the truth was forgotten. If they knew the truth about what I'm telling you now; they would have never omitted a thing about this amazing man. The Son Of God. Jesus is and always will be "The Truth."

Beside herself, Mary pleaded with him and as she clung to his feet and kissed them, she looked up with puffy, swollen eyes and told him that she was with child. He had known the day that his sperm impregnated her and he fell to his knees beside her. As he kissed her forehead and smoothed the hair from her brow, he was more sure than ever what must be done to ensure her and his unborn child's survival. He knew that the men coming to kill him would do the same to Mary if they knew that she was carrying his seed in her womb. He made her swear that she would wait two sunsets, bring the stone to his dead body and lay it upon him. He would then raise from his death tomb and be gone. But the stone would remain behind and she was to take it, go far away and have his child. He told her that the stone would protect them both. She gave him her oath and swore her eternal love. He swore the same for her and his offspring and at last gave her a very old scroll that she was to hide with the stone once she was safely away.

Mary looked at what was written on the scroll and became terrified. When she asked him what the words of doom meant he told her that it was called Revelation. He told her to write down exactly what was written therein and to give the copy to John. She was never to part with the scroll or the stone and she was to keep them safely away from the world. Confused, Mary gave him this additional oath. Her final instructions were to sign the scroll upon him taking his last breath and to become the possessor of the gift.

After I had told Amber, Rick and Judy the truth of the history of the stone and the fate of their planet, Rick and Judy looked at me like I had grown a second head in the short amount of time that had elapsed. Rick started to laugh and the Planet Perfection began to emit red beams of light, marking its target, the center of Rick's forehead. "Perfection! Reposition now," Queen Cyforah yelled. Rick had no idea how closely he had come to meeting an untimely death. Left to its own devices, the planet was about to blow his arrogant head off. "What is this shit Carmen, what do you want from us," Rick asked me. "We need your help to battle the Soulless Slaves." "Soulless slaves, Senzoval, Jesus married to that whore, you have to be making all this shit up. It's too crazy to believe otherwise." "You can believe that outside my dreams, the Rapture has just ended." "It began last night once you all entered my dreams and all of the children's souls have been taken. There is not one innocent one left alive on your planet." Judy began to cry and Amber put her head down, ashamed because she knew it was partly her fault that this set of events had been put into motion. It wasn't entirely her fault, but she wasn't blameless either. She screamed and fell to her knees, tearing out her hair by the root full. "It's all my fault, why did I make such a wish," she keened. Judy looked at her incredulously, like it was now Amber that had grown the second head and she asked her, "You made this wish Amber? Why? How could you?" "No, no, I didn't want this. I just wanted to see the Creator." "And you shall have your wish my dear," Cyforah said cryptically. "No! No God, No," Amber cried. "Perfection, transport us at once," Queen Cyforah demanded. The orb began rotating wildly, calling upon the cherubim Pavilent. This angel of transportation can take you from one universe to another. They were all headed to the world of Nab'ee, where the Mayan people had relocated and it was simple enough. Out of the hole created by Perfection came strange bubbles of light. The bubbles were clear and had rainbows within their core. Beautiful were they to witness and Judy reached up as though she would touch one. As soon as her finger skimmed the surface of the bubble she was engulfed within it. Four bubbles remained, one hovering over each rider. Cyforah asked if everyone was ready and I told her that we were. "We must hurry," Cyforah insisted and then the remaining bubble shields engulfed the rest of us and we were all transported down through the hole. Into the sea, the unknown world of planet earth. The forth hour in my dreams has begun. The Hour of Salvation.

Scripture 20: The Angel of Mimic

In Spanton, Sonya and Carlos were lost. Not only did they have no clue as to where they were, they didn't understand why they were there or what was about to happen next. Sonya just kept wondering why their mother would do this to them. They just kept walking, walking through a thick light blue mist; that smelled like cotton candy freshly spun. Carlos kept trying to eat the mist and as he reached into the mist to tear off a piece, his fingers would close on nothingness. He settled for sticking his tongue out and letting the mist fill his mouth as he walked along. Just the same way you might let the first snowfall of winter fall onto your tongue. Snowflakes have substance though, but the mist was there just as surely as they were and Carlos was sure he would be able to catch some to eat. He told Sonya, " "It smells like candy Sonya and it's good too." Chubb Chubb was barking at the mist. Sonya looked down at her little brother and could only smile. Overwhelmed with the situation herself, she tilted her head back and followed her brothers' lead. The mist did indeed taste good. "Where are we Sonya", he asked her. "Carlos, I don't know but when we get home, I'm going to let mom have it." "This note she gave us makes no sense, I wish she would have just left us at grandma's house. How are you feeling anyway." Sonya remembered that before all of this he was complaining about not feeling good and she looked down at him worry in her eyes. The last thing she needed is for him to start feeling sick again. "I feel fine," he said. They kept walking forward until the light blue mist turned red. They had no idea where they were headed because if they did, they would have turned around right there. Chubb Chubb was still barking at the mist. They were on the road to what the Spantonites call the Path of No Return. This path would lead them to The Forest of Deadlife.

In the forest, evil takes on another meaning. The children had no idea what was about to happen to them. Whispers warning the children could be heard. The voices were soft but crystal clear; and persistent. "No children go back, please children go back." Carlos grabbed Sonya's hand and she pulled him close to her. Chubb Chubb started crying out. Things were starting to get really spooky and Sonya wished again for their mother. When the whispering voices came again they stopped in their tracks. Before them they could see a forest that looked almost like the great rain forests on earth. Almost. This was no rain forest and they knew they were definitely not on planet earth. They started walking tentatively forward because Sonya didn't know what to do. Go forward or turn back like the whispers were telling them to. So she kept them moving forward. When they came to a giant gate, they stopped and looked inside. Rolling towards them was the biggest and prettiest cherries they had ever seen. It just so happened that cherries were both of the kid's favorites. Chubb Chubb was going to eat a cherry but did not;it didn't smell right. The gate swung open before them and Carlos ran forward and scooped up one of the cherries. Holding it in both of his hands, he raised it to his mouth and was about to take a giant bite; Chubb Chubb started barking at him and Sonya knocked it away from his mouth. The cherry went flying and tears welled in his eyes. Seconds later he was crying like the eight year old baby he very much was. "I'm so hungry Sonya," he wailed. "I want mom," he sobbed. Sonya felt bad about hitting his hands like that but she was responsible for both of them. She couldn't bear to hear him crying though and she bent down on her knees and gave him a hug. "Carlos, I'm sorry about that," she told him. "But you have no idea if they were safe to eat right." Carlos' sobbing subsided a little bit and he shook his head no. "And they were dirty, rolling around on the ground right," she asked him. His sobbing had stopped altogether and now just a few tears were still trailing, "Yeah," he said. "So it's probably not a good idea to eat the dirty cherries on the ground that Chubb Chubb wouldn't eat; right." He raised his big brown eyes up to his big sister and said, "Right!" Just like that his tears had stopped and Sonya gave him another hug. She was nine years older than him and she loved him almost like he was her very own baby. Looking into his baby browns, she knew he trusted her to keep him safe and that meant the world to her. Keep him safe was exactly what she would do. Chubb Chubb started licking Carlos's face.

With that very thought, a strong gust of wind blew. Sonya and Carlos tumbled to the ground and a dark shadow appeared over them. Sonya grabbled Carlos and threw her arms around him and he gripped her with every ounce of strength he had in his little body, hiding his face in her chest. "Leave us alone," Sonya screamed. Chubb Chubb started to bark at the shadow! The dark shadow turned to light and floated up through the red mist and into the sky. Sonya looked up to where the shadow of light had gone and what she saw was the most beautiful thing she had ever laid her eyes on. Chubb Chubb stopped barking. "It's okay brother, look." They both stared up and became to mesmerized to look away. They had been entranced by Julie, The Seraphim of Distraction. The glow that came from her shined colors of profound beauty up into the heavens. Julie was in possession of the spirit of Larishta. With it, she can become an amazing angel that has the ability to distract the most darkest of evil ever known to Spanton. Julie flew back down to where the children were and ordered, "Children, come quickly," They got up off of the ground and ran to her. At that moment, tree branches swooped down at them and knocked them back down. Chubb Chubb grabbed the tree branch. Carlos screamed but Sonya stood back up, grabbed Carlos and they kept running towards Julie. The tree branch started a second assault on them but Julie intervened first. She spoke the spell of Ardent Bush. Beaming flames shot from her and seared the branches as they reached again for the children. The trees backed off then. "Touch my wings so you can float behind me," Julie said. Sonya and Carlos did what she asked and when they touched her wings of light they too became light. Sonya picked up Chubb Chubb. Children of light, floating along behind Julie, leaving the Forest of Deadlife behind.

In New York City, below the streets, the number two train was in route to Forty Second Street and Times Square. The few hundred passengers on the train all looked terrified. They wanted to get home, home to their families. The train operator in front was the most worried. He had heard from passengers boarding that children were dying all over the world and he had two small children that he wanted to get home too. His cell phone never worked underground and more than anything, he wanted to get home to them. It was never going to be however because right before his very eyes, a giant black hole opened within the tunnel. He slammed on the emergency brakes but it was too late. The train was going too fast, was too heavy and momentum carried them forward. The train operator was the first to go into the black hole, praying that somehow he would come out of it alive. The passengers on board were screaming for their lives because when he had thrown the emergency brakes, it had thrown them all forward. Fear and terror are a heady mixture when combined. This is what I feared would happen. The Them were robbing souls from the earth because of Mistress Pat's betrayal. All two hundred thirty seven people on the train were gone. The souls at least. The bodies would be falling across the globe all night and the news reported it all.

Tatisha Battles was setting in her living room in Jacksonville, Florida. She was scared and shaking and watching the news was making it worse. Her mother Debra was talking to her on the phone, "The government is asking for all Americans to stay in their homes." Reports were coming in of more dead bodies falling out of the sky and people once again were looking up. "Ma, did you hear that it's started again, the bodies," and Tatisha's voice trailed off. Just then Tatisha heard a huge collision on her roof and seconds later, the roof caved in. The body of William Dumbar a store owner in Queens came crashing to her floor. She screamed and ran out her house calling for help. In Belgium the body of Bertha Harmon a beloved wife and mother of two small children who also lost their souls to the Gofogen: crashed head first into the windshield of a patrol car cruising the streets. This was happening everywhere. Once again everybody was looking up at the sky. Portals was opening up all around the planet dropping bodies everywhere. Mistress Pat kept the T.V. on to hear and see what's going on outside her home.

Passing through the ocean, safely inside of Pavilent's' sub shields, we were in a world that was a part of Earth, yet it seemed to be completely separate. A world that people will never see. Rich blues, purples, oranges and yellows decorated the sea creatures that we passed. As we went deeper into the abyss, creatures unknown to man came up to us. Curious creatures they were, perhaps some of the very things that life on earth evolved from. Wherever Pavilent was taking us, I knew it would be out of this world. "Yo, this so cool you guys," Judy said awed. I was happy to see that she wasn't still suffering from the shock of what Rapere had done to her. The human mind is a miraculous thing when it is allowed to be. Rick, however, was not doing so well. He had a green look about him and he startled when Cyforah asked, "Are you alright?" It must have cost him dearly to turn and look at her because the next thing you know, he was double over, regurgitating. Nothing but a yellow, frothy foam came out and I saw the bemused expression that crossed Cyforah's' face.

What we saw next was never to be seen by human eyes. The waters started to glow and two creatures appeared in the light. Creatures that scientists on earth believe to be extinct; but truly on we went deeper. We all stared at two sixty foot megaladon sharks. Ancients beasts from over one and a half million years ago and as we stared I realized that it was not the water that had begun to glow, but the sharks that were emitting a radiant green luminescence causing everything around them to be cast in this same greenish tent. As we moved through the waters, the sharks became agitated and darted at us, ready to gnaw at our bones. I could sense that they wanted to stop us from reaching our destination. We were intruders. Foreigners in their land and if not for Pavilent speeding us along, they may have made a meal of every last one of us.

Streaming up and behind the mega predators, we saw three more crafts, submarines of light, coming toward us. The Planet Perfection stood guard and began emitting it's warning beams of light, aiming directly for the hearts of the threat. It began to spin so fast that the ocean water couldn't touch it's surface. The crafts were not deterred however, they paused briefly and scanned Perfection. They sent some kind of light messages to Perfection that only it could understand because as they passed, Perfection ceased aiming at the sharks. Much like a barking dog being told to heel. It began following them into the greenish glow. What we entered next was the most amazing thing that can ever be seen on your planet. You would call this the ninth wonder of your world if you were allowed to look upon its glory. It is the great world that vanished over ninety six hundred years ago and here it was standing before us in mystical wonder. Protected by its impervious surface. Perfection and Pavilent passed us through the shield of diamond unfazed. As we passed through it, I could feel the substance of the shield breathing around me as though it was alive and it knew. Knew what we had come for and had been waiting for us.

Once we had docked the subs and gotten out, we were greeted by Atlantis' leader, Chinowa. He is the master of the world's ocean and it is he that many people see on earth but think it is a ufo. It is he who passes over us to inspect the world and see how far we have come. Or perhaps how far we have fallen.

"Greetings your highness, I'm Carmen, the Seraphim of Dreams. We come for your help please." King Chinowa looked at us all and shook his head. He wouldn't help us. "It is not the time the Great Book has spoken of. You must leave my domain immediately and are never to return, never to speak of anything that you have seen. Go now and you all may leave." His voice was like that of a raging sea and he looked like that as well. A being of water in the shaped of a man over eight feet tall. The harder you try to look at him and make out his characteristics, the harder it became to see him at all. Some things are meant to be seen; witnessed but not seen. Try to see too much and madness will surely follow.

Rick clapped his hands and said "This is crazy Carmen, please wake us up now!" Perfection bumps Rick upside his head and zooms around his body. "O.k. I'm awake, I'm awake get this thing away from me!" Rick screamed."From here on you will be silent Rick. Cyforah commands.

Overhead flew an image that I knew I could trust. It flew around and brought a smile to my face that I haven't used in eight years. The glowing apparition landed among us and I started to cry. It was my beloved cousin Kim. She shined like the sun and had the glow of the moon at her stomach. Upon her head a crown of seven stars; she had become a angel of light. She was with child and I cried. We embraced and cried in each other's arms. "Carmen I missed you so much, why me Carmen why me?" "Kim this all must come to pass. You are very lucky that they took you." I explained. "Carmen in my mind I see and hear very strange things. They talk to me in my mind." Kim cried. "They tell me that I have some damn spirit inside me and they're waiting for this night to happen for it to appear." "Interesting." Cyforah said. "It's all true Kim, you have the spirit of The Man Child who is to rule the new earth with a Rod of Iron. Your bringing forth a gift for God himself; you should be very honored Kim." "I guess so Carmen".

Once again, I tried to talk to the king. This time I reached out to his mind with the power that I now own and spoke to him in the manner that befitted King Chinowa. He had denied us before and I needed him to understand that we were here for a cosmic purpose. Whether he liked it or not he was part of it and the Earths' fate was ultimately in his hand. After seeing what had just transpire between Kim and I, I wasn't sure that he would help us or not but I had to try. I asked him for his help once again but this time, he shook his head yes. He turned slowly, and walked towards a set of giant doors that I would have sworn weren't there before. "Follow him Carmen, He will take us all to the Lamp of Jinni," Kim said.

In Spanton, Julie had taken Sonya and Carlos to the Assembly of Seraphims. "Here we are Sonya; Carlos, you will wait here." Carlos looked around at her and a broad smile crossed his face. He was in a grand banquet hall surrounded by everything that an eight year old should desire. A huge table full of meats, pies, cakes and even vegetables overflowed on one side of the room. On the other side, a huge playground with all the works waited for someone to play on it. Little angel children just about his size were there already, swinging and sliding, singing and playing. They beckoned for Carlos to come and play with them but Sonya stopped him. She innately knew they were safe here. They had been since Julie got them from the Forest of Deadlife and so she would let him play. But first she told him, "I want you to eat your meat and vegetables first, then you may have some cake or pie. Then you can go and play, little brother. Save some fun for me okay." She bent down and hugged him, then gave him a kiss. When she let him go, he shot off like a rocket to the banquet table, Chubb Chubb ran behind him to play and eat to. All the while eyeing the playground and the angels that seemed just as eager for him to come and play with them as he was.

Sonya on the other hand had a worried expression on her face, "Where are you taking me to Julie." "No harm can come to you here child, you and your brother are under the protection of the Angels of Spanton. I swear your safety." "Ok, if you say so," Sonya said. "Tell me Sonya, do you believe in angels?" "I don't know, I guess I do, I mean I'm looking at them right?" Julie laughed at Sonya's smart response and she said, "Just making sure sweetheart. Just making sure."

When this curse first came upon me, I met some of the greatest souls that ever existed in the universe. One of these was the Seraphim of Mimic, Elishela. She comes from the Neferdum galaxy, in the outer reaches of the farthest unknown universe and she was formed from the matter of ionic metal. It is said that I AM himself breathed life into her. Her power is a dangerous one because she possesses one of the greatest Spanton spells ever called into creation, the spell of mimic. With it, she has the power of duplication. She can steal any angels spell and use that very magic against them. This would make a very powerful ally during an epic battle or the fiercest of foes.

Sonya was being brought to Elishela so that she would become the second being of matter in the entire universes that would be able to perform this spell. She would have to learn this spell first so that she would receive the Sound of Madness spell from Nika, keeper of the Mirabilia Stone. Very, fearsome spells to fight against but necessary for the war about to be waged. Seraphim Elishela is breath catching to behold. Her body is a lattice work of ions held together by some invisible compound. Like crystal, her color changes to match that of her surroundings. She can be as solid as a human being or as fluid as water and even has the ability to turn into gas. It really depends on how pissed she gets. When Julie brought Sonya to Elishela, she took Sonya by the hand and first gave her the ability to understand truth. The universe is a mystical place and the eleventh grade education that Sonya had so far just wasn't going to cut it if she was going to perform the work set out for her. She needed to comprehend that all matter can flex if giving the will and what she sees is just an illusion. After Sonya could understand the mystery of image, Sonya's old body became no more. She was able to shed the shell that was keeping her full power at bay, like a butterfly emerging from a cocoon.

She had become a beacon of light that will be honored in all of Spanton. As Elishela changed her spells, Julie watched as Sonya kept up with her. It didn't take long before Sonya was stealing the spells from the Seraphim of Mimics' mind before she could even think of what would come next. After Sonya destroyed a wall with her new found power, both Julie and Elishela knew she was ready. They took her from where she had been and training and brought her to Carlos. "Wow, Sonya, you look really pretty." "Thanks baby bro," she replied. A little afraid in spite of himself, Carlos turned to Julie and asked, "Why does my sister look so different?" "She is now an angel of Spanton Carlos; she will be able to do great things for the universe." "Cool," Carlos said. "I'm going to take her now, back to earth so that she can do the work of the lord. You must wait her where you will be safe my love, trust that no harm will come to you here." " If you say so Distraction Lady," he said. "I can still play with all my new friends right Sonya," he said. Looking up with hooded eyes at his big sister because she looked so beautiful, too beautiful to even look at. Sonya took his chin, "Of course, go and play." He started to run away to the playground but then he stopped and turned around. He ran back to where Sonya stood and hugged her and said. "I love you so much Sonya." Then off he ran. Free to be the little boy that he still very much was, would always be in Sonya's eyes. Chubb Chubb stayed with Carlos to watch over him. "I am ready to do the lord's work Julie."

Scripture 21: King Chinowa and The Lamp of Jinni

When the great doors opened, behind them was the amazing Lamp of Jinni. With the spirits of the Three Cursed Virgins from Heaven floating upon its beauty. They are the protectors of the spirit of Jinni. Next to this spectacular lamp stood The Kodiller, a magnificent blade of sacrifice. The victims of the lamp must spill their blood in the lamp and die by the accursed blade. When the soul has departed the body, Jinni will collect the soul and be able to manifest himself in the flesh. After I explained this to everyone, Judy asked, "What are you saying Carmen?" She scoffed, "Someone has to kill themselves in order to help you?" "I'm not saying anyone has to do anything Judy. The lamp contains the Spell of Suetonius, the Twelve Caesars to help in the battle. Cyforah spoke then, "Our goal is to stay alive until the eighth hour. Then, we will see the truth for our own eyes.

It was now three thirty-two am in Spanaway. President Hillard had issued new orders that the entire state of Washington was to be evacuated. The secret service had also begun the process of transferring him and the new first family to the underground vault that had been prepared for a day such as this. Most presidents had been lucky enough however that they never had to use it. The world was in chaos and your world leaders had waited for this forsaken day. Strange orbs were seen over Los Angeles and anywhere people could look up into the sky, they saw what looked like shooting stars in the sky.

It seemed the dying of the young had stopped. Every innocent child that had been alive less than four hours ago was now dead. At St. Mary's Community Hospital in Nebraska, Dr. Anesha Berry was doing the best she knew how to do. But the need was too great. She and her staff had never seen anything like it before. Parents lined the hallways taking up every inch of available space so that there wasn't even room to move. Holding their dead babies, their precious ones, in their arms. The wails of the heartbroken seemed to echo throughout the hospital and she herself couldn't stop the tears from falling. The grief was immeasurable. Many of her staff had just walked or ran out of the hospital at the onset of these events because they had small children at home. She understood. She had three of her own. She stayed at her post though because she knew she could somehow help more where she was than to go home and grieve her own loss. She had stopped trying to pry the dead innocents out of their parents' arms and left them there instead. Somehow, it seemed right for them to hold on to all they had left. She treated the ones she could for shock but it was the parents who were waiting for operating rooms that broke her heart most of all. No birthing room for them. No bouncing baby at the end of their tenuous labor. No screaming infant to hold covered in vernix caseosa. She would be forever known by these expectant parents as Dr.Anesha Berry, deliverer of dead babies.

Anesha's cell phone had been ringing all night long. She had been ignoring it with fear in her heart; no news was good news, she wanted so desperately to believe. All thirty of the missed calls had been from her mother. Her mother is babysitting her three small children. When the cell phone started ringing again, she stopped and looked around. There was nothing that she could do here until she dealt with her own tragedy. She couldn't ignore the inevitable any longer. She went to her office, took the call and her own wails then joined the thousands outside her door. She held the picture of her babies that had been on her desk and cried her heart out.

At Mistress Pats' mansion, the army had started to pull out, leaving only their most heavy equipment. Looked like they were in a hurry too. Thousands had been loaded on buses and special carrier planes to get them out of the state. "Devy, it looks like they're leaving, what's going on?" "Master, the soulless slaves are now entering your stratosphere. Your planet is readying itself for war."

On the television, reports were streaming across that there was a fleet of glowing orbs hovering over the Temple Mount in Jerusalem. Fear was also mounting at the sight of massive war ships in the sky around the world. Each a mothership with its own fleet of orbs. The host of people praying at the Well of Souls in Jerusalem was frightened by images of screaming ghosts from the well. Powerful beams of light from the mothership there had fixed upon the Temple mount. People there witnessed the unthinkable taking place. The temple was being rebuilt in minutes. The bibles truth was unfolding: Armageddon was taking place. Muslims ran out in the street and took aim at the ships and the orbs hovering around them. The religion forbid the building of the third temple and this was an act of war to them. A mothership broke formation and headed over Mistress Pat's home. Four orbs descended from it and the hovered in front of the diamond shield; scanning it. The shield responded and scanned them back.

Rick was staring at the Lamp of Jinni, deep in his thoughts. He asked me, "Carmen, the world is doomed right?" "Unfortunately, that is correct," I told him. "Is it just our planet that's doomed or is it the entire universe? Will you survive," he asked me with a somber look in his eyes. "Though we can exist on Earth, we are not part of your world Rick. The Revelation will have no affect on us or any other universe; save your own," I explained. "What about the genie? It will be on earth when it is being used right, so will it, the genie I mean, survive?" I could see Rick had come to believing. As I told you, we all must come to believing: some sooner than others. " "Jinni is not of your world so yes, he will continue to exist." "So if I become the genie of the lamp, I will live through all of this and I'll get to fuck those virgins from heaven right? I didn't try to hide the disgust I felt for him at that moment but I did swallow back the bile that rose in my throat at the thought of what perversions were driving the questions that Rick had asked me. After all that he had just been through, I decided to give him the benefit of the doubt. Perhaps there was a greater motivator for him than just getting to lay a couple of virgins.

"Well, yes Rick but the virgins aren't what you think." "Hell, a virgin is a virgin to me. What else does a guy need to know." He stood there with a smug look on his face and a hard-on in his pants. He was despicable. It would have probably been a good idea to intervene after he had castrated himself, instead of before. Hell, forget probably. It would have. Queen Cyforah answered him for me and I was grateful, I could barely stand too look at him at that point. "The Cursed Virgins feed off the low." "Yeah, yeah, yeah. I get it," he interrupted. " The bottom feeder's right, poor people, bums and stuff like that. So what does that have to do with what I asked. Do I get to fuck the broads or not?" Perfection had apparently had enough of his bullshit towards the Queen and the next thing you know it dotted towards Rick and hit him smack in the forehead. It was unfazed, Rick, not so much. The skin on his forehead split open and blood was streaming into his eyes. "What the fuck," he yelled. No one made any move to help him and Amber said under her breath, "What the fuck, exactly" Guess Perfection and I weren't the only ones who had had enough.

As the blood streamed down from the cut, the three Cursed Virgins awakened. Hovering by the lamp, they had appeared to be asleep but as the blood from Rick's body poured, they had awoken with a ravenous look in their eye. They smelled fresh meat. A portal opened in front of Rick and a man fell out of it. He was alive, disheveled, but alive. He looked around at us with a wild look in his eye asking, "Where the hell am I? Who the hell are you?" In unison, the Cursed Virgins said, "Show us his crime." Like a hologram projection, we saw what the man Bevis Dickson had done. He had been molesting his five year old daughter when she died. Along with the rest of all the innocent children, death had come and rescued her from the hells to come. If that wasn't bad enough, he hadn't stopped when he realized she was dead. He had gone back and forth to her death bed and committed such crimes against the child that we all had to turn away. Judy fell to her knees, compulsively vomiting and the Planet Perfection was spinning so rapidly that the wind it created had the hair on our heads blowing as though a hurricane would strike at any moment. "It is enough" the three replied. At the same time, they all attacked the man. Hands became talons that tore every limb from his body and from the open wounds, their razor sharp teeth began to suck him dry. By the time his screaming stopped and their sucking ended, there was nothing left but dehydrated piece of flesh that you couldn't even tell had been a man. Judy had fainted by the end and Amber was screaming at Rick, "Don't worry buddy, they only drink the blood of the low." "Fuck you, Amber," but there wasn't any feeling to it. In fact, Rick was as white as a ghost. "No, Rick. Fuck you. Go ahead and try to have sex with them now," Amber was goading him but there was a glaze in her eyes that let me know she was either in shock or something very close to it. Human minds were never meant to see all they had seen thus far and they still had a long way to go. Shock was the least of my concerns for her. Kim had a pained expression on her face and she was rubbing her stomach. Pretty sad that Rick could even manage to upset an unborn baby.

"All of you can kiss my ass, you don't know me, and you can't judge me. I want everybody to know," I think by everybody he truly meant the three virgins because his eyes kept going from them to the shriveled corpse of the child molester on the floor, "I want everybody to know that I am doing this to help our planet fight the intruders of evil." He picked up the Kodiller and with one swift slice, cut his own throat. The blade of the Kodiller can slice through any matter on earth and we all watched as Rick's spine gleamed in the light. He had nearly decapitated his own self, both his jugular veins were wide and open and flowing. Blood gushed from his neck, spraying us all. King Chinowa quickly grabbed Rick's head and put it over the lamp, ensuring that not one more drop of his blood would go wasted. He said, "May the new Genie of Jinni be absorbed and his spirit used to wreak havoc upon those who intrude upon the earth." As the last of Rick's life force, drained from his body Chinowa threw his empty carcass to the side. "May your death serve a better purpose than your life ever did, Rick." A bright green fog came out of the lamp and the King said, "It has been completed."

The virgins entered the lamp and the bright green fog followed behind them. King Chinowa closed the lamp and handed it to me. "Thank you your highness. I promise to use it wisely." Cyforah looked at me and said, "We must go Carmen. The fifth hour of your dreams had fell upon us. It is now the hour of Battle." Judy had finally come to. I was glad because I would need her to use the lamp. I grabbed her arm and said, "Judy, you are to take this and hold on to it until you have to use it. You will know the time. Be very careful, the Lamp has celestial power now that Jinni's spirit has been resurrected. Go with Cyforah back to the mansion and aid my mistress. Amber and I will follow shortly." I heard a gasp and I turned and saw Kim doubled over. She would be giving birth, soon. I walked over to her. "Kim, you know what must be done. Go with them to the mansion and wait until it is time. You will be protected." She must have been in the middle of a contraction because she could only nod her yes. "Queen Cyforah, please send us to where we must go next." "Perfection, Mount Alfa Omega; transport them now," she commanded. Lightening struck and thunder clapped. One minute were who knows how deep under water and then next we were being transported by the Stone of Perfection, on our way to the Divine Cave of Spanton.

The Them knew that there Soulless Slaves had reached the location of the Stone of the Hubriser. There are passages in your bible that tell of the dead walking the earth. Now, I see that the prophecy is true. Jumping out of the orbs, the walking dead poured upon the earth. The Army could only stand back and witness the horror. The voice with the sound of many waters screamed around the Earth in every tongue saying "THE PROTECTOR AISSEN IS BEING FREED OF A DEADLY VIRUS." The realization that what they had been told by their leaders was downright false. Grey, almond eyed bodies were everywhere. They huddled in a huge mass in front of the Diamond Shield and began to undulate. From the mass of bodies, a high-pitched, banshee like scream began to radiate. "GIVE YOUR SOULS TO OUR COLLECTORS."Later it would be said that it was heard the world over. No one knew it at the time but The Them were stopping the rotation of the earth. Time had ceased to be because we were no longer moving forward. The earth was now a still blue marble. A sitting duck in the fabric of the universe. Everyone could feel the horror that had come to be but it would still take a few minutes for the scientists to realize exactly what had happened. They had no hope to understand how it happened, only that it had. Because The Them had stopped the clock, so had they locked the door to my dreams. They thought that it would delay me, us, the vicious force that comprised the Angels of Spanton but how wrong they would be. In Mistress Pat's library, Judy, Cyforah and Kim appeared out of the portal in the fireplace. Kim walked out slowly, doubled over by the pain that gripped her. She looked like she was literally going to drop at any minute. Judy raced to give her a hand. Heaven help them, help me help them. Help us all.

Scripture 22: The Battle Of Revelation

The trip through the portal seemed to do Judy good. Not only did she look much better but she was wearing the legendary suit of the city of Nab'ee. It was made from the strongest fibers ever known, dragon skin. Mistress Pat, alarmed, yelled, "What the hell is going on? Judy what is this?" "Carmen sent us here to help," Judy said. "Good, I needed help. The soulless slaves are parked outside my damn front door. Judy, what the hell is that, what did you bring into my home?" "Sorry Patricia, this is Queen Cyforah: the Queen of Perfection." Mistress looked the queen up and down and all she could see is herself in the Cyforah's reflection. "Charming. Devy, show yourself," Mistress Pat commanded. Devy appeared in a deep red mist blazing with fire, outfitted in war gear. "I am here master." My army of black death is at your service; we battled the Soulless Slaves in the Nelle Universe two eons ago: they are but a waste of matter to us. Five foot high and stupid. We will obliterate them easily. The walking dead are but a pawn for the original evil that follow behind them." "Good Devy, use your army at will," Mistress Pat ordered.

Out in front of the mansion, the ground started to shake. The trees around them started to pull their roots out of the dirt. A gigantic sink hole opened and out of it appeared. Montuorus; Ruler of the Deadlife Forest. The humanoid giant made of the most ancient of woods looked to have over a million branches swirling about him. His roots emerged in hundreds of snake like coils out of the ground. He used some of his giant "tentacles" to lift some of the heavy tanks and launch them at the army scrambling on the ground. The army power that remained scrambled for an aerial attack. The jets circled around high and opened fire with guns blazing. The bullets hit Montuorus but didn't even faze him. The Mother ship released four more orbs and they landed in front of the mansion. The fighter jets took aim at the orbs but before they could take aim, the jets exploded. The mother ship took aim and blasted them from the sky with an unknown cosmic power.

The slaves exited the orbs; forty of the walking dead from each. They shot at the Diamond Shield with guns of solar rays, technology unheard of on earth. The rays shot out of the guns with the blazing brightness of the sun but still the shield protected the mansion. Mistress Pat saw it all in the Stone of the Hybriser and she asked Devy, "Will the shield hold up?" "Yes my master, you haven't begun to witness the true power of the shields protection. It will present itself when needed, right now they are using toys to the protector."

Back outside, Montuorus swept down and grabbed some of the slaves. He threw them back in the direction they had come from. You could hear the bodies hit the orbs. The mother ship shot beams of fire at Montuorus and some of his many branches started to burn. The master of The Forest of Deadlife vanished back into the hole he had come out of. Trees started shaking and homes and buildings began to tumble to the ground. Devy burst from the ground in a terrible wonder and the trees shot out their sap of blood. They sky rained blood. With a giant, red head he seized the mother ship and yanked it right out of the sky. He was an amazing sight to behold at over twenty stories tall. The ship came crashing to the ground and splashed a great wave in the river of blood that had now formed. Mistress Pat watched it all safely from inside the shield and she was impressed. The walking dead tried to attack him with their insignificant weapons and he laughed at them, "You are still foolish dead things, I will show you true power!" The Master of Darkness raised his bloody red hands and from the bottomless pit in front of the mansion crawled out what Spantonites call the Unknown.

This creature eats grey flesh and it crawls along its' belly with six; roach like legs. Over four railroad cars long and just as thick, it began swimming through the river of blood in search of its favorite meal. It have a mouth for a face and it will search and feed on Soulless Slaves living or dead and was called into creation just for that very purpose. "Do you remember one of my pets from the last battle," Devy raged.

Some brave news station had one lone helicopter in the air, broadcasting the most shocking thing every seen. Those still watching television watched in horror as the things from their nightmares came true. Those of the army left on the ground were safe inside of the few remaining tanks, those that hadn't been sent flying through the air and Sergeant Drinkwater ordered his men to retreat. "We can't do anything here ladies and gentleman, head out." The tanks drove through the streets of blood, away from the battle, fearing for their life.

Countries around the world were preparing to mount a defense of their own but when they saw the battle being waged in Washington state, they thought better. If the most powerful country in the world was pulling back, then what chance did they have. Still they prepared. Maybe, just maybe, they could do something later.

Another huge ship entered the airspace over Mistress Pats' estate and released eight more orbs. These were different than the metallic ones released earlier. They were made of sparkling light and inside Queen Cyforah ordered, "Perfection, aid Devy." The planet took action and shot out of the house and passed through the diamond shield unfazed. On the other side of the shield, the planet began to give birth. From its planisphere, came the Profective. This perfect, golden angel stood over one hundred stories tall. It looked like a living, breathing version of the Oscar Academy Award. How the Planet Perfection housed such an immense idol is unfathomable to me. His head turned as he purveyed his surroundings and it parted the cloud with it. After looking down at the chaos around him, he gave a nod. Rapere, from Judy's nightmare appeared busting out of the planet's clouds with his evil sadistic laughter. I couldn't help but be afraid for Judy. That beast had a serious thing for her and I hadn't been sure that he had been ready to let her go. Hopefully, we weren't about to find out how deeply his love for her was.

Now Rapere was a mass of compacted violence, made out of living crystals from the land of Rachelle. "So Pretty-So Pretty." He said looking at himself. He went about crushing any slaves he found in his path. He shot crystal daggers at the ones he couldn't crush with his feet and from the tips of his fingers, death came to many. Their bodies falling as soon as the dagger had it; their lifeless bodies fell to the ground. Profective didn't speak at all, he just nodded his head slowly, again.

Jumping out from dark lightning clouds came Rick's father yelling, "You've been baaad!" He landed on his feet standing half as tall as Profective, as tall as the trees. He had become the perfect eating machine. His broken body of flesh jerked and spasmed as he swooped down and grabbed the Soulless slaves. Giant hands seized on around their almond heads and shoulders and threw them in his mouth. Like grabbing a hand full of peanuts. He chewed with an expression of sadistic delight on his face and an odd colored bloody pulp ran down the sides of his mouth; pulpy pieces of slaves oozed out with it. "Come here slaves, you know what the fuck you did," he yelled and across Spanaway the slaves heard.

The blood in the streets started to recede and Queen Cyforah knew it was almost time. "Judy, soon you must release Rick to serve his purpose." "What do I do, rub the lamp or what," she asked. "No Judy, you don't rub it. Just wait until I tell you what to do."

The Them had stopped time, stopped the planet from rotating and we were now frozen in the fifth hour of my dreams. Everything was on hold. The power they had displayed was incomprehensible. I would be lying if I said I wasn't worried; how could we ever defeat such madness.

In front of the White House, three red hummers pulled up. The Secret Service approached them with caution. The windows rolled down and out flowed The JenSiege from the far away Nelle universe. This dancing dark angel of superfluid plasma swirled in a liquid bound light. The Spantonites say she has been seen dancing on the stars. She shot a dark, viscid gelatin at the secret service and it enveloped their entire heads. The sticky substance flowed into their throat and nose and drowned them standing on their feet. The harder they tried to breath, the deeper it flowed into their lungs. After they fell to the ground, twelve men dressed in red suits exited the hummers, four from each one. The leader was Losou. His skin was dark as night, blue- black and the only thing that served to break up all that darkness was a silver bone hanging from around his neck. Somehow you knew the bone once belonged to a human. You couldn't be sure of it, but something about it said real instead of good fake. As he exited the first hummer, he brought a platinum armatura with him, fastened to his wrist by a platinum cuff. He opened it and the JenSiege returned inside. Back to where she dwelled inside the Blazing Lake of Sotteros.

Across the street, the New World Law was watching. This is who they had been waiting for. The eleven men who were with Losou had already went inside. They had lain waste to the secret service men there. They had placed the cooks and caretakers under a trance. Each of the staff stood with a gun in their hand, staring off into blank space. Losou entered the White House and told them to finish it. Shot after shot rang out until every living person inside the White House was dead. Losou and the eleven humanoids went about the business they had came there for; to gain total control, for the Anti Christ, of the official residence and principal workplace of the President of the United States.

A black cloud materialized in the sky and overshadowed the White House. The scent of brimstone filled the air and the sulfuric stench began to suffocate the citizens of Washington D.C. The voice of many water sounded and the evil cloud parted over the white mansion, then vanished. "I know thy works and where thou dwellest: even where Satan seat is," the voice boomed. The ground beneath the mansion shook and rumbled as though the earth would open up and swallow it whole.

Losou' team had been busy. In the Oval office they were standing nude, in the shape of a hexagram. At each of the six points an entity stood and also at each intersection of the inner hexagram. One of them laid in the middle of it while Losou stood outside of it and spoke an unknown language. They were conjuring. When Losou had reached the end of the chant, he expelled from his mouth a long dagger. Coated with blood and other things he walked in the center of them and split the man laying down into two. The body sunk upon itself, as though any bones providing structure had just melted. The mass steamed and began to change. Out of the carnage rose Christina Deanvilt, the recently deceased former President of the U.S. Light streamed from her body as though it was trying to tear through the surface of her skin. The Anti Christ had risen in the morgue and now that it had been conjured, knew it had to act quickly. She could not hide the truth of what she was any longer. It had been necessary for Deanvilt to die in order for the original ruler of darkness to come to the surface.

"My brother is coming, we must go now," it commanded. It was the voice of a demon serpent that spoke. Losou asked her, "Your brother, my lord?" "Yes," it slithered. "Senzoval, we must hurry." Losou opened the armatura and inside was the Gunung Medallion. The medallion was as old as Satan was, made of Kingfisher jade and white marble, it was encrusted with small, pebble sized meteorites. It is able to open the door to other worlds without going through Spanton first. It is one of a kind and only true evil could ever control it. This is the great segregator of the cosmos: the division, the key, between good and evil. Losou reached for the medallion and it seared his hand completely through. The Anti-Christ flicked it's wrist and knocked Losou off of his feet. "You have the audacity to touch that which is not yours," she raged. The human-like beings all fell to their knees, praying not to incur the wrath of their master. Losou castrated himself upon the floor and begged for forgiveness, "My God, please forgive me, I have forgotten myself in your absence, " he sniveled. He was about to be hit with another blow when seven golden objects appeared over the White House. Seven unrecognizable shapes that just hovered above the white-domed roof. Next a voice, the sound of majestic wisdom spoke, "I will come to thee as a thief and thou shall not know what hour I will come upon thee." The Anti-Christ clasped it's hands about its ears as though that would keep the voice out. "We leave now!" It picked up the Gunung-Medallion and summoned a gateway to appear. The Anti-Christ and her eleven remaining disciples left the building. The police and back-up secret service had been trying to call the Oval Office since no report had been given by those stationed inside. They had sent a team to check out what could be causing the delay. They arrived just in time to hear the voice of many waters speak it's mystical words. They were struck instantly deaf. They had heard the true voice of Senzoval and that is forbidden until his triumphal return.

Time had been at a standstill and the planet was beginning to feel the effects of it. With no rotation there was no wind and many cities relied on the power that the wind turbine plants provided. The power was going out in cities all around the world. The air started to smell rotten and it felt thick to the lungs, almost as though you should drink it instead of breath it. The world was suffocating. Trimmers were felt all around the globe. No birds were flying through the air because they had all died. Trillions of insects fell dead upon the earth. Land animals were dead, fish and other sea creatures were washing up on the shores everywhere. The planet wreaked of death.

At Fort Greely, the launch site for the US Army, Captain Pierre Garrysand and Captain Justin Alexander were called into special duty. They would launch the bomb of all bombs if needed. So it was on a frigid cold night in Fairbanks, Alaska that caused Pierre to be staring up at the winter sky, and the glow of the mother ship off in the distance. He looked like he was about to lose his soul to the devil. Justin was staring up with him smoking a cigarette, maybe the last one he would ever smoke. He inhaled it long and deep, to hell with cancer. They had bigger things to worry about. Perspective is a bitch.

"I don't like this Justin. They have us sitting here, knowing my kids are dead and the world is going crazy." Tears welled in his eyes and like a good soldier, he choked them back. No use in giving in to the grief now. He had already cried his eyes out, it hadn't helped. "Why are we the ones that got picked for this suicide mission. If the world is about to end, I'd rather be with my wife." "You might not have a wife pretty soon," Justin replied under his breath. Pierre looked at him, "What was that," he asked. "Nothing." Justin said. Justin was a soldier's soldier. He would do what he was told. He understood that he and others would have to die if it meant killing those motherfuckers that were hovering in the air around the world. Only the strongest survived. He had no qualms about pushing the button. It was one of the main reasons he had been selected for the job. His superiors knew that he would get it done. Pierre on the other hand was a liability. He talked to much and wasn't very well liked. Justin was just waiting for the alarm to sound. That would be his cue. He knew his superiors didn't place much faith in Pierre. He had been giving instructions to get the job done at any and all cost.

"Guess you don't talk much," Pierre asked Justin. "Nope," he said. He didn't want to get to chummy with Pierre in case he had to blow his head off later. "It's fucked up that our superiors are safe underground somewhere, hundreds of feet below ground and we don't even have a radio or TV. They don't want us to know anything that's going on. If we're going out, let's go out with a bang!" "What do you have in mind," Justin asked. They had gone back inside the building by then and Pierre reached inside his duffel bag and pulled out a bag of weed and cocaine. He dug around deeper and pulled out a bottle of scotch. "Let's party," he laughed with a stupid grin on his face. Justin had seen enough, he pulled out his service pistol and said, "By order of the US Army, I am placing you under arrest and holding you for court marshal! You are a disgrace to the uniform solider! Hands behind your back! Now!" Caught red-handed and with nowhere to run, he did as he was told. Justin sat him in a corner after he was cuffed and left him there. They were in a small out-house with nothing but the bomb, themselves and a makeshift table. The alarm bell mounted on the wall was the only piece of equipment in the room. After about a half hour of silence between the two men, Justin asked Pierre, "You want to see what Major Colon did when they built the nuke?" " I don't give a fuck," Pierre responded.

Justin laid down on his back and crawled under the housing that held the bomb, "Come look," he said. Curiosity got the best of Pierre and he scooted to where Justin was and laid down. Justin pointed up with a bizarre smile on his face while his eyes started to glow a blazing red. Pierre crapped his pants and in spite of himself, he looked up. The word 'WORMWOOD' had been scrawled in big capital letters.

We had made it to Mt. Alfa Omega and were walking out of a thin mist inside the Cave of Divine Matter. Even Spantonites dare not walk on this holy ground. Looking around, we could see small cerulean blue orbs flying near what looked to be a tomb made out of light. The orbs sensed their approach and attacked us. I covered myself and Amber with my protective wings. Coming out of the tomb of light we saw a beautiful, electric blue vision of celestial matter. It transform in front of us into the very first seraphim: Nika, Daughter of I AM. She was the watcher; keeper of the stone of Mirabilia.

"That will be," Nika commanded and the brilliant blue orbs flew to the entrance of the cave. They hovered there; blocking further entrance or exit from anyone. "I've been waiting for you Seraphim of Dreams. The final battle between my brothers is nearing the ultimate conclusion, we must act quickly," she said to me.

I would be lying to you if I said I had not been somewhat vain during my time on earth and had become even more so since my transformation, but my beauty paled in comparison to Nika's. The daughter of I AM was more than anyone should be blessed to see. It was more than a physical beauty, which was quite dazzling, it was her presence. She radiated a goodness and mercy that I had only read about in the book of the Bible. Blessed by her Father, her feet had never touched the soiled dirt of any universe. Nothing had ever touched her in fact. She radiated that blue aura and from it, you felt safe, loved. As though you could come to her and tell to her any woes you may have and she would solve them all. She had wings made of the same blue light that surrounded her soul and they reached from wall to wall of the cave. They were encrusted with every jewel known in the universe and the blue glow bounced off those jewels and turned them into a living spectrum of colors. And for some reason, you felt compelled to walk into them. I knew that if I walked to her, she would envelop me with those beautiful wings, gifted to her by her Father, and all would be right with the world. The only problem is that I knew I would never want to let go. Her wings were the ultimate shelter. Amber must have felt the draw too because she started walking forward and I grabbed her arm. We had come too far to surrender to the power of Nika's warmth now. Though I couldn't dream of a better place to be than with Nika at that very moment. It felt as though I had waited forever to be here with her. I knew that she had been waiting too, for over two thousand years, for this day to arrive.

"Nika, we are honored to meet you and are blessed to be in your stately presence. I feel as though I AM is with us at this very moment," I told her. Amber tried to speak but she could not find the words, I couldn't blame her. She settled instead for falling upon her knees before Nika, touching her forehead to the cold floor of the cave and weeping. "You honor me with your words Dream Angel and I am more honored by your tears Amber, please stand. We have much to do," she said. Amber pulled herself from the ground and composed herself. There was a light to her that hadn't been there before. As though she had been touched by the very hand of God. "Do you have the stone your holiness," I asked. "Nika will do just fine and yes, the Mirabilia Stone is in the crypt with Senzovals' human remnants. Jesus Christ is what he was called on Earth, correct." Amber looked shocked.

"You're telling me that I'm going to see the remains of Jesus Christ," Amber asked. Nika answered her with a beatific smile and led us towards a covered alcove. As she walked deeper into the cave, the light coming from it started to dim and she started to glow brighter. We came to a hewn rock door which opened without anything or rather, anyone touching it and I knew that she bid it open with her mind just like I did with the door to my sleeping chamber. As the door slid back in the cave wall, right before our very eyes laid the greatest man who every walked the Earth. He hadn't decomposed at all in over two millennia and in fact, it looked as though he lay there sleeping. The afflictions that his body had undergone upon his martyrdom were still present. Amber and I both fell to our knees and worshiped the risen Lord, in thanks for washing our sins away.

Next to Him was the Mirabilia Stone. Nika willed it to come to her and it dismounted it's pedestal and floated to her blue image of light. "Jesus daughter gave it to me and I have not willed it into use since then. It was a gift to her from her mother Magdalene," Nika told us. "Daughter? Jesus had a daughter? So you were telling us the truth then Carmen," Amber asked. "Your worlds existence grows short even as we speak Amber, do you think we have time for mistruth's," I answered her crossly. "Amber, you are to take the stone and use it when your universe wills it," Nika instructed. "Carmen, it is very important that you get back to where the other Celestial Stones are. When they are put together, Nueden will open so that Senzoval can enter your world. You must be on watch for my other brother Denfulus." "Who is that," Amber asked. " Your bible call him The Anti-Christ," Nika said with a look of shame. Amber looked like she had seen a ghost. She glanced at the Mirabilia stone in her hands and with a worried expression and asked, "This will have the power to stop Denufulus, right Nika." "No child, that will open the door for Senzoval, this is what will stop the Anti-Christ," and Nika held up the Eutarpa. "This what my brother Denfulus needs to keep Senzoval from stopping him: use it before he does." This exquisite blue lyre is able to create the spell of the Sound of Madness. This is what Sonya will need. Seven golden trumpets held by seven angels will bring forth Senzovals Fold Of Sheep That You Know Not Of. It is a very crippling display of cosmic power. When the soulless slaves tried to steal the lyre before, for their own purpose in the Tunguska wilderness, it caused a great explosion. Still a mystery to this day on your planet."

"Have you both read the great book before today, before the last of animated matter ends," the daughter of God asked me. Before I could answer her, Amber said, "The Bible? Of course we have read it. Carmen was human before all of this happened to her and I was brought up in a very religious family." "That is what you call: The Bible, on your planet. A very interesting book. That is not the book I refer to Amber." "Well what book is she talking about Carmen," Amber asked me. "Nika is referring to the Book of Spanton, Amber. Keep in mind that though you have seen a lot, there are still a great number of things that you will never come to know." "Will you give me the lyre to take back to Sonya," I asked. "No Dream Angel," she answered. She will be here in a very short time, in fact I hear her approach as we speak. It would put you both in grave danger to be in possession of two of the Celestial Stones at one time and we cannot risk they fall in the hands of evil. We must use a Angel of my father's." Amber looked like she had so many questions, so much that she wanted to know but even she knew that now was not the time. Her world was on the brink of collapse, we had to return.

"Nika, thank you for your knowledge and wisdom and the great honor that you have bestowed upon us, " I said. "You are welcome Seraphim of Dreams, go now, the time is upon us," Nika commanded. The blue orbs parted, Amber and I left the cave but we knew we never forget this day, never, no matter what was to come.

The sound of a thousand thunderclaps, of universes colliding filled the Cave of Divine Matter. Another portal opened and over Nika's head flew the Angel of Distraction with Sonya flying in essential formation. Julie and Sonya's inherent power was pure beauty. The blue orbs tried to attack them but Nika waved them off. Julie and Sonya landed and knelt before the Daughter of I AM. Nika handed the Lyre of Eutarpa to Sonya and she held it close to her face in disbelief. Nika held up her hands and called upon her father with a voice sounding like a hundred tsunamis crashing at the same time, "Father, I have done what you asked!" At the same time the Spanton Spell Tranise appeared. "Tranise, you were not summoned, why are you here," Nika asked, a hint of anger in her voice. " I was sent by your Father Nika to cleanse the planet Earth of impurities. I no longer respond to anyone's, not even yours Nika, command." "You all must leave now, the Revelation has begun," Nika told Sonya and Julie. The instant she said it, the earth's rotation started again. A greater force was coming to shed light on this epic war of prophecy. It was now four am and within the fifth hour in my dreams. The hour of climactic battle has begun.

Scripture 23: Senzoval's Return

The Anti-Christ and its followers entered the Temple Mount in Jerusalem through the Gate of Darkness. Here is where they would set up to do battle; the place that is believed to be footstool of God's presence on earth.

The ground shook in fury and out from the holy dirt came a temple of granite. Denfulus and his two most powerful angels of sin appeared: Genmoz and Losou. Both of them stood as dark shadows in the light of the day. Jews that were praying at the mount ran in terror. Muslims would rather die than give up control of the mount so they stayed in battle, shooting their weapons at the third temple, seeing that prophecy had finally become real.

As they shot at him, Denfulus' human skin began to peel away and revealed the first Seraphim of Original Evil. Everyone stopped and to behold him. They each saw something different, an illusion of themselves. They could see the crimes and lies they committed throughout their own lives and most turned and ran in shame while others stayed to fight. Looking at Denfulus, you saw yourself, and not many people are able to kill themselves. Losou opened the platinum armatura. Bursting out of it while screaming with the sound of death came the JenSiege. She shot her dark matter at both Muslims and Jews and then watched as the spell engulfed their heads, she watched as they drowned and fell. Several golden orbs appeared over the granite temple but in the blink of any eye they were gone. One moment there, the next not. Denfulus knew what this meant. His brother Senzoval was near and had called upon the Seven Seals of Nueden.

Tranise appeared in the middle of the Caspian Sea. She knew that the Seven Seals had been called upon and it was now time to enact the judgment. She shot down in the water and started the biggest tsunami ever recorded on earth. The Caspian is the largest enclosed body of water on Earth and some classify it as a lake while others say it is a sea. Bordered by Iran, Russia, Kazakhstan, Turkmenistan and Azerbaijan, their coastal regions would soon be devastated.

The ancient inhabitants of its littorals had thought the Caspian was an ocean because they thought it to be boundless. They were close, it is the source to the world's oceans. As Tranise churned through its depths, sea water propelled in the air at an amazing speed. Reaching over ten thousand feet into the atmosphere, the wall of water created a dark shadow and a roar never heard before on the planet. It hit first over Yuzhny okrug, the southern federal district of Russia.

The inhabitants there could see the wall of water rushing towards them, high in the sky. People ran for their lives but it was too late. The wall of water came crashing down, washing away the sinful. Sirens sounded in Iran, the eighteenth largest country in the world. With no remorse, the tsunami was coming to wash it away too. The people their thought it was an air raid or a terror attack. They were gone and had no idea what had hit them. Tornados and hurricans swept the world over. At a unbelievable speed; blowing away countries around the world, Afgh anistan, Germany, Canada, Nigeria and America to name a few. Look at you now, running for your pathetic lives. Is it really that hard to stop living in sin and just believe in him! Your body is just a matter of space that make manure to fertilize the grass! I AM do not want them, let your soul free and pay the price!

At Mistress Pat's mansion, five tornados could be seen in the stone of Hubriser headed for Washington state. The soulless slaves were trying their best to penetrate the Diamond Shield. People who were left or that had decided to stay in spite of the danger, came out and started to defend themselves. To fight for their souls. Motherships hovered over every country on earth. Hundreds of them could be seen roaming the skies and air forces all around the world were trying to battle these monsters. Your planet wasn't ready. It would never be ready to battle against such imminent power. The walking dead entered homes and searched for living beings to rob them of their souls. There was no place to hide, the slaves of The Them would have what they had come for.

Parked inside the vacant garage of an abandoned house, hiding in the limo, sat James and Paul. The sound of death was beating at the door, the Soulless could smell living souls and wanted the two of them badly. They were listening to the radio and a reporter was saying, "NASA has confirmed that thirty three object have landed in the seas around the world. No explosion or tsunami has been experienced from the events and it is said that the tsunami that devastated the coastal regions of the Caspian Sea were completely unrelated. Radar picked up the location of the objects but it is unknown at this time, their purpose." After that the radio went dead, no more news will be heard over the radio. A tornado brought down the last station working in Washington." James clicked off the radio and the men just stared at each other and listened to the pounding on the garage door. It sounded like a lazer was going across the door. They would have their souls very soon.

"James, I just thought of something. If this is really the end, I think we may be on the wrong side of the fence," Paul said, his eyes bigger than saucers. "What do mean Paul?" "I mean Mistress Pat. I don't know what the fuck has happened to her but I think we might be safer at the mansion. She has this huge glowing diamond and I believe it is the cause of all this madness. I say we go back there." A look of sheer fright passed across James' face and he yelled at Paul in the dark of the garage, "First, you said there is no place to run. Let's park here and die you said. Now you're saying let's go back to the mansion and die! Make up your damn mind Paul!" "Mistress Pat, we must get back to her so that she can protect us," Paul urged. "Fuck it! Looks like we die one way or another, better than in here shivering like a bunch of pussies."

James started the sedan and put the car in reverse. He punched the petal to the floor and the limo screeched backwards out of the garage. The aluminum door burst outwards showering the soulless slaves with debris and killing those standing in the way. Once on the street, he threw the car in drive and sped down the road, running over any slaves that got in his way.

Mistress Pat was watching the battle going on outside from the Hubriser Stone. Devy and Rapere, the Giant along with Perfective were killing many of the soulless slaves. You can hear Rapere's crazy laugh screaming in the air. Devy smashed them to the ground like toys with his powerful bare hands. Rick's father was picking the orbs out of the sky and shaking the slaves from them into his mouth. " "Yum yum, come out slaves; you know you've been bad." he said. He pulled out his giant leather belt and used it like a giant whip. Smashing it to the ground, scattering slaves as he did so." "Don't you run from me slaves; I'm putting you on time out," he screamed.

Pat could see the limo approaching through the stone. "James," she said incredulously. "What is he doing back here?" Directly behind the limo, the Unknown was on his tail. James looked in the rearview mirror and started to scream like a little girl, "What the fuck is that! Good Lord, please help us!" The unknown caught up to the car and pounded on it. It chased the sedan on its large roach legs, looking for a meal, and eyes gone black with hunger. James pressed the gas pedal harder but he was already pushing it at one hundred sixty miles an hour, so he started swerving, trying to evade the beast. Paul was blubbering, crying for his life in the seat next to him. Mistress Pat wished them inside the mansion and the next thing either man knew is that they were on the floor of the living room, crying like children. "What the hell is happening? " James asked once he had regained control of himself. "You took the words right out of my mouth. Hell is happening," Mistress Pat answered. The lost spirits that had never been turned over to them were floating around freely, they didn't bother James so much as they had before because he didn't go running from the house. It would probably take Denfulus himself to come and get James out of the mansion at that point. Though he wasn't leaving the mansion, the spooks were spooking him so he ran to a closet to hide. He screamed when he opened the door because Kirk Bailey was kneeling and praying. Bailey screamed at him yelling, "Close the fucking door already!" James jumped inside the closet with him and slammed the door shut.

Streaming across the sky, the mother ship took aim at the mansion with its ultimate weapon. It blasted at the shields core, the shield reacted and brought down the Spell of Reflection" an invisible coating of reflective protection. The shield launched the diamond missiles that contained the spell at the mother ship and when the ship took aim at the shield once again, the power was turned back on it. The ship exploded in the sky and the falling debris killed many of the slaves.

The Queen and Judy were now standing outside of the mansion, but still safely behind the shield. Cyforah commanded Judy to release Rick. Judy looked at the lamp and started shaking it. "No Judy, just ask him to appear. You are his master now." "Awe shit, that's what's up," she squealed. Judy sat the lamp down on the ground and said, "Rick, I call on you to help us." Out of the lamp, three jet streams of cherry colored smoke zoomed around Judy's body. Transforming in front of her was the Three Cursed Virgins: the protectors of Jinni. Jinni let out a powerful jolt and it was felt by everyone in the mansion as a painful shock in their chest. "Quickly Judy, wish Jinni on the other side of the shield before he lets loose another jolt," Cyforah ordered. Judy did as she was asked and Jinni and the three virgins materialized on the outside of the shield. A powerful jolt went throughout the city of Spanaway, any orbs left in the sky came down crashing to the ground.

Legend has it that the Iblisarn from Sotterus created the lamp an hid an evil spell inside of it. Many spells can be placed or hidden in the lamp of Jinni. One of his most spectacular spells is that of Suetonius, the Twelve Caesars. This spell contains the souls of every Caesar that ruled the earth, captured because they were headed to Sotterus when Iblisarn stole their souls away and entwined them together to create the spell. Once the twelfth Caesar had died, he sold the spell to the spirit of Jinni for a favor. No one knows what this favor was but it was granted and now the spell lives on inside of the lamp.

Focused on the mother ship; Jinni cast out The Spell of Julius Caesar, the Daggers of Casca. The soul of Julius appeared out from the green fog; busting out around him were flaming giant daggers that tried to assault the ship but it had no effect. Many daggers landed upon the slaves and killed them on the spot. Devy jumped high at the mother ship and it dotted out of the way in light speed. The unknown started eating every living thing it saw. Slaves and humans were being swallowed whole. Soulless slaves ran toward the Lamp of Jinni. The three cursed virgins flew towards the slaves and with a snap of their fingers, the slaves froze. The Virgins attacked them by eating their flesh and sucking out their blood. Blue liquid stained the virgin's mouths. Rick's father stomped on the walking dead and peeled them off his shoes and ate them; slapping some with his belt screaming. "Now go home slaves, it's getting late!"

Jinni called upon Augustus Caesar and the Ivory Coach. Giving out non-stop bolts of electricity. The bolt sounded like a giant anvil hitting the ground from far above. Out from a green fog came powerful horses with carriages ,pulverizing the slaves where they stood. The Evil Eye of Jinni finally appeared and slithered around in its pus colored fog; gazing: watching! Rick's two red eyes could also be seen. Four chains of submission with sharp hooks shot out of the fog and locked on to the four orbs in the sky bringing them to the ground and they exploded. Hundreds of submissive chains came out of the fog next, grabbing anything that moved; hooking them and bringing them back for the cursed virgins to feed on. The Them had had enough.

They sent their most powerful spell, Defender of the Them. The moon went dark. Devy had seen this before, those two eons ago. He knew it wasn't good. The spell had earned the name Defender of The Them for a reason. It was very powerful, very powerful indeed. The Them were no longer playing. "Cover yourselves," Devy yelled. The unknown crawled back into the hole from where it had come from. Devy grabbed the Lamp of Jinni and passed through the Diamond Shield. Obviously, he wanted to protect his own ass as well and Prefection flew back to. "Devy, what is everyone running from," Mistress Pat asked. "The true meaning of Calamity, mistress: witness." The soulless slaves started to run back to their orbs and took cover themselves: Crocruell would kill all!

Rick's father and Rapere chased the slaves back to their orbs. The Shell puts up it's Dark Moon armor remembering the last time this battle took place. The light inside the shield got brighter around the mansion. It brought upon itself the spell; Light Of A Hundred Suns. Now nothing can look upon the Protector without going blind: you are only safe within the shield. "Devy what's going on?" Pat asked." The Diamond Shield is preparing for the ultimate battle my lord." The wind started to gust and the city of Spanaway was abandoned by the earth. Every country feared they would be next. Flying out of the portal, Sonya and Julie appeared. "Sonya my baby!" Mistress Pat yelled.

Right behind them, Amber and I walked out. The moon seemed to come closer to the earth. It was so close that standing from the mansion looking out all you saw in the sky was darkness. The moon was blotting out the stars in the sky. You could see a spot of light shining on the moon from the Diamond Shield's brightness. Busting out of that spot of light on the moon surface, was Crocruell. Flying through our atmosphere with incredible speed; with wings eighty feet across. The beast landed in front of The Diamond Shield. With the body of a pit bull and the head of a dragon; it sits sixty feet tall. His tail waved back and forth and grows: at the end of his tail is a mouth with the teeth of many sharks. It was slithering through the streets; looking for anything that moved; catching people and soulless slaves, eating them whole. The Spell of a Hundred Suns had no affect on the beast. The plasma power the Crocruell produced can shatter the Diamond Shield in time. The Spell of Calamity his destroyed many Diamond Shields. Releasing energy from the cosmos, Crocruell shook Washington State; the mansion stood unfazed. Rick's father and Rapere fell to the ground in pain. The shield fired back with the spell of Metallous; a pulsating clink that knocks out the senses. This clink could be heard as far as Oregon, Idaho and Montana. Rapere and The Dead Father held their heads: another powerful clink sounded and their heads imploded. People and soulless slaves started to implode where they stood! Everyone in the state of Washington, Oregon, Idaho and Montana imploded. Building crashed to the ground. Crocruell felt nothing. The Planet Perfection shot plasma lightning bolts at the beast; zooming around it in light speed. Crocruell was unfazed. The Golden Angel of Perfection opened his mouth and set free a swarm of moscas. The swarm flew over Spanaway. The giant beast blows the spell Abiding winds at the Planet Perfection; causing massive tornados on the small planet: knocking it back through the Diamond shield. The moscas attacked the beast; until his body was covered by moscas. They bit and sucked, trying to bring down the monster. They entered the creature's mouth eating inside of him. Out from beneath Crocruell comes Montuorus. Montuorus grabbed the beast and tried to bring him underground. The two stone deities of lions in front of the mansion came to life and attacked the beast feet. Crocruell gave out a burst of heat and the moscas all fell to the ground burning in flames; Montuorus held onto the beast and his branches burned around him. Crocruell lift up his feet and smashed the deities.

"Carmen, put the Celestial Stones together." Cyforah said. Carmen, Judy and Amber lined the stones together. "Mistress Pat, bring over the Hubriser stone quickly." I said. My master did what I asked and lined up the Hubriser Stone with the others. Amber placed down the Mirabilia stone very carefully. All the stones started to irradiate together. The Mirabilia stone started to rise above the rest. It's now four forty-four am; the sixth hour in my dreams. The True Number of the Beast. Your so called mark of the beast was changed in your bible, and St.John knew this. The true number could not be told in fear of worship of the true Anti Christ Denfulus. It's not a six- six- six mark on your body: but a time, and the time is the sixth hour of my dreams: St.John knew this fact and changed it around. Anyone still alive at four forty-four am on December twentieth, two thousand twelve is marked for Sotterus. The Gofogen did its job of collecting the innocent and left your universe: leaving behind time marked souls for hell.

The four gates of the cosmos are open together once again. Kim fell back in her chair in pain. Her water had just broke. Paul ran to her aid. Kirk and James were still in the closet crying to God. Julie and Sonya flew through the shield and confronted the beast. Crocruell burst the burning tree from around him. Julie paused in front of Crocruell and distracted the beast. He couldn't take his eyes of the beauty of her light. He's mesmerized by her image. Sonya hit the beast with The Spell of Ithina. This powerful spell breaks down atoms inside matter. The Beast shook in a rage and the spell was cast off of him. Crocruell saw Sonya and brake out of Julie's spell: he shoot dark plasma at Julie. Sonya caught the plasma and mimicked it. She shot it back at the beast; blasting him with his own power. Then Jinni came out from behind the shield; the virgins were by his side carrying the lamp. Jinni released a jolt of cosmic power that tumbled Croculell.

Jinni call upon Gaise Caligula Caesar and the Chaerea Swords. The ghost of Caligula appeared over Spanaway and thousands of spinning swords fell from the sky and landed in and around Crocruell. Jinni let loose another earth shattering jolt. Sonya picked up the powerful jolt and mimicked Jinni. She shot out a jolt of energy and knocked Crocruell down again. The stars in the sky seem to move closer to the earth. The night was hosting the light from the stars of the galaxy. Crocruell had had enough. He was ready to release the Spell of Calamity. "Take cover!" Devy yelled. Crocruell shots up to the sky and vanished. The Galactic Alignment formed and the milky way and all the planets in your solar system shot powerful beams of plasma at the mansion. Meteorites came down upon Washington state. Croculell returned to the ground with fury in its eyes. The Diamond Shield of Atlantis can't take much more.

Just then the light of the moon turned on like a light switch. Sonya pulled out the lyre of Eutarpa. She played the harp and the Sound of Madness was heard. The Mirabilia stone shot a magnificent ray of light in the sky and a massive dark hole appeared. The sound of many trumpets blew. Seven Angels of Nueden appeared out of the brightest spectrum; blowing their trumpets: the sound could be heard around the world. Denfulus and his angels of evil put their hands over their ears in Jerusalem. Kirk and James peeked out of the closet to witness the wonder. The sky opened and in the whole sky was the light of the brightest suns: A Fold of Sheep We Know Not Of appeared; and one hundred and eleven millions angels flew off around the world to battle and kill the Soulless Slaves.

With a various continua that resembled some unfathomable color, a thousand and one angels stayed behind and guarded the door to Nueden. After these things I looked, and beheld, a door opened in heaven. And the first voice which I heard was like a trumpet speaking with me, saying, "Come Up Here, and I Will Show You Things Which Must Take Place After this day." We all stood there with our mouths open. "Look like your wish is coming true Amber." Judy said. Amber couldn't take her eyes off The Return of Senzoval. Immediately I was in the Spirit; and beheld, a throne set in the light, and Senzoval sat on the throne.

And He who sat there was like a king and a sardius stone in appearance; and there was unknown colors around the throne, in appearance like an birth of a star in its dust. Around the throne were twenty-four thrones, and on the thrones I saw twenty-four Seraphims clothed in light; and they had crowns of gold on their heads. Croculell saw the image and started to back up. And from the throne proceeded lightnings, thundering, and voices. Seven golden orbs of light were burning bright before the throne. Senzoval stood up and put his hands to the heavens and said "Father I Feel Your Presence." The sun shot a solar flare at Croculell; the sky was on fire around the world. The beast couldn't take anymore and flew through the flames back into the moon. And I saw in the right hand of Him who sat on the throne The Secret Book of Spanton written inside and on the back, protected by seven golden orb seals.

Then I saw Julie proclaiming with a loud voice, "Who is worthy to open the Book of Spanton and to loose its seals?"

And no one on the earth or under the earth was able to open the Book of Spanton Spells, or to look directly at it.

So I cried, because no one was found worthy to open and read The Secret Book of Spanton, or to look directly at it.

Scripture 24: The Four Seraphims of Apocalypse

Hell broke loose in Jerusalem: Literally! The third temple stood tall and anarchy set in around the world. All countries of the earth lost control of their government. It was every man for himself for those still left alive. "You will now worship me ,you will all take your own life so I can claim your souls. Your souls have nowhere to go but with me to Sotterus: amuse me with repentance. The time of my mark is upon you!" Denfulus screamed. People were running into the sea. They had nowhere to go; they had all been marked as of four forty-four am, the sixth hour in my dreams. The Hour of The Beast!

Lake Tiberius is best known for its association with the lives of Jesus Christ and his disciples. In the Bible the lake is referred to as the Sea of Chinnereth or the Sea of Galilee; a name that has survived in the modern Arabic Bahrat Tabariye. The vicinity of Lake Tiberius was well populated during ancient times. Now with no hope to live, people knelt at the shore begging God for forgiveness. Like a flash, busting out the middle of the lake is Tranise the Angel of Cosmic Wind. People cowered in fear as the wind made of light came back crashing down upon the waters. The lake came upon itself; and the waters started to part: The ocean floor started to appear. The separation of the waters is a very powerful spell in The Book of Spanton. It was done only once before in your planet history. When the ocean floor was revealed; massive arks, thirty three in number, in thirty three locations around the world was revealed; one ark at every shore. Waters started to part all over the world. Each ark was two hundred feet long. Made out of red rubies coated with a shield of diamonds from the universe E'ly to be impenetrable to the earth ocean's pressure. Marching out of the first ark in Jerusalem was the Mayans. Wearing the ancient war gear of Nab'ee: they prepare to defend the arks around the world. Shooting out the earth seven seas was thousands of Unidentified flying objects. For the second time in your Earth history the Mayans will team up with the Atlantians and fight the invaders of Earth in a epic battle in the sky. Hovering over the waters was the craft of Chinowa leader of Nab'ee. Speaking the language of the people of Israel. "Come and join our world for your world is no more." People looked back at the devil and ran towards the ark to keep their souls. This angered Denfulus and he ordered The JenSiege to stop them. The dark angel shot out of the armatura and rained down dark matter at the head of the Mayan soldiers; some was caught and drowned on their feet. The highest power had set Tranise free from ridding the earth of viruses. She now had a will of her own. Tranise flew down at the JenSiege to confront its cosmic spells. They both flew high over the ark in front of the craft of Chinowa in epic battle. People still running down in the parted waters for their lives being helped by the Mayans around the earth shores.

The risen Senzoval had paid the purchase price to be the kinsman redeemer and all power and authority over the earth had been restored to this second coming. Had the rulers of this world known about this plan of I AM to redeem the earth they would not have crucified his beloved seed. Amber start to also cry standing next to me. Paul was in amazement at what he had witnessed but was still helping Kim have her baby. "Push madam push!" Kim screamed out in pain as the baby's head started to crown. The elders around Senzoval stood and chanted the word of God. They are redeemed from every tribe, tongue, people and nation to become kings and believers that will reign on the new earth. Senzoval purchased them with His own blood. Senzoval is not coming back to take everyone up into Nueden for eternity after this marked day: the human race will be evaluated for the last time.

I beheld till the thrones were cast down, and the Ancient of Spirits did sit, whose garment was bright like the sun, and the hair of his head like the full moon: his throne was like the fiery flame, and his wheels as burning bushes. His skin was as the color of many stars. A brilliant rainbow reflecting a shade of skin that shows of mixed DNA throughout the universe. A fiery stream issued and came forth from behind him: the judgment was set, and the Secret Book of Spanton was opened by him. Just then Kim's son passed from her womb. Paul caught the child in his arms: Julie flew down and cut the glowing cord and took the babe from his arms. She held the child up and Senzoval took him. Kim looked at her son in his arms and cried. When the babe looked in the eyes of The Son of God: the ground shook and right before us all: was The Third Temple. Denfulus was standing tall on the mount: are we in Jerusalem or is Jerusalem in Spanaway? "Carmen, I'm a little confused, is this my wish? Who is the creator? Amber asked. It was now the seventh hour in my dreams. The hour of Repent.

To the readers of Carmen Dreams: Your Government made me give this warning and I must cooperate. If you wish not to know the truth about life stop reading here: The eighth hour is upon you in my dreams: you have been warned!

Now I know it's all true: I believe! Senzoval kept alive only the wicked that believed in him. They are not worthy to go to Nueden: but they will live on under the world's oceans until they grow old and die; They're bloodline will forever be known as The Last Believers. Whoever died by chance this night by any circumstances are non-believers of Senzoval; and their souls will forever be lost in the metaverses until they learn. Only those who died by the Gofogen went to Nueden. While Senzoval held the babe, Amber walked to the front of the Diamond Shield, still in its protection and asked Senzoval: "Are you the creator?" "Amber No!" Cyforah yelled.

Just then all power on earth was neutralized: the planet was in darkness. The sun started to dim and the world started to get cold but not freeze. Over the planet was the most hideous and perfect sight of matter that my eyes have ever seen. It appeared to be two of them. The eyes alone was the size of the full moon. It's right hand could hold the earth: right away I knew it was The Them from section zero. Remember that section zero is the size of a million Jupiter's; anything so massive must be to accommodate it's host. Hundreds of people running for the arks around the world looked up and just died from fright; the Mayans warned them not to look up: thousands more kept running to safety. Kirk and James ran back inside the closet: Mistress Pat fell to the floor and cried for Sonya and Carlos. Julie left Carlos and Chubb Chubb in the world of Spanton safe with the Seraphim of Mimic. "This is your wish Amber: be careful what you wish for, you just might get it." Judy said. Every bat of The Them's eyes brought with it a gust of pure air from the zero section of space. The thought went through all our heads and we heard like a sound of a dragon. "WHERE ARE OUR SOULS?" Amber screamed and ran inside the closet with Kirk and James. "We are the creators, you broke the celestial law: give us the Stone of The Hubriser."

I looked at Julie and Sonya floating over Senzoval and the babe. They shook their heads no at me; letting me know this is not the true creator of all. Looking at Senzoval how could such a wonderful image come from the likes. Just then Nika, the Daughter of God appeared next to me; she did not look at me at all. She just said "This was the joke of Nueden for many supernovas. Even at this moment a Nuedener is laughing about them thinking there God. Mistress Pat was not amused. "If they are not the creators who are they?" Pat asked. "Their only the creators of your universe. In other universes their known as waste matter collectors. "WHAT! Isn't that garbage men." Judy yells. "Everyone prepare for battle, they are not God." The mistress orders. The Them set off Yellowstone Park and a super volcano erupted. Many people already left Wyoming this morning in fear of a eruption. How right they were; even though they didn't make it far enough in time. This event will destroy the United States of America and put the earth in an ice age. The skies over Wyoming turned fiery red; The caldera had erupted with tremendous force several times in the last two million years but nothing like this. The one thousand and one angels held up one thousand and one Rods of Iron. Senzoval held up the babe to the first sealed golden orb hovering over the throne.

And I saw when the first orb opened it seal; four Seraphims coming toward the earth from the door of Nueden: and I heard, as it were the noise of thunder, one of the four beasts saying, Come and witness. Everyone started to walk closer to the protective shield to behold the unbelievable. Kirk, James and Amber also came out of the closet to witness.

And I saw, and behold a horse with wings and a horn of light sticking out from it's head shinning as the full moon: and the Seraphim who sat on him had a bow; and a crown was given unto him: and he went forth conquering, and to conquer. The Mayan got many people inside the arks around the world's shores. It was time to take the people who were left on earth to their new home under the sea. Denfulus swore at The Them. Senzoval held the babe to the second sealed orb. And when the orb opened the second seal, I heard the second beast say, Come and see me.

And there went out what look like a dragon that was made of fire: and power was given to him that sat thereon to take peace from the world, and that they should destroy one another:

and there was given unto him a mighty sword. The Seraphim of Destruction passed the sword to the Them; the two of them took the sword and started to mutilate themselves.

Back at Fort Greely missile base; Pierre and Justin were sitting and waiting. They felt the explosion from Yellowstone and the phone did not ring. "Why has no one called yet Justin?" "Their all dead man." Justin looked like he was in a trance. Looking in the security cameras Justin saw a red sky. " "What do you think is causing that?" "You know Justin they left us here to die man." Turning the cameras around they can see the glow from the park high in the sky. "Pierre let's do it man; things are out of control." "Shit I'm down, I just want to get the fuck out from underground Justin." " Let's blow that fucking state off the map."

At the battle site The Them repeated "We are the creators; give us The Stone of the Hubriser." The fake creator chopped off a piece of its finger with the Sword of Destruction; under the sword's spell: and it fell into the ocean and it turned the sea to blood. Blood rained over all the earth! "Give them the damn stone!" James screamed. "No mistress Pat we won't have to; trust me, time is running out for them. It's almost the eighth hour of my dreams."

The Them was tired of the games and started to shift the poles slowly on earth. The cataclysmic pole shift hypothesis is the conjecture that the axis of rotation of a planet has undergone relatively rapid shifts in location, creating calamities such as massive floods and large scale tectonic events. This means that the North Pole will be changed into the South Pole. Scientifically this can only be explained by the harmonic cycle of the magnetic fields: but know you just learned how it will really happen.

Senzoval held the babe to the third sealed orb and when the orb opened the third seal, I heard the third beast say, Come and behold. And I beheld, and lo a Lion with wings as dark as deep space; and the Seraphim that sat on him had a pair of balances in his hand.

And I heard a voice in the midst of the four Seraphims say, A measure of wheat for a price, and three measures of oats for a price; and see thou have not the oil and the wine. The thunder clapped and the Mayans work was done. Before the pole shift, they were able to save four hundred and forty four thousand people of the earth out of the seven billion that were alive just yesterday. The battle between Tranise and The JenSiege continued over the parted blood red sea. Tranise will keep the dark angel at bay until everyone is safe. Denfulus said to his brother; "Brother you know father said that the planet Aissen is mine to rule." "Yes Denfulus he did say this; but he also said just for a thousand years. Your time is up; the humans have been marked: your job is done here." "NO!" Denfulus screamed.

Then Senzoval held the babe to the fourth sealed orb; when the orb opened the fourth seal, I heard the voice of the fourth beast say, Come and believe. The trumpets blew!

And I looked, and beheld a Gargoyle made of bones: and his name that sat on him was Death, and the door to Sotterus followed with him. The power was given unto them over the fourth part of the earth, to kill with sword, and with hunger, and with Spanton Spells, and with the beasts of the earth.

The spell of death cut down Denfulus and his two apostles Genmoz and Losou leaving behind the Gunung Medallion. Sending Denfulus below the earth oceans to test the faith of the Last Believers for ever more. The JenSiege was sucked back inside The Blazing Lake of Sotterus: with the Key of Segregation to the universes. Tranise stood undefeated and witnessed.

The Mayans were ready to depart. Scores of parted waters around the earth is ready to seal back the ocean. Senzoval nodded his head and said " WHO DARE NOT BELIEVE IN THE SON OF I AM?" Just then the oceans closed, covering the thirty-three arks around the world; they took the Last Believers to their new home in Nab'ee. The Mayan and Atlantians with powerful ships hovering by sound waves went crashing down back into the oceans.

Kirk and I walked over to console my cousin Kim. "Carmen what does all this mean." She asked. "Kim it mean that the human race was wrong; their way of living and their lust for greed is not the way of God." "Yes my child; you gave birth to the babe with The Rod of Iron: he will now rule the new earth." Bailey explained. The Them spoke with blood gushing out of their body; dying as they speaks. "Where is the keeper of the Hubriser stone? Show yourself to your creator." Mistress Pat walked up to the shield to show herself. With the planet shaking and shifting but well protected by the shield she said. "What I did with the souls; I did because this is wrong." As she spoke; the lost souls floated around her in fear. "They do not want to go with you." she said. "Who are you to question the law of the cosmos?" "I'm Patricia Brewster; I am The Angel of Dreams."

Just then Senzoval held the babe to the fifth sealed orb and it opened. I saw under the altar the souls of them that were slain for the word of God, and for the testimony which they held:

And I looked at the lost souls in the mansion and they cried with a loud voice, saying, How long, O Lord, holy and true, dost thou not judge and avenge our blood on them that dwell on the earth? They swirled around the mistress and cried.

And robes of light were given unto every one of them; and it was said unto them, that they should come hither, until their fellow servants also and their brethren, that was killed as they were, should be fulfilled on to him. All the lost souls of the mansion pass through The Diamond Shield and hovered around the Throne of Senzoval. Senzoval held up his head to the sky and set the spirits free; to travel through the metaverses until they also learn.

Senzoval held the babe to the sixth sealed orb. And I beheld when it had opened the sixth seal, and, lo, there was a great earthquake; and the sun burned out, and the moon became as blood;

The cosmos of heaven fell unto the earth, even as leaves on a fall day, when she is shaken of a mighty gust of wind.

Nueden departed like a scroll when it is rolled apart; and every mountain and island were moved out of their own place. The poles are now shifted and the earth is calm.

Kings of the earth, and the non believers, and the rich men, and the evil men, and the greedy men, and every jailed man, and every free man, is dead. For the great day of his wrath has come; and no one shall be able to stand again?

Amber walked back to the protective shield; The Them moved down closer. All you could see was its giant bloody eye: inside it's eye was an unknown world of slavery. Blood spattered on the diamond shield from its neck. Senzoval called upon Amber; she disappeared from behind the Diamond Shield and appeared before him. Senzoval hands Amber the seventh seal; "What is this my lord?" Senzoval answered to Amber. "This is your wish my child; open it." Amber trusted Senzoval and took the orb in her hands.

Just then the whistle of all whistles came roaring down out of the air. Pierre and Justin sent the nuclear bomb from Fort Greely to end this madness. They are now also dead from the pole shift; buried alive underground. It was now six forty-three in the morning, one minute before I awake; Amber and Judy had no world to go back to and Rick was dead. I yelled to Amber; "open it Amber and behold your wish." The nuclear bomb will hit in 15 seconds. They sent the one marked "Wormwood." Amber opened the seventh seal and everything went pitch black and silent!

Scripture 25: The Creator

Your galaxy is a massive, gravitationally bound system that consists of stars and stellar remnants, an interstellar medium of gas and dust, and an important but poorly understood component tentatively dubbed dark matter. Every star in your universe went out: all suns went cold. There was no light in space. True darkness fell at this time; and the other universes pause and wait for the judgment of your planet Aissen. All planets must be judged and this is your time: recycling is a non-stop process.

I truly am sorry for the people who believe that man was created in God's image. That is the ego of your race; you are not perfect. How can you be in his image. You are created to live only for your world. Some universes don't need eyes to see. They don't need a mouth to communicate. Some species hear by feeling. Why can't they be in God's image? You humans are very stuck on yourself, everything is about you, you, and you. Sorry to tell you this, but when you look at the whole true picture of the cosmos; you are a virus and your planet is going to get a shot in the ass to rid itself of you; so to speak.

Did you ever here the saying that God is everywhere? Dark matter is what you call The Creator; very interesting: upon Amber opening the seventh seal. It vibrated through all of us at the same time: Every animated and non-animated thing felt it's presence. There was no light like the way you know light to be. Light is in the eye of the beholder; the true light is in the darkness. Energy pass through our brains not of words; but of knowledge. Then out of the darkness comes the light. The Secret Book of Spanton was adding it's last chapter for the end of days; the results! We can hear the word of God not through our ears but through our atoms of matter; speaking to every cell in our body.

We all could feel him say, "I am with thee and you are with me always. I am everywhere and nowhere at once. You are what was and are to be again. You are a part of me and all of me must be perfect or we shall be undone: you must be reborn. You have judged my seed; now you have been meted judgment. I am truth without name or reason. The gift was given unto thee and now it has been taken away by me."

Everything in all universes that can be seen or touched and thought of; did not move. The Creator told you his True Laws Of Life. Take heed to this message, or go by your own fate. Just remember that time is running out for you.

ONE: You will Respect me

TWO: You may not imitate me.

THREE: You must believe in my son.

FOUR: Every day of your life must be Worthy.

FIVE: Cultivate your seeds, their seed and the needy.

SIX: Do not give unto me those that are mine.

SEVEN: Do not destroy half of your Soul for Lust.

EIGHT: Learn to Respect what is not yours.

NINE: Do not destroy another life out of Envy.

TEN: Learn to love one another as a whole; I will bless thee much more.

ELEVEN: Beware of false religions; you need not die and kill for me: I love you all the sameTWELVE: Follow my scrolls given to you by My Seraphims.

Just then enigmatic energy struck the Diamond Shield. A light brighter than the sun destroyed the area around us. It's now The Eighth Hour in my Dreams! The Hour of New Madness.

I woke up out of my dream state screaming and thinking; what kind of crazy nightmare was that. It's was all a bad dream; maybe I'm back home in my own bed and my mother is going to yell "Coffee's ready Carmen." Just then I could hear Mistress Pat screaming to the top of her lungs. "My babies; Sonya, Carlos where are you: dear God no!" I looked over from inside my diamond bed of glass; and there was Amber, Rick and Judy sitting in their chairs dead as can be; blood dripping out of Rick's neck. Then there bodies vanished before my eyes; Mistress Pat came running, busting through the door with an ax. She start crashing down on my protective chamber in anger and fright. "I don't want this; go away: die!" Just then coming out of the closet was Kirk, James and Paul and they grabbed the ax from her. It's true what they say about dreams: sometime dreams come true. "Bailey you bastard; get away from me!" she screams. "Wait Mistress Pat; now you can undo this. The door to Carmen Dreams is now closed: you can find The Replacer." Mistress Pat looked at Kirk like he lost his fucking mind and yelled. "Look outside man; the world is destroyed. All this shit really happened, it wasn't no fucking dream!" "Yes Mistress Pat; but don't forget my child: you are the Angel of Dreams." "That don't mean anything to me now, I lost my children because of you." "No Pat, your children are safe in the World of Spanton; Sonya is now an Angel of God: and Carlos wants to come home to you. Also don't forget, you have the power of the cosmos in your hands." "Yes, your right Bailey; I almost forgot: I can go back in time and undo this." Kirk looked at Pat and said. "Yes my child, it will be like it never happen." Pat wiped her tears and yelled for Devy. She got her sexy walk back "Devy show yourself." "Yes my master." "Yea thanks a lot Devy some help you was." Devy looked worried and start begging forgiveness. "I'm sorry my lord; but you was dealing with matter unheard of: please forgive me master, what is your Desire? Pat looks over at Kirk with an evil look in her eyes and said. "Take me back four years from November twenty ninth, two thousand and twelve. " "Yes my mistress, your wish is my command." Kirk looked in shock and screamed, "Your Crazy! Impossible! No you bitch!.."

It is now ten thirty pm November twenty-ninth, two thousand and eight in New York City; at seventy second street west end. The streets are crowded and the children of the city are going to bed. At a private home, a dark mist hovers over the city. The wind is blowing at fifty mph. Traffic was running steady; a cab pulled up to the estate and Mistress Pat steps out. She looks up in the air and screamed. From a hole in the sky fell the bodies of Amber, Rick and Judy. They splattered in the middle of the street and sidewalk bringing traffic to a standstill; people get out of their cars screaming in horror pointing to the sky. Amber felled on the side walk in front of Mistress Pat; she look at Amber's splattered body and say. "I see you got your fucking wish bitch!" She walk over Amber body like it was a pale of shit. Rushing to the doorman Mistress Pat is holding the Gold Armatura with the Gold Handcuff secure around her wrist. "Yes I'm here to see Kirk Bailey; tell him Mrs.Brewster is here." "Yes he's waiting for you, follow me this way. Mistress Pat notice the doorman had strange colored eyes; a color she remember from the Mist of Darkness: "They know." she thought to herself. Mistress Pat looks around Kirk's home and realize this man have great taste in fine arts and stones: he is a true collector. Kirk was waiting in the study. "Yes Mrs. Brewster, so happy to finally meet you." Kirk heard police sirens and looked out of his window in the study. "It gotten real cloudy out there, that's strange; what's all the drama in the middle of the street? Was it an accident?" He looks at his doorman Greg. "Greg are you wearing contact lens. Mistress Pat closed the door in Greg's face and locked it; she ran over and put the Scroll of Spanton on the coffee table. "Here Mr. Bailey please sign, I am running out of time." Kirk look confused. Not aware that his beautiful brick home started to bleed from outside. "What deadline are you trying to beat?" Pat looked at her watch and it was ten forty-two pm. "Good lord man; please just sign the damn thing: I got what you asked for." She yelled. Mistress Pat opened The Armatura and The Stone of the Hubriser was shining it's madness of light. "Spectacular!" Kirk yelled. "Is there anything I need to know Mrs. Brewster?" Kirk's eyes opened wide in amazement. Pat look Kirk straight in his eyes and asked. "Do You Believe In God Mr. Bailey?" Kirk looked at Pat and said. "No I don't believe in such things Mrs. Brewster; but I'll sign!" Kirk put the pen to the scroll and signed. A clap of thunder with the sound of many bombs shook New York City. The voice of many waters sounded." TO SHEW UNTO HIS SERVANTS THINGS WHICH MUST SHORTLY COME TO PASS." Pat fell to the floor in relief crying; she can now go home to her beloved children.

My name is Carmen Dreams and I am forever the Seraphim of Dreams. There are only three humans responsible for getting this scroll to your planet Aissen. I entered their dreams and showed them the truth. There will be more Seraphims of Spanton coming out to tell you the truth about life and the universe you reside in. It is up to you to believe what you cannot see: but believe me it's there. The proof has been all over your planet for thousands of years;open your eyes! YOU ARE NOT ALONE! Man was not a problem thousands of years ago. All you seek was the truth and knowledge. Now you have weapons of masdestruction.

They do not want to start a war that you can't win! The Mayans are the Superior Race around your planet. They've been watching over you for over a thousand years. They don't come from another planet,this is their planet and your in the way! There will be a Great OIL SPILL in the GULF OF MEXICO,that will kill billions of sea life. The Mayans can't take no more;you are destroying the world's oceans and the Mayan's home with your silly ways of conducting energy. If you are reading these pages; you are a survivor of the end of days. They are now thirty three new scrolls concealed around the new world left behind by the arks of E'ly. They will be able to be found by clues around the new planet what you call Earth. Let us show you the way to go. This will be not for the human race, sorry you fucked up; you're not getting out of this alive! The survivors of the human race will be branded deep below the ocean surface until the day of rebellion that is told in the thirty three new scrolls. You still have a chance to be among the few that live: all you have to do is believe in him! This will be an epic battle for the new world between you and the new seed. The scrolls will be for the new seed of matter that the creator will bring forth in my dreams. This will be their Bible. I who testifieth these things saith. Surely he came quickly. May The Grace Of Who You Believe To Be God Be With You All: Amen.

Would you like to enter my dreams before it's too late human? You might find a way to escape all this Madness. I'll allow you one wish: How May I Serve You Master, What Is Your Pleasure?

Is It The End Or The Beginning?

-end-